OWNING COREY

A
Novel

MARIS BLACK

This novel was written for the people I love.
You know who you are.
You make me good.

1

(BEN)

FUCKING hospital Christmas parties. I hate them with a passion. From my lonely spot in the hallway, I've got a good view through the open double doors and into the crowded cafeteria, where everyone is stuffing finger foods into their faces and talking about God only knows what.

Don't they get enough talk time spending twelve hours a day with each other?

My head is starting to feel light as I down my third cup of sour pink punch. One of the nurses brought it in a spouted 10-gallon cooler, and we're tearing it up, though certainly not for the taste. It's helping me tolerate the obnoxious lights and tinsel, and all the chintzy red and green decorations the day shift taped up this afternoon. Fortunately for me, doctors don't have to pull decorating duty. One of the perks of the job.

In fact, this is a Tuesday night and I should be working, but I got someone to cover for me so I could bring Christina to this miserable event. Now she's all the way on the far side of the room, tossing her white-blond hair and getting way too friendly with that new asshole EMT who's training on day shift.

Look at him. Thinks he's God's gift to women.

There's a rumor going around that they're going to stick him on night shift with me. Not something I'm looking forward to at all. The thought of having to see him every night churns my guts, because at the moment my girlfriend has got her perfectly manicured hands all over his biceps, and she's giving him that cute little smile she gives me when she wants my cock.

I lean back against the wall, cross my arms across my chest and try to imagine what I'm going to do about it. We haven't been dating that long, so I don't have a whole lot invested. Kicking her to the curb immediately seems the right move to save myself the future headache. I can put up with a lot, but that kind of blatant flirting is not something I'm willing to tolerate.

"Hi, Dr. Hardy." One of the floor nurses approaches me cautiously, like I'm some sort of cornered wild animal and she's afraid I'll bite. I can't blame her for being wary. With my slim, Hollywood tailored charcoal suit and what I imagine is the flintiest stare in the room, I'm even less approachable than usual, and that's saying a lot. Not to mention I'm her superior.

The girl pauses in front of me, teetering on her functional black pumps, and I think she's going to chat me up. In my mind I'm cheering her on, though I do nothing to make it easier for her. If she succeeds, maybe I'll take her home tonight, since it looks like a good possibility I'll be dateless soon.

But she doesn't succeed. Instead, she veers silently off toward the restrooms, and I can see the defeat in her eyes.

As soon as she's out of sight, Dr. Hannigan sidles up to me with a drink in each hand. I wonder if he expects people to assume he's holding one of them for someone else, or if he just doesn't care if he's seen double-fisting alcoholic beverages.

"She's cute," he says.

I look toward the restroom the nurse has just disappeared into and shrug. "I guess so."

Hannigan laughs his pretentious boom of a laugh and barely avoids sloshing punch on me as he and nudges my shoulder with a freckled hand. "I meant *her*." He gestures toward Christina. "Aren't you two dating now?"

"Yeah. Right now I'm wishing I hadn't let her drag me out here. I'd rather be working."

"Oh, I know what you mean." He attempts a soulful expression that doesn't quite hit the mark. "I almost don't know what to do with myself when I'm not on duty. You and I are both married to the job, Ben. Men like us are built to lead rather than follow, but that comes at a hefty price, doesn't it?"

He raises his cup toward Christina and her handsome companion, as if he's taunting me.

"I don't mind it so much," I lie smoothly. "What I do mind is a dull party. I'm thinking I need to go home and pull out the good cognac I have stashed away in my office drawer. I don't drink often, but now that I've gotten started, might as well finish it off right, you know?"

"Absolutely. I do love a good cognac now and then." His dull eyes sparkle for a beat, and I realize he's angling for an invitation. I've also heard he's angling for my job, but the bastard had better not hold his breath waiting for either one.

"Would you please excuse me?" I mumble. When I don't make a move to go anywhere, Hannigan shuffles awkwardly away.

I've had just about all I can stand of this party, and I'm just about to march over and drag Christina out of here when she turns and looks straight at me with that same cock-licking smile on her face. Dammit, I can't help it having an effect on me. I'm definitely going to break up with her, but I'm considering postponing it until tomorrow. The liquor has got me worked up in more ways than one, and since I don't know how long it will be before I get laid again, I'm thinking about grabbing one for the road.

Besides, Christina is looking especially tasty tonight. The contrast of siren red lipstick against her translucent skin creates the most startling impression of a juicy apple, and I'm thinking I want to get out of here and take a bite.

But then *he* looks at me, too, all dark and dangerous with blazing blue eyes, lightly tanned skin and wavy black hair that curls slightly around his collar. He commands the room effortlessly, drawing attention and energy like he's some brilliant electrical thing, and everyone and everything else in the room is dust. His apparent obliviousness to his own magnetism makes him all the more despicable.

Italian designers would fall all over themselves to get this guy in their blue jean and cologne ads. With his deadly mix of confidence, rebellious sophistication and fuck-all attitude, it only takes one look at him to know that hearts— and panties— are about to be dropping all over our little town.

Hell, he's so good-looking, he's got me thinking how nice he and Christina look together, and she's *my* girlfriend.

The two of them come straight toward me, parting the crowd like the red sea as nurses swoon in his wake. I'd love to sneer at his inappropriate attire, which consists of a black t-shirt, faded blue jeans, and biker boots, but the truth is he looks fantastic. He could probably get away with meeting the queen of England in camouflage shorts and flip-flops.

In contrast, I feel like a bit of a dandy in my trendy tailored suit. At least my hair is its usual rakish mess on top, but I run my fingers lightly through it just to make sure. I shift my body into a subtle slouch so as not to seem too formal, but I'm finding it difficult to figure out what to do with my hands.

Why am I so self-conscious? I'm the freaking Chief of Staff, and he's a nobody.

"Ben," Christina purrs to me through those red lips, curling her slender white fingers into the crook of my arm. "This is the new EMT, Corey Butler." The way she says his name makes me want to punch one of them in the mouth, and I don't even care which. "Have you two met?"

"No," I say.

At the same time he smiles and says, "Yes, we've met."

I shrug. "I don't remember it, sorry."

Corey's smile turns to a faltering laugh, and he shoves his hands nervously into the pockets of his jeans.

Score one for the home team. He's obviously not used to being

5

forgotten.

"We met on my first day, Dr. Hardy. Remember? You were still here late that morning catching up on your charting when they gave me a tour of the hospital."

"Yeah, okay." I nod, irritated that he's trying to force me to remember him. Because of course I do. I just don't want to admit it.

"You looked awful that morning." He winces, realizing he's just insulted me. "Uh, I didn't mean that in a bad way. I only meant that you'd had a rough night... two codes, a seizure, and a couple of bad COPD exacerbations. But you were still here charting away when most people would have said *screw it* and gone home already. I really admire that."

Hmmm, getting better.

He may be trying to snake my woman, but at least he's stroking my ego. Against my will, I start to like him just a little bit. One curse of being a doctor is that we need our professional egos stroked... a lot.

"Wow, you remember my day better than I do." I finish off the last of my warm punch and toss the cup toward the trash can inside the cafeteria doors. When it bounces off the rim, Corey scrambles to retrieve it and drops it into the bin for me. "You give me too much credit, though. In this business, we all live by the same code, or at least we're supposed to. Would you have said *screw it?*"

"Hell, no. I'm new, but I take my job very seriously. I would have been right there beside you, charting with my eyes half closed." He laughs. "Doing a good job is almost like a compulsion with me."

"Ben is compulsive, too," Christina says brightly, squeezing my shoulder. "The man is a total workaholic. It's almost impossible to get any private time with him. You know, big important doctor, always in demand."

"Oh, I'll bet he is," Corey says. "I'm finding it hard to adjust to twelve-hour shifts and being on call for the ambulance, so I can't even imagine what it must be like for a doctor. I'm surprised you get any rest at all, Dr. Hardy."

I open my mouth to answer, but Christina pipes up first and cuts me off. "He's very dedicated. Did you know he's the youngest Chief of Staff they've ever had in the history of the hospital?"

Why do I feel like she's trying to sell me to this guy? I hate to tell her this, but from the look on his face, he's already starstruck. It's so funny how people automatically bow down to doctors, even though most of them don't freaking deserve it. Sometimes I wonder if I deserve it, even just a little bit.

"I'm about to be finding out first hand just how dedicated he is," Corey says with a conspiratorial wink in my direction. "They're turning me loose to work on my own. I start night shift tomorrow, Monday through Thursday, same as you, Dr. Hardy."

Rumor confirmed. Fan-fucking-tastic.

Christina gasps. "Already? Boy, that was quick. People usually have to train at least a few weeks. I can't believe they're letting you go on your own after only one week. You must be *good.*"

The way she says *good* sounds like she's talking about something other than work.

"I *am* good," he says. "Damn good."

It's obvious that he's joking, but I can tell by the glint in her eye that she's not. Jesus, why doesn't she just fuck him right here and get it over with?

I've got to hand it to the man, though. He hasn't glanced at her tits once, and that has got to take a will of steel. They are perfectly displayed in her sparkling silver mini-dress, and the lacy edges of her red bra peek out of the low cut neckline when she moves just right. It's giving me wood, so I don't know how he can resist at least a glance. She's wearing those red high heels that she knows make me nuts, and suddenly all I can think about is stripping her down to nothing but those shoes and fucking her against a wall.

Maybe the bathroom is empty now...

I must be having a reaction to the young wolf who's just been introduced into my pack, because I've definitely shifted into alpha mode. I eye the shoes deliberately, feeling even more blood rush to my dick. "Let's get out of here."

"Okay," Christina and Corey both chime in unison. I stare open-mouthed at Corey.

His lips turn up in a sheepish grin. "Oh... You meant just the two of you. Shit, that's embarrassing. Okay, you kids have fun. I'll just go eat some reindeer cupcakes and get plastered. " He gestures toward the dessert table, where three portly nurses are stalking the goods.

Christina laughs, a sultry sound of feminine delight that gets the attention of nearly everyone in the room, especially the men. Of course it gives me a sense of pride that she's so desirable, but sometimes it can be quite the annoyance... like now.

"Ben, I've already invited Corey back to my place with us." She trails her fingernail down my arm. "He and I were discussing it earlier, before I introduced you. I hope you don't mind."

"Guilty as charged." Corey nods, and an errant lock of wavy

black hair falls across his forehead. "We talked about the three of us getting a twelve pack and a movie. She said you like psychological thrillers, same as me. And stout beer."

"Jesus, how long have you two been talking? Has she told you my underwear size, too?"

Corey smiles and looks at the floor, his face coloring slightly. "Um… we've actually talked a few times, Ben."

Christina slips her arms around my waist, trying to pry me away from the wall. "Come on, Ben. It'll be fun." She's using her sexiest voice on me now, the one she knows will almost surely get her what she wants, but I'm still not sold.

"Look, I know what you're thinking," Corey says quietly, leaning in so close to my ear I can feel the heat coming off of him. He glances meaningfully at Christina, then back at me. "It's not about her. I just don't have any friends in town yet, and it sounded really good to have a beer and watch a movie— get to know each other. But if it's not cool with you, I totally understand."

Against my will, I'm starting to like this guy. I don't have that many friends, either. It's hard to make friends when you work like I do. Truth be known, I'm not great friend material. Not with all the shit I carry around inside me. Being a doctor isn't the glamorous job people think it is. It can seriously fuck you up in the head.

"Alright." I hold up my hands in surrender. "It sounds fun. I think I'm just in a bad mood from this horrendous party."

Since Christina hasn't been drinking, I let her drive my car. She's been annoying the hell out of me to drive it for the entire two months we've been dating, so she's thrilled.

What is it about a Porsche that gets women so wet? Between the car and the doctor title, I'm a walking chick magnet. Which is not as great as you'd imagine, by the way.

In the beginning it was awesome, but after a while you get tired of the fake shit. Most of these small town women get dollar signs in their eyes every time they look at me. I'm their rock star, their Prince Charming. You can see them get all nervous and fidgety, desperate to say the right thing. They're all in a contest, and I'm the first place trophy, which makes me extremely uncomfortable.

Maybe I'm two-faced. In fact, I know I am, but I can't help it. I crave admiration and respect, but not for having money. I certainly don't want a woman who considers me some sort of financial conquest. I suppose you could say I have a fear of being some woman's bankroll.

That's what I like about Christina. She appreciates nice things, loves the car, loves dating a doctor, but she's much too impressed with herself to consider me her superior. If anything, she thinks she's bringing more to the table than I am, and that I'm lucky to have her as arm candy. She is a pretty hot piece of ass. But the main thing is I don't feel like she's desperate to land me. That means a lot.

I wonder how it would change things if she knew how much

money I actually have, and that being a doctor is just something I do to have a sense of purpose. My real money was handed down from my grandfather, but almost no one knows about it. Money earned through hard work is a source of pride for a family, but that's not the case with my money. It's more like a dirty family secret.

As we drive from the hospital to the convenience store, Christina and I are comfy in the cockpit, but Corey's substantial bulk is literally folded into the backseat, and it's got me rethinking my choice of vehicles. The Porsche isn't exactly conducive to having friends.

Christina drops the windows, and I let my head fall back, feeling the icy wind whip through my hair and into my nose, stealing my breath. We all shiver and howl in the wind as if we've lost our minds, high on adrenaline. It's exhilarating, and for a moment I'm a school boy again.

"Think it's gonna snow?" She yells over the rushing of the air.

I laugh. "If it does, we'll freeze to death before we get to your house."

"Bring it on," Corey growls, pumping his fist up through the open sun roof like some misplaced teenage football star. "Woo-hoo!"

By the time we get to the store a couple of blocks down the road, our faces are made of flesh-colored ice. Christina's long blond hair has been whipped until it looks like white cotton candy. Corey's longish dark mane is similarly disheveled, though it does nothing to diminish his looks. I wonder what my hair looks like. It's shorter than both of theirs, so there's a chance I still look fairly respectable.

We stand shivering just inside the store for a long moment, waiting for the warmth to penetrate our frozen bodies, before we can bring ourselves to go near the drink cooler to grab the beer.

"Hang on," I call as Christina and Corey make their way to the cash register, Corey holding the twelve pack hoisted on his broad shoulder. "Let me get some Boston Baked Beans. I'm craving something sweet."

"Ooh, ooh," Christina cries, running back to join me on the candy aisle, her red heels clicking on the terrazzo floor. "I want some lemon drops. Will you buy me some lemon drops, baby?" She gives an exaggerated flutter of her false lashes.

"I don't know, Chris. They're a quarter a box. That's pretty steep."

She laughs, grabs two boxes, and kisses me on the cheek. "I'll pay you back," she whispers, and there's promise in her green eyes.

"Mmmm, I think I'll take it out of that sweet ass." I slap her on the rear, eliciting a cute little squeal that makes my dick jump in my pants. *You'll have to wait, buddy*, I tell it. *We've got company.*

"Hey man, what's your favorite candy?" I call out to Corey, who's waiting at the counter. "I'm buying. Sky's the limit, as long as it's not over a quarter."

His face blanks out while he tries to decide if I'm serious or not.

"Just kidding," I tell him. "What do you like?"

"Um… Nerds. Or anything with toffee. I'll pay for the beer."

"No, hell, you won't. I'm getting it all. You're our guest."

I grab a box of Nerds and a chocolate covered toffee bar and head up to the counter. The clerk eyes the three of us over the top of his glasses like we're a bunch of rowdy teenagers with the munchies. Christina pokes me in the side and giggles, and Corey is stifling a laugh. As for myself, I've got a mile wide grin on my face. It's like the store is piping in nitrous oxide through the air ducts. Or maybe we're still delirious from the cold air. Or maybe it's just the Christmas spirit finally kicking in. Whatever it is, I'm liking it.

2

WE'RE on the road again. This time we've kept the windows up and the heater is going full blast.

"I'm stopping at the movie store," Christina announces as she pulls up to the curb and leaves the car running. "You guys sit here, and I'll surprise you, okay?"

I groan and hand her my credit card. "As long as we don't end up with *Steel Magnolias* or *He's Just Not That Into You.*"

She laughs and sprints up the steps, giving me— or us— a sexy flash of ass cheek from beneath her short dress as she muscles the heavy glass door open and a gust of wind blows her inside.

Corey turns to me after she's gone. "I still can't believe you guys have an old-fashioned video store. Everyone in Atlanta rents their movies from a box."

"Yeah, we have one of the few remaining mom and pop video stores in the state, probably even the country. But that's how things are in towns as small as Blackwood. Businesses aren't corporations around here; they're someone's livelihood. The family who owns this store has lived here for generations, and everybody knows them. No way some damn box is going to come in and put Mr. And Mrs. Leroux on welfare. Besides that, they have an unbelievable inventory they've been building for decades. If you can't find it at Leroux Video, you won't find it anywhere."

"I know, man. I went in the other day to see if they had a cheap used player, and I couldn't believe it. Two huge rooms of wall to wall movies. One full of DVD's, and one full of old VHS tapes. It's a movie lover's paradise."

"Three," I correct.

"Three what?"

"Three rooms." I'm looking intently at him now, because I sense he doesn't know what I'm talking about, and that means I'm about to have a good laugh at his expense.

His eyebrows draw together, and I can see the cogs turning in his brain as he tries in vain to remember a third room.

"The back room," I whisper with a sneaky smile and watch as realization dawns on his face. His embarrassment is amusing to me, and I prod him a little just to watch him squirm. "You know, triple X movies. Porn. *The Devil in Miss Jones*—"

"Whoa, you had me at *back room*." He holds up a hand and laughs. "But how long has it been since you've watched porn that your example is an obscure movie from the eighties?"

I cock an eyebrow at him. "It's from the seventies. And you recognized the reference, so I guess you don't have much room to talk. Which is interesting, because you're really too young to know that movie. What are you, twenty-five?"

He laughs. "I guess you're right, doc. And I'm twenty-six. Well into manhood, thank you very much. How old are you?"

"Thirty-three, which officially makes me your superior in all things. And that reminds me… Night shift is my domain, you know. Maybe you want to reconsider working with me. I've heard I can be a real bastard."

He smiles, showing boyish dimples that counter his manly physique. I work out, but this guy looks like he belongs in action movies or something. His muscles aren't bulky, but he's broad and cut like hell. And tall. He's got to be six-foot-four if he's an inch, because I'm exactly six feet, and he makes me feel pretty small.

It's embarrassing for me to admit this even to myself, but he's the most amazing looking guy I've ever seen in my life. It's no wonder Christina is barking up his tree.

"Some of the nurses have actually warned me about you, Dr. Hardy. They say you're anal retentive, and that you'll chew me up and spit me out if I don't do things just so."

He waits for me to respond, but I'm having trouble finding my tongue. No one, not even Christina, has ever had the gumption to say such a thing to me. The truth stings a little, but I'm impressed by his candor.

"Does that make you nervous?" I ask. "Do *I* make you nervous?"

He shrugs, flashing the dimples again. "Yeah, a little. But I have a plan." He rubs his hands together evil villain style. "I figure I'll watch a movie with you, drink a few beers, ply you with my charm… You'll be putty in my hands before morning."

16

Before I can deliver a smart comeback, Christina climbs back into the car, bringing with her an arctic chill that makes my teeth chatter. "What movie did you get, babe?"

She shoves a plastic bag between the seat and the center console, hands me back my card, and puts the car in gear. "*Return of the Living Dead.*"

"What is this, seventies movie night?" Corey asks.

"Eighties," I correct, and he rolls his eyes.

"Guys, it's a fun movie. I want to get wild and crazy." Christina tears away from the curb a little faster than I would like, barking the tires loudly, and I fear for my Porsche as well as our lives.

"You'd better enjoy driving my car tonight, young lady, because it's the only time it's ever gonna happen."

She pouts. "You're such a chauvinist."

"I certainly am not. I believe women are great at lots of things. Driving is just not one of them. See? You almost clipped that curb. Jesus, slow down. You're about to give me a heart attack."

"Ben, quit being such a control freak. I'm not going to wreck your precious car."

"I'm less worried about the car and more about our well-being. I don't want to end up in the hospital as a patient, okay? Let me enjoy my night off."

Christina's house is only a few blocks further, and I hold my breath most of the way there. She's driving erratically on purpose, trying to push my buttons.

I snatch the keys from her and stuff them in my pocket as we cross the threshold of her small but immaculate house. Inside it is sleek and modern, and expensive. I have no idea how she can afford to decorate and dress like she does on what she makes managing the hospital human resources department. But she's childless and has few obligations other than overindulging herself, which she does well and often.

"Nice place," Corey says.

"Thanks, hon. Have you got an address yet? I need to get it updated in our system when you do."

He shifts uncomfortably on his feet. "I haven't found a permanent place. I'm still living out of the Blackwood Motel."

Christina grimaces. "Ew. Are there bugs?"

"Not that I've noticed." He swings the twelve pack down from his shoulder and scans the room. "Where's the fridge?"

"Follow me," she says.

While they put things away in the kitchen, I make my way over to the pristine white leather sofa I helped her pick out only recently. It was the best thing they had at Peebles Fine Furnishings. I usually try to shop locally, but in the case of furniture for my own house, I was forced to order online and visit tons of antiques shops. After putting so much money into remodeling and updating an old home, it would be a travesty to destroy it with trailer furniture.

This sofa is nice enough for Christina's stark contemporary decor, though, and the leather feels soft. As I sink down into it, I'm instantly glad we left the party early. The room is dark, illuminated only by the glow of the street lamps through the white curtains, and what little light filters in from the kitchen.

When I close my eyes, my thoughts take a dark turn, and I'm remembering the night Christina and I christened the sofa. We'd planned on watching TV, but fifteen minutes into the show I had her

18

bent over the back of the couch, skirt hiked up to her waist and panties around her ankles. There was no romance that night, no politeness or niceties. I held her down by the nape of her neck, her firm alabaster ass presented in the perfect position, and watched my cock sliding between her legs, felt her sweet warmth gripping me...

The sound of laughter jolts me, and I realize I've been dozing and having one hell of a dream. I'm hard as a rock now, and I reach down to adjust myself, rubbing ever so slightly, wishing she and I were alone so I could do something about it.

Instead, she's giggling with Mr. Muscles in the kitchen. I can't hear what she's saying to him, but I recognize the low, sexy tone of her voice. She's flirting with him again.

"I'm still here, you know," I call out, instantly regretting my words. I'm really not myself tonight.

Corey comes out first, carrying two beers. He tosses one to me and sits on the other end of the sofa. Christina pops the movie into the player and lowers herself gracefully between us, crossing her legs and dangling one of those infernal red shoes from the ends of her toes. She slides her hand across the leather seat toward me and rests it against my leg, but she doesn't come closer. She sits at an even distance between me and Corey, and I wonder if she's baiting me, trying to tweak that alpha aggression that's been threatening to surface all evening. I have to resist, though. There's no sense in making a scene over a woman who's about to be my ex-girlfriend.

When the first grainy scene of the movie comes up, Corey chokes on his beer, spewing a trail of foam across the carpet.

"Sorry," he gasps, still struggling to catch his breath.

One look at the screen tells me what's got him so shocked.

There's a naked woman standing in an under-decorated bedroom just letting it all hang out when her doorbell rings. She tries to look surprised, but I've seen better acting in a high school drama club.

"This isn't *Return of the Living Dead*," I say.

Christina shakes her head slowly without looking at me, and I can see her confidence ebbing.

"You went to the back room, didn't you?" Corey asks, his voice raspy from his choking spell. He wipes beer from his lips with the back of his forearm.

"Christina, look at me." I grasp her chin in one hand and force her to face me. "What is this all about? What were you thinking?"

"I just thought… we might…" She seems to search for the right words. "Well, I have this fantasy of… being with two men at the same time."

She waits for a response, but I don't know what to say. I've been totally blindsided by this. Here I am thinking she's trying to replace me, but what she's actually trying to do is… God, I can barely even bring myself to say it in my own mind.

Corey lets out a low whistle and shakes his head. "Didn't see that one coming." He leans forward with his elbows on his knees and looks around Christina to catch my eye. His expression is serious at first, but then the corners of his mouth twitch upward, and I realize he's about to laugh.

Suddenly I have the urge to laugh, too. In the midst of this situation, it seems absurd, but the sound bubbles to the surface before I can call it back. Corey tries to hold his laughter in, but it bursts out through this closed lips in a noisy blast of air. He barely gets his beer settled on the end table before he rolls off the couch and onto the floor in a twisting fit of laughter.

Within seconds we're both giggling like a couple of schoolgirls. Christina looks back and forth between me and Corey, her mouth hanging open. I almost feel sorry for her, but I just can't help laughing. I can tell it's a defense mechanism, because it doesn't feel like normal laughter. It's more hysterical than humor-induced.

"You guys think this is funny? Are you laughing at me?"

I grab her hand and try my best to stifle the laughter. It's hard to stop, because it keeps welling up and tickling my belly. It doesn't help that Corey is still rolling around on the carpet. He's definitely lost it.

"Christina, I'm sorry. It's just quite a shock." The laughter threatens again, making it hard to speak. "I've just never really considered doing anything like that. Not for real, you know?"

On the movie, the woman has answered the door and invited two shabby looking men into her bedroom. One is a plumber, the other a carpenter. You can tell by their dollar store Halloween costumes. But then they won't be wearing them for long.

"It's just a fantasy of mine, Ben. I thought maybe you would be game. You seem so up for anything in bed. You're the one who started tying me up, and you taught me how to do anal…"

I clear my throat and glance nervously at Corey, feeling more than a little exposed having my sex life aired in front of a stranger. Unfortunately, he's calmed down and hanging on every word we're saying.

"You can't just pop a porno in on a couple of unsuspecting guys, honey. Corey and I have barely even met, and now you've got us…" *imagining being naked together, fucking alongside each other.*

I shudder. Those are not really the kind of thoughts a guy wants to have in a room with another dude.

"This is a seriously bad movie." Corey's attention has shifted to the television, where one of the men is lying on the bed, cock in hand. The woman is climbing on top of him, awkwardly positioning herself with the help of the second guy. For a moment, all of our eyes are glued to the screen, watching to see how it all unfolds. The volume isn't loud, but we can hear the exaggerated and unmistakable sounds of porn sex commencing.

"Have you ever done that?" I ask to no one in particular, staring blankly at the screen.

Both Christina and Corey say *no* and shake their heads.

"Me, either. I came close once in college, but only because my roommate and I were drunk and horny as hell, and there was only one girl. We were a study group, supposed to be cramming for a Biology test, but that fifth of Jäger said otherwise. My roommate ended up passing out, and I screwed the girl." I smile to myself at the memory. At the time, it had seemed like some great victory.

"So if you considered it for her, why not me?" Christina is now on the verge of tears. "It took a lot for me to ask this of you. The least you can do is think about it." Her brows crease. "I thought this was every guy's fantasy."

I open my mouth to speak and close it again. I don't even know how to respond to that.

"Um… I think you're confusing that with two girls and one guy," Corey says quietly. "A threesome with two girls and one guy is a popular straight male fantasy, at least if the porn industry is any indication."

"What, are you some kind of porn aficionado?" I ask, suddenly irritated enough to lash out.

"Hell, no, Ben. Are you?" He meets my glare with one of his own. "You're the one who knows all the seventies porn titles by heart."

"Hey, you knew it, too."

"Boys," Christina yells. "Please don't start. This might have been a bad idea on my part. I just didn't know how to go about bringing it up. I'd envisioned this going down a lot differently, like the two of you would start drooling and staring when I turned the movie on."

"Men are not mindless sex zombies, Chris. We don't just trance out every time sex comes on the screen. Besides, you and I are supposed to be dating. I know it's not official, but you could've had the courtesy to warn me before you brought someone else in. We don't even know who this guy is." I point at Corey, who looks patently offended. "He just blew into town, lives in a freaking motel for God's sake. Was this his idea?"

"Alright, now," Corey says, standing up and towering over us. "I don't have to put up with this bullshit. I'm just as shocked as you are. I thought I was coming over for a movie and a couple of beers. Why would you think it's my idea?"

"I don't know. Everything was fine before you showed up. For all I know, you've got a hard on for her. Or me. Maybe you're trying to use Christina to get to me. What were you two talking about at the party, and in the kitchen? Were you plotting this thing out?"

Corey's mouth presses into a tight line, and the veins on his neck bulge. "That's a messed up thing to say. It's your girlfriend who's propositioning me for a threesome. As I see it, I'm the least to blame of anyone in this room. Maybe you're the one with the hard on."

"I'm not gay," I say.

"Yeah? What makes you think I am?"

"Well you could certainly pass for it looking like that."

Corey's mouth drops open. "What the fuck is that supposed to mean?"

I've just taken a nosedive into social impropriety, and I can tell I'm about to drown in it. Maybe I can fix it. "Uh… I mean you look like one of those queer underwear models, with their pretty-boy faces and perfect bodies, and your mouth…"

Fuck. What am I saying?

"Did you just say my mouth looks gay?" he asks incredulously. "And as for the pretty-boy face and perfect body…" He rakes me with an exaggerated once-over, his manner so heavily tinged with aggression it gives me chills. "I could say the same about you, doctor. Are you sure you're not queer?"

"Hell, no," I roar, hoping to intimidate him like he has me.

Christina jumps between us just as we're about to square off. "Please," she screams. "Would you guys please just sit down and watch the movie? This was all my idea, and neither one of you are queer. You're both gorgeous, muscular, virile, intelligent men whom I happen to find very attractive. But if you're going to act like this, maybe I should just go to the bar and pick up a couple of random guys. I probably won't find any with your pretty-boy faces and

24

perfect bodies, but at least maybe they'll be interested in some kinky sex with a beautiful and willing woman."

That gets my attention, and the buzz of anger running through my body begins to subside. "You're right." I take a couple of deep breaths and step backward away from Corey. "We're probably overreacting. I'm just a little taken aback by this whole thing."

"Me, too," Corey agrees, offering a little dimpled smile.

Pretty-boy faces and perfect bodies. Jesus, I feel like an idiot.

We sit down and try to watch the movie. The threesome is going at it hot and heavy by this time. The chick has a dick in each hole, and she's loving it, or at least acting like she does.

"I guess it might not be so bad," Corey says. "Maybe we wouldn't have reacted so badly if we just knew each other better, Ben. I mean, I've never thought of a threesome as being gross or anything, have you?"

I struggle to come up with an appropriate response. "I suppose not. I've never thought of it as gross or shameful, or even that particularly kinky. It's just different when it's… imminent."

"Imminent?" Christina squeals. "That means it's going to happen, right?"

I look at the screen again, then at Christina, then at Corey. She's made it perfectly clear how she feels, but I can't read his face at all. "Give me a couple of days to consider it."

She smiles, then looks expectantly at Corey.

He nods once. "Yeah, let us have a couple of days to get a little more comfortable with each other, and then we'll decide."

Christina bounces up and down on the sofa. "Yay. I'm gonna have three-way sex with two of the hottest guys on the planet." Then she looks guiltily at me. "If you decided yes, that is."

I'm a little disturbed that my girlfriend looks so damned excited at the prospect of bringing another man into our bed, and even more disturbed that I'm considering it. Especially when I had planned on breaking up with her tomorrow. There's a current of foreboding humming just below the surface of my consciousness, like something bad is coming, and there's nothing I can do to stop it.

3

I DON'T budge until well past noon the next day, and by that time Christina and Corey are gone. I am so glad I don't have to face him and try to make small talk. I wonder if Christina gave him an early ride on her way to work, or if he walked. His motel is only a few blocks away, as is everything in this rinky-dink town.

On my way home, I pass the Blackwood motel, a horrible little place that looks like it hasn't been updated for several decades. I've never paid much attention to it before. It's one of those pieces of the scenery that you've looked at all your life but never truly *seen*. Now that I'm finally seeing it, all I can think about are drug dealers, prostitutes, and killers. I shiver to think of Corey sleeping on a dirty bed in that wretched, dark place.

A little girl with long brown hair skips down the breezeway, looking fresh and lovely and completely out of place. It's like a scene in a horror movie when you know something awful is about to happen. It breaks my heart to see her there. No decent human being

27

should have to stay in a place like that, least of all a child.

I look away, because I don't have time to worry about shit like that right now. I need to go home, shower, and mentally prepare for my night at the hospital. I owe it to my patients to be a hundred percent. Hung over, reeking of beer, and worrying about neglected children and group sex is definitely not a hundred percent. I've got to pull it together.

My house is empty and quiet, much too large for just me. I hope to have a family someday, but at the moment my house feels like the Grand Canyon. A big, hollow echo chamber with nothing in it but air, furniture and silence. I shower and dress, then relax on the sofa with a book, and as usual I'm relieved when it's finally time to go to the hospital.

It's not particularly busy in the ER tonight. I make some rounds, visit with my patients that have been admitted in the last few days, chart their progress. I release a couple of them, then I return to the ER, where it's still relatively quiet. No real emergencies yet, and I cross my fingers that there are none. I would never wish anything bad on another person just to relieve my boredom.

"I'm headed to the on-call room," I tell the nurses. "Let me know if you need me."

"Oh, Christina wanted you to call her when you get a chance," says Julie, one of my best night nurses.

Nodding, I trudge off to the spartan on-call room and collapse onto the bed. I pull out my cell and dial Christina's number, dreading talking to her. Maybe I should have just stuck with the plan to dump her today.

"Hey, babe," she says in a cheerful voice that doesn't exactly jibe with my mood. "Just checking to see if you've made a decision about Corey yet."

"Jeez, woman," I laugh. "Is that all you think about?"

"Hmmm…" She is quiet for a while, and the moments stretch painfully between us. She's not a terribly scintillating conversationalist, but she's hot. Hot women can get away with being a little dull, I guess. And she's good at being social, which is a good quality for a doctor's wife.

Stop making excuses for her, Ben.

"Have you ever looked at the Blackwood motel?" I ask. "I mean *really* looked at it?

"Yes, and it's disgusting. I can't believe Corey is actually living there. He's going to have to do some extra washing before he touches this body."

"There's a little kid staying there, Chris." My heart squeezes remembering her innocent beauty surrounded by the darkness of that horrible place.

"Probably some whore's kid. Look, I have to go to the store before bed. There's a dress I've been wanting, and they close in twenty minutes, so I don't really have time to chit-chat."

"By all means, focus on the important things. I'm going to watch a little TV before the ER starts hopping. You know it usually breaks loose after ten."

Sure enough, ten o'clock rolls around, and with it comes a rash of hypochondriacs, or *regulars* as we call them. Something about knowing everything in town is closed brings them to the emergency room. Maybe it's plain, old-fashioned boredom. Right now I know exactly how they feel, but I'm also uncharacteristically restless, which gives the boredom a sharp edge that's hard to handle.

"Hydrate Mrs. Watson," I tell Julie. "Put her on two liters of O2, and give her a room for twenty-three hours. And get a blood gas on Mr. Frank."

"Yes, sir," she says and hurries off to tend to my orders.

Right when my butt hits the chair behind the ER desk, the emergency radio buzzes to life. *"We've got a possible heart attack in progress. Arriving at the patient's home now. Stand by for ETA."*

I recognize the voice on the radio as Corey's. This might be a hell of a first night for him.

We all rush to prepare the ER for the possibility of a code, rolling the crash cart out and getting the defibrillator in position. This is how it is some nights. You're bored to tears for hours, and then suddenly all hell breaks loose and it doesn't seem like you can get things ready fast enough. One night we had two gunshot victims and one gut stab wound in the ER at the same time. All from separate incidents, and all fatal, which is really freaking odd for such a small town.

A woman's voice buzzes over the radio shortly after we've gotten the room ready. *"ETA one minute."*

"Damn, that was quick," I mutter to the nurse nearest me. "Must be bad."

"Patient is unconscious, not breathing, no pulse. CPR has been initiated," the female voice continues.

So Corey is performing CPR. I find myself trying to picture him doing it, wondering if he's got good form, or if I'm going to have to chew him up and spit him out like he said. I chuckle bitterly to myself. We medical workers have sick senses of humor that surface at inappropriate times. One of the hazards of the job.

The swinging door to the ER bursts open, and the stretcher is wheeled in by the regular female EMT they have on night shift. I don't remember her name, but she's been working here for a long time. She's bagging the patient with an AMBU bag connected to an LMA tube that's inflated and lodged snugly into the back of his throat, and she's trying to wheel the stretcher at the same time. Corey is walking alongside the stretcher doing chest compressions. A sheen of perspiration slicks his face and throat, probably more from nerves than exertion.

I meet them just inside the door and help push the stretcher into the prepped area and draw the curtain. In my mind, I feel very distinctly the dropping of what I like to call my ice shield, and my brain shuts down to everything but the task at hand— saving this man's life. Corey is pounding out perfect chest compressions at a rate of more than a hundred per minute. He's a machine, and his muscles are made for this kind of work. There's no vanity in him whatsoever, only the desperation of a man trying to force another to live.

The respiratory therapist rushes in and hooks the AMBU bag tubing to the oxygen flowmeter, cranks it to a hundred percent, and takes over bagging the patient. Julie is getting the IV in the patient's arm and administering epinephrine. I have my night staff trained well. Mistakes cost lives, and we can't afford that, especially at our little underfunded hospital.

"How long has he been down?" I ask Corey as I slap the defibrillator pads onto the patient's chest.

"Two minutes," he pants. "Wife called 911 for shortness of breath and chest pains. He collapsed the minute we pulled into the yard. He had a pulse when we loaded him up, but one minute out, he coded… I just had time to tube him, strap it, and get CPR started."

He continues pumping the man's chest with a shocking intensity. He's strong. Stronger than any medical worker I've ever seen, and just as determined. He gets a good compression and full recoil every time, which is surprising, because I was under the impression he was new to the field.

I hear the patient's wife in the waiting area crying, begging someone to tell her if her husband is okay. "He's not dead, is he? Is he *dead*?" she screams. I hate dealing with the families, but I feel so responsible to them. It's easily the most painful part of the job. In a case like this, the family members are the ones hurting, not the patient. The man on our table has no idea what's going on, but his wife is in the worst agony imaginable.

"It's lucky he waited for you to get there before he coded, huh?" I ask Corey.

"Yeah, he might just have a chance."

"We've got a rhythm," Julie calls, and I check the defibrillator screen.

"Yep, he's in V-Fib, guys. I'm going to shock." I press the button on the defibrillator, listening to the familiar siren-like whooping sound of the machine charging to deliver its juice. "Everybody clear," I call loudly, and everyone stops what they're doing and steps back from the stretcher. The patient's muscles contract, tensing his entire body as the electrical current runs through him. Even after years of working codes, that body spasm still gives me the creeps every time.

"Resume CPR," I call as soon as the shock is over, and

everyone jumps back to their spots to continue chest compressions and bagging for another sixty seconds. "There's no change. Give him the amiodarone," I tell Julie, who already has it at the ready and pushes it into his IV.

"I'm shocking again," I tell them after a minute still with no change. The machine whoops and charges again. "Everybody clear." They jump back, and the patient's body tenses again. Corey is always the last to let go, pushing right up to the last second. That's good. He knows his job is the most important.

At this point, I begin to worry. It's been five minutes. The pallor of death is creeping over his skin, a look I know far too well. We're smack dab in the middle of the danger zone now, the time frame when death starts to take hold. After ten minutes, there will be very little chance of getting him back. My heart is beating hard and fast, as if it can make up for the lack of activity in his. *Dammit.* I open my mouth to order more CPR when suddenly the machine beeps, and I look at the screen.

"We've got a sinus rhythm." I hold up my hand to halt CPR. "He's breathing spontaneously. Put him on the vent on assist-control." The respiratory therapist fires up the machine and fiddles with the controls. Relief washes over me like cool water, and I can see the same relief on the faces of my team.

Corey wipes his forehead with the back of his forearm as sweat slides off of him. He's worked hard for this man, and it's paid off.

I turn to Julie, whose face still hasn't quite let go of the worry lines. "Go tell the wife we're stabilizing him. He's on his way out of the woods, but he's not quite out yet. Tell her she did great calling

911 so fast."

"Yes, sir," she says, moving quickly out of the room.

I look at Corey. He's not worn out, but I can see he's winded from exertion and stress. Like a runner recovering from a lap, he has his hands on his hips, and his breaths are coming fast and hard, his chest heaving slightly. I clap him lightly on the shoulder. "You did good."

"Does that mean you're not going to annihilate me?"

"I thought it was chew you up and spit you out."

He smiles. "They said that, too."

"Damn. Does everyone around here think I'm a monster?" I glance at the respiratory therapist, who looks away nervously, and I throw my hands up. "I guess so."

Corey crinkles his nose and laughs, but quietly so as not to get the attention of the family of the man we're trying to stabilize. If families only knew what kind of stuff goes on behind closed doors in a hospital, they'd think people in the medical profession were the most insensitive bunch on the planet. But we need our defense mechanisms, our quirks of survival. It's not easy dancing with death day in and day out.

Julie pokes her head in through the curtain. "The ambulance to County is on its way, Dr. Hardy. Should be here in half an hour."

"Good. Come check his vitals again, and keep a close eye on him."

"Yes, sir," she nods and pumps the blood pressure cuff.

"Where are you sending him?" Corey asks, and I remind myself that he's just learning how we do things around here.

"He's going to the county hospital forty miles north of

Blackwood. We don't have an ICU here. We're what they call an urgent care facility, which means we can admit non-critical patients to our floor, but anyone who is critical is transferred out."

"Wow," he says. "I think in Atlanta they don't send anyone out, except maybe to the Mayo Clinic or Vanderbilt Children's Hospital, in which case they're flown out."

"Oh, it's big news when the helicopter comes here. Half the town shows up to watch. They stand in a huge circle around the front parking lot, which doubles as a make do heli-pad. If it's the middle of the night, some of the ladies even show up in their robes and slippers. It's really pretty insane."

"Do they bring popcorn?"

I cock an eyebrow at him. "You think you're joking, but I wouldn't be surprised if they did."

"How do they even know the copter is coming?"

I shake my head. "Police scanners? Phone calls? I have no idea. That old saying about word traveling fast in a small town is true. You'll learn that lesson soon enough, I'm sure. Everyone knows everyone else's business around here, and sometimes they just make it up."

After we load the patient onto the ambulance and wish him and his wife well, we all retire to the ER where we can finally relax and reflect on what we were able to accomplish. Corey's ambulance partner sits in a chair in the corner, leans back and closes her eyes. Julie takes off her gloves and throws them into the trash can.

"I figured we ought to initiate you right, Corey." I lean casually against the nurse's desk.

"Oh Ben, you arranged all of this just for me?" He covers his mouth with his hand in feigned surprise. "How sweet. I always wanted a surprise cardiac arrest. You really know how to roll out the red carpet."

"Well at least now we know what you're made of."

"And what's the verdict?"

"Hmmm… So far, so good. I think maybe we'll keep you."

"Yes, definitely." Julie giggles and smiles sweetly at Corey, obviously smitten, and I'm struck again by the effortless power he has over women.

"What's your name?" he asks with a smile.

"Julie."

"You did very well tonight, Julie. How long have you been a nurse?" His voice is smooth, his eyes sparkling, and the little half smile playing at his lips is an invitation. He's a smooth operator, that's for sure, and fascinating to watch.

"Two years," she gushes, twisting a finger in her straight brown hair. I think she would drop her panties right now if he told her to. "But I've been a year with Dr. Hardy. He's like the best around, and I'm one of his."

Corey looks quizzically at me, and I shrug. "I'm particular about who I work with, so I hand-pick the nurses on my shift. I had no idea working with me was a bragging point. Now I'm flattered."

"But you don't pay us any attention, and you're terrible with names." She pokes her bottom lip out. The nurses aren't usually this forward with me. Seems Corey has a tendency to lighten the air when he's around. Or maybe it's because I'm hanging around and talking for a change. At any rate, I do know Julie's name, but I enjoy teasing her in my own subtle way.

"I can't be expected to remember everything, Julia."

"Julie," she corrects.

"See? I have far too much knowledge stuffed into this brain to bother with names. If I were to store your name in here, I would have to get rid of something else to make room. What would you have me trade for your name? My drug dosage chart? The protocol for placing a chest tube? The lyrics to the Beatles' *White Album*?"

Julie stares at me wide-eyed, as if she doesn't know if I'm being serious or not.

Corey tips her chin with his index finger. "Lighten up, Julie. He's only joking. And I'll bet he'll remember your name from now on, won't you Doc?" He glances over her head and winks at me.

"Oh, okay" she breathes, blushing from the contact. Unbelievable. He's melted the poor girl with one finger.

Now that I've seen Corey's seduction skills in action, I'm absolutely green with envy. Charisma radiates from his skin, I think. He doesn't even have to try. Women respond to him before he's even said or done anything. Maybe it's just his looks they're responding to. I have to admit the guy is GQ as hell. He makes me want to run to a mirror and check my hair, or go to the gym and lift some weights.

"Wanna get a coffee before I get called out again?" he asks me.

"Sure," I say. Julie looks surprised at my answer. I guess everyone around here knows I don't have friends.

"Sorry, no Starbucks here," I apologize as we make our way down the hall, which is eerily quiet at this time of night. "Getting a coffee in our tiny hospital means going to the cafeteria on day shift, or making it yourself in the coffee pot in the doctor's lounge on night shift."

"Sounds good to me. At least you don't have to pay for it. And I'm sure the doctor's lounge is cushy compared to the ambulance shack we stay in. A desk, a squeaky metal bunk bed, a hot plate, a twenty-inch TV, and a bathroom. That's it. Our coffee pot only makes four cups at the time. Even so, I guess I shouldn't complain. It's still better than the motel."

We enter the doctor's lounge through the swinging door and I discover someone has already made coffee. Occasionally, one of the nurses will sneak in and make a pot if I haven't gotten around to it, and I'm really glad of it tonight.

"I wanted to ask you something," I say cautiously as I pour us each a styrofoam cup of coffee. "Why exactly are you staying at the motel? Is it money?"

He sits in a chair at the table and leans back. "I had to move from Atlanta suddenly, and I didn't have much money saved up. But even if I did have the money, I don't have great credit. Plus it takes a while to find a place, you know. It's not so bad, really. I've stayed in worse."

I get the feeling he regrets saying anything to me about his living arrangements. He's trying to downplay the whole thing, but I can tell it bothers him.

"There's a little girl staying there." I sit across from him, taking a sip of the bitter coffee and grimacing. "I saw her today when I rode by. Do you know anything about her?"

"Yeah, her name's Tyleah. She's two doors down from me. Her mama stays inside all day, no father that I can tell. She comes out and plays on the sidewalk every now and then. I've been worried as hell about her. I told her not to come outside alone anymore, but she still does it, and how can you expect a little kid to stay closed up in a room all day? I leave my door open when she's out just to keep an eye on her, and she knows she can come over any time she needs me. Only problem is I'm about to be sleeping during the day. What do you do about something like that? I told the manager about it, but I don't think he cares as long as he's getting his rent."

I consider for a moment while we both sip our coffee. "I don't know. I think we should contact child services. What do you think? Is the mom really that bad?"

"Yes. I think Child Services sounds like a great idea. In the meantime, I can try to stay awake as much as I can during the day to keep an eye out."

"You're not going to be sleeping there anymore, day or night." I swirl my coffee around the cup, watching his face for a reaction.

"Huh?" He's truly bewildered, has no idea where I'm going with this.

"You're staying with me. I have an enormous house. Four bedrooms, five and a half baths, over five thousand square feet, a pool, a hot tub... Plus a really killer pool house with its own kitchen and bath."

"Good lord," he gasps. He's either impressed or appalled, I'm not sure which.

"You can stay in the pool house until you find a place of your own. It doesn't make sense for you to be living in that miserable dump when I have so much extra space."

"I'm shocked, Ben. I don't know what to say. I feel guilty

accepting your offer… but at the same time it's awfully tempting." He looks lost in thought as he sips his coffee. "Do you really not mind? I don't want to say yes if you have any reservations at all. I know you're not really the communal living type."

"It's fine. Two people is far from being a commune. And besides, I'm not one to put up with anyone's shit. You get on my nerves, I send you back to the motel. Got it?"

He smiles. "Got it. You know, this coffee is really bad."

"Yeah, I think it's burnt."

The lounge door swings open, and we both jump in surprise as Christina gusts in wearing a cream cashmere Burberry coat over a pair of designer pajamas and furry Ugg boots. Even in the wee hours, she's the walking embodiment of couture overkill.

"What the hell?" I jump up from the table and face her while Corey grabs a paper towel and soaks up the coffee he's just spilled on the table. "What are you doing here in the middle of the night?"

"The ambulance service said Corey was still at the hospital, and when I got here the nurse said the two of you had come back here together for coffee." Her normally pale face is flushed from the cold. "I was wondering, you know, if you guys were having a discussion without me."

I laugh, and then it hits me. "You called Corey first? In the middle of the night? That's fucked up, Christina."

At least she has the decency to look embarrassed. "Oh… I just wanted to ask him if you'd said anything to him. If you'd decided."

"Chris…" I run my fingers though my hair and cast an exasperated look in Corey's direction, and he mirrors it right back at me. "You really want this to happen, don't you?"

"Yes," she says. "And you know I can be a handful if I don't get my way, once I've got my heart set on something."

"Obviously," Corey says under his breath.

"Well, I've already put myself out there and sacrificed my pride to ask you guys to do this, so there's no turning back. The least you can do is humor me." Her voice is strained, and for a split second I think she's going to cry. "If I don't go through with it now, I might never have the courage to ask anyone again."

I look at Corey, and his expression is unreadable. I'm feeling more than a little awkward, because I can't exactly speak for both of us, but she's looking to me for an answer.

"Shit." I run my hand through my hair again. This is the most fucked up thing I believe I've ever had to say. "I'm okay with it if he is. As long as we're only pleasuring you, like they did in the video."

We both look at Corey, but his face is still a mask.

"Bring it on," he says lightly and smiles.

"I just love those dimples," Christina says. Then she comes to me and puts her slender arms around my neck. "You've made me very happy, darling. This is a fantasy come true for me. Thank you for being secure enough in your manhood to let me have it."

She seals her mouth against mine, and her tongue darts out to tease my lips apart. I let her in reluctantly. It feels really strange kissing her like this in front of Corey. But then I just agreed to fuck her in front of him, and to watch him fuck her, too, so I guess it's a bit late to be coy.

I push her to arm's length. "I'm not sure about protocol in

this situation. How do we proceed from here?"

She laughs. "It doesn't have to be by the book, Ben. It's sex. Just do what comes naturally."

I bark out a harsh sound that is supposed to be a laugh. "This is your fantasy, not mine. Nothing about this feels natural to me."

"Ben, you're usually so… aggressive. You've always taken charge, and you've done so many amazing things to me in the bedroom. That's one of the things I love about you. In fact, you're the one who gave me the courage to ask for this." She looks away. "I truly thought you'd be more open about it."

"I thought I would be, too," I confess. "I don't know what's wrong with me. You're right, it is a dream come true. Group sex… who hasn't jerked off to that fantasy at least a time or two? But they don't tell you what it's really going to feel like, you know? Nobody does. The porn movies, erotica stories, people who have tried it…. No one mentions the awkwardness of it, do they?"

"Well, I don't feel awkward at all," Christina says. "I just want you both."

"I do," Corey says quietly from the corner. "I feel awkward, Ben. It's not just you." He approaches us slowly, where we still stand facing each other, my hands on her shoulders.

"Really?" The knowledge that he's feeling the same way floods me with relief, as well as an odd sense of camaraderie.

He nods and moves up behind Christina, removes her coat, and tosses it across the nearest chair. Then he reaches slowly around her from behind with those incredibly strong, tanned arms, cupping her breasts through her pajamas. She closes her eyes. Her lips part, and it's plain to see how aroused she is at his touch. He keeps his eyes trained on me, as if he's gauging my reaction.

My cock has been reluctant until now, but seeing his big, dark hands on her, the way he teases her nipples through the silk fabric of her pajamas, brings me up full force just like that.

Corey moves one hand up to her jaw, pulls her head back to expose the pale throat beneath, offering it up to me. "Mark her." His voice is rough with passion, his blue eyes silently commanding.

I close my mouth over the sensitive spot in the hollow just above her collar bone and bite down, feeling a dark passion descend over me, and it's like I'm touching her for the first time. She moans loudly and shivers as I suck the blood to the surface like I haven't done since high school. I feel rather than see that Corey is doing the same to her other shoulder, and it makes my cock a blade of steel knowing that he's doing the same thing I'm doing, that we're partners in this wicked game.

Christina cries out in pain or ecstasy, or maybe both, and she squirms and shakes her head from side to side. I pull back, my full on erection pulling the blood from my brain, and with it my sanity. Corey pulls away, too, and we share a meaningful look. His eyes are hooded and full of need. I have the sudden urge to look at his pants, to see if he's just as wound up as I am, but I won't. And anyway, I don't have to look. I already know from the look on his face that he is.

"Now you're claimed," he half whispers to Christina, who looks like her knees are about to give. He guides her over to the tiny bathroom, turns the light on, and shows her in the mirror, moving her head first to one side, then the other. Oblong blood red stains mar the alabaster perfection of her skin on each side, mine slightly larger and higher than Corey's. "These marks mean we're both going to fuck you. Together. Every time you feel them, see them, or think of them, you'll remember what we're going to do to you."

Her eyes widen and she puts a hand to her throat.

"Now go," he says gruffly. "Don't call us. We'll find you when we're ready."

She nods and leaves the bathroom on unsteady legs, pausing to fumble her coat back on. Neither Corey nor I make a move to help her with it. When she leaves through the swinging door, she doesn't even look back.

As soon as she's gone, Corey clears his throat and drops back into his seat, adjusting his pants. I'm still not looking, but I think I see his eyes flash to my crotch then look away. I move quickly to stand at the coffee maker, hoping he hasn't seen the evidence of my arousal. Now that Christina is gone, my wood is inappropriate. Unfortunately, it doesn't seem to have gotten the memo.

"More coffee?" I squeak.

Damn traitorous vocal cords.

"Yeah, sure." He crosses his arms on the table and rests his head on them while I pour the coffee.

"Are you tired?" I slide his second cup of crappy coffee in front of him, and he raises up to drink it.

"Tired?" He's got a funny little sarcastic smile on his face. I don't know what it means, and I'm afraid to ask. "No, Ben, I'm not tired. I'm pretty fucking far from tired. How about you?"

He leans back in his chair in that languid way he has, legs sprawled to either side of the seat. His blue scrub top stretches tautly across the muscles of his chest, and the sleeves band around his biceps. Hospital issue uniforms are clearly not made for a man of his proportions.

His hand drops to his thigh and rests there, the sudden movement drawing my eye, and I can see from the way his scrub pants fit that he's still very much aroused. He doesn't even bother trying to hide the bulge, which is intimidating enough to make my mouth go dry.

Jesus, is he even wearing underwear?

When I look up, he's staring calmly at me with narrowed eyes, and I know he's caught me looking. It's a straight guy's worst nightmare, and I have to turn and pretend to fiddle with the coffee pot just to escape the awkwardness of the moment.

"Somehow I can't bring myself to be as open about all of this as you are," I say. "You have such an easy going nature, and I... well, I chew people up and spit them out, as they say."

"You haven't chewed me up yet."

"It'll happen. You can't understand what it's like to be unapproachable, when everyone is so intimidated they're walking on eggshells every time you're around. Everything comes easily to you simply because people get a freaking endorphin rush just from looking at you." I pour the rest of my coffee into the sink and drape my stethoscope around my neck. "Hell, all you'd have to do is crook your finger at Christina, and she would leave me. Of course at this point, I don't even think I give much of a shit."

Corey stares at me without moving. His blue eyes are burning a hole through me, and I feel like I've just made the biggest asshole of myself.

"Sorry," I apologize. "I should keep my feelings to myself. I'm better at being a hard ass."

"Endorphin rush from just looking at me, huh?" Corey muses with a smile, as if I haven't just had a meltdown. "So what are you saying, you think I'm hot?"

"Fuck you, Corey," I growl, sticking my middle finger up as I leave the room. Through the swinging door, I can hear him laughing.

4

THE rest of the night is uneventful, so I take the opportunity to cat nap a time or two between bouts of charting and seeing patients in the ER. It's a good thing, because I get the feeling I'm going to need my both my energy and my wits for what's coming.

About a half hour before time to knock off, I make my way to the back of the lot to the old ambulance shack. Through the little window in the front door, I see Corey leaning over the desk and writing something on a piece of paper. A doorway at the back of the room reveals the flicker of the television and part of a metal bunk bed frame. I never realized how much this place needed updating, or how dreary it was, since we doctors don't often have reason to visit the ambulance shack.

I knock lightly and wince as he comes up too quickly and bumps his head on the old fashioned light that hangs above the desk.

"Sorry, I don't have your cell number," I say. "Is your head okay?"

He waves a hand dismissively. "Fine. And I don't own a cell. You could've rung the ambulance phone, though." He gestures toward the old black push button phone, a perfect twin of the one in my on call room.

I shrug and notice he's wadded up whatever he was writing and thrown it in the wastebasket beside the desk. I give it a pointed glance, but I don't want to ask. Probably none of my business.

"I was writing you a note," he says quietly. "To leave at the nurse's desk on my way home."

I frown. "Didn't we agree you would stay at my house from now on?"

"Yeah... I'm not so sure about that. You don't really know me that well. I don't want to cause problems between us, Ben."

"My instincts tell me you're okay. You might count yourself lucky I've even offered to share my place with you. It's not often that I... put myself out there." I wait through a heavy silence, and an embarrassing thought occurs to me. "Oh God, do you just not want to stay with me? Am I putting you on the spot, harassing you into doing something you just don't want to do? You don't know me that well, either."

"No." He shakes his head emphatically. "Absolutely not. I really appreciate your offer. I just... there are things about me that you don't know, that you may not like. I don't want you hating me is all. This is my chance for a fresh start, and I don't want to ruin it."

The pain in his eyes is genuine, and a lump forms in my throat. I don't like to see people in pain.

"Listen..." I move closer to him, resting my hip on the desk.

"I don't like the idea of you in that motel, okay? Can we leave it at that? You can stay in the pool house and pretend I'm not around if you want. I won't get into your business, as long as there's nothing illegal going on or you're not destroying property. I mean, if you're selling drugs out of my backyard, or if I find chloroform and a bag of lime in the closet, we're going to have a problem. Otherwise, everything will be fine."

"Well, I can't very well pretend you're not around if we're going to be sharing your girlfriend, can I?" His smile is back, and I'm relieved.

"Come on, get your car. You can follow me."

He flashes a big, cheesy grin. "I don't drive a car, Ben. How do you feel about really loud motorcycles?"

With his ragged Harley tucked away in my garage, Corey emerges for a tour of my home. We checked him out of the motel on the way over, and the scruffy duffel bag he retrieved from his depressing little room is now slung over his shoulder. I try to imagine how a person can exist with so few belongings.

"Let's start the tour in the main house," I say. "We'll save your new place for last."

We return to the street, because I want to take him through the wrought iron arch and up the front walk. In my opinion, it's the only way to view an Antebellum mansion for the first time.

As we come up the brick walk, he's a bundle of energy,

talking fast and asking questions. "This is really where you live? The whole thing is yours? I've always wondered what one of these old white houses with all the columns would be like on the inside. This is a real antique mansion, isn't it?"

His enthusiasm delights me, makes me laugh. "Yes, it's an Antebellum mansion. Greek Revival style. It belonged to the town banker, and at one time it was the grandest home in town. Might be still, but who am I to say? I'm biased. When I bought it three years ago, it was in pretty bad shape, but I restored it."

"It reminds me of *Gone with the Wind*," he says.

"Well, don't expect any slaves or Southern belles."

"Whoa, " he breathes when we enter the black and white marbled foyer. His mouth unhinges as his eyes follow the curve of the grand wooden staircase all the way up to the original crystal chandelier that hangs from the two-story foyer. The kitchen thrills him with its stainless steel Viking appliances, glazed vanilla cabinets, and leaded glass doors. "This place is totally old fashioned, but so modern at the same time. I love the high ceilings, and those rectangular windows above the doors— "

"Transoms," I interject. "They were very common in houses of this era."

"It's unbelievable. Is that the living room over there? You could have a freaking masquerade ball in there."

" I kept as much of the original feel as I could without sacrificing modern amenities."

"You definitely have amenities, Doc, I'll give you that. Jesus, this place takes my breath away. I've been in a mansion before, but not an old one. Those new ones don't have character like this."

"Come see the master suite. There used to be two smaller bedroom suites downstairs, but I knocked out the walls and combined them into one. I also installed a huge walk-in steam shower with wall jets. I love old things, but I couldn't bring myself to sacrifice comfort for the sake of conservation. The old plumbing was for shit, and I despise claw foot tubs. Some of the folks in town would like to have my head for what I've done to this place, but... It's mine, and I'll do whatever I damn well please."

Corey leaps onto my high four-poster bed and bounces like a kid in a mattress store, which is funny because he looks nothing like a kid. "Nice bed." He sprawls onto his back. "Hell, nice everything. Look at that crown molding. You don't play around when you fix up a house, do you? I could never do something like this. You're like everything I wish I could be."

I continue, purposely ignoring his compliment. "I got the house at a foreclosure auction. If you haven't noticed, the economy is not so great around here. Since hardly anyone else could afford it, I was able to get it cheap. When you pay next to nothing for a house, you can sink some money into it." Explaining how I can afford things is a habit for me after years of hiding my true net worth. "I'll show you the upstairs another time. Three bedrooms and bathrooms up there, and another living area. I rarely even go up there, myself. I want you to see everything eventually, but I'm far too eager to show you the pool and the pool house."

Through the glass doors off the living room, we exit to the pool area, and I flip the outdoor lights and start the automatic pool cover opening. The pool is a narrow rectangle lined with colorful tiles of blues, greens, and yellows. Warm mist rises from the surface as the cover slides back. "The pool was pretty boring before, but now I think it has an old Hollywood flair. I couldn't bear to close it up for the winter."

"I don't think I could possibly be any more impressed with your house, Ben. I feel like I've died and gone to heaven, especially after being in that moldy motel for weeks."

"Save the praise until you see where I'm putting you. Maybe you won't like it."

The pool house is mostly glass across the front, and the golden lights shining from the eaves give it a magical feel in the gray glow of early morning. I unlock the door and flip the light switch, illuminating it from within, and watch as Corey's eyes go as wide as saucers. Of course I've always known he would love it.

"This is like the perfect cottage," he breathes, running his hand over the arm of the white slipcovered sofa. A small glass dining table is tucked into the corner beneath glowing paper lanterns and set with two sparkling place settings of white china and crystal. All of the walls are natural stained wood, broken up only by the glass windows and a few abstract paintings. Corey peeks into the back, where I've added on a small but well-appointed kitchen and bath. "You'll have to drag me screaming back to that motel, Doc. I'm just telling you up front."

I laugh and point to the entertainment system. "Your TV and stereo. Just make sure you turn off the outdoor speakers, unless of course you're having a pool party. Definitely make sure they're off if you're watching porn."

"It's a little cold for that." He laughs. "I mean the party, not the porn."

"Not necessarily. The pool is heated and has a hot tub."

"Of course it does," he sighs.

"I don't want you to think I'm bragging, Corey. I've hardly shown this stuff to anyone before, but… well, I just want you to like it. I'm feeling kind of stupid right about now."

"There's a difference between pride and superiority, Ben. I can't imagine you ever trying to make someone else feel inferior because they have less than you. Honestly, this is the nicest thing anyone has ever done for me. I really mean that. You have a good heart." He presses his hand against my chest right over my beating heart, and I force myself not to squirm away or to let him know that this kind of thing makes me uncomfortable. It seems absurd anyway, considering what we're planning to do with Christina.

"So when are we going to do the deed?" I ask, wondering why I'm deferring to him when she's my girlfriend.

"This afternoon before we go to work. We've got to get this thing out of the way before it drives us both crazy."

"I was under the impression that you were unfazed by it all."

"God, how did you ever get that impression? I'm at least as messed up about it as you. Though I'm sure for different reasons."

"I don't know." I shrug. "Maybe you just know how to play it cool better than I do."

"Dr. Ice doesn't know how to play it cool? Somehow I have a hard time believing that."

I laugh. "Dr. Ice? Did you just make that up, or is that what they call me at work?"

"Do you even work at that hospital? You must go around with blinders and ear plugs. Do you really not know they call you

53

that?"

"I'm there to save lives and help people get well, Corey. I don't pay attention to all that gossip bullshit." I don't tell him how it really makes me feel to know that people talk about me that way, or that on the inside I'm about as far from ice as it gets. Or that I work the late shift because I have trouble sleeping at night after all of the death I've seen.

"You know they all worship you like a god, right?" He cocks his head to the side and bends slightly to catch my eye. "You're their hero."

"Get some sleep," I say quietly, holding down a button on the wall near the door and watching the gauzy white drapes swing across their track to cover the front windows. "Let me know if it's too bright for you to sleep during the day in here. The sofa is a pull-out. Not one of those cheap ones, either, so it should be pretty comfortable. But if you'd rather have a bed, I'll buy you one."

I take my leave before he can say anything else. It's been a long day, and I'd like to draw my blackout shades and lie cool and naked in my bed for a while and zone completely out. As I drift away, wrapped in the cold sheet and seeing nothing in the blackness, I'm thinking that I really hope it's not too bright for Corey in the pool house. Maybe I should have let him sleep inside.

5

COREY is doing push-ups with the drapes open when I get down to the pool house just after three o'clock in the afternoon. When I knock on the door, he startles and jumps up to let me in.

"Couldn't sleep." He's wearing nothing but a pair of ratty dark blue sweat pants, and sweat glistens on his tan skin.

"Was it too bright for you with these white curtains and all the windows?"

"No, no," he assures me. "I'm just a little wound up. It's all good. I haven't been able to get a gym membership yet, so I'm going a little soft." He pats the ripples of his six pack, and I roll my eyes.

"Yeah, I see what you mean. I don't even know how you can stand looking in the mirror with all that flab."

He laughs and grabs the blue hand towel that used to be on the towel bar in the bathroom. "Nothing like a good sweat." He rubs his skin briskly with the towel, giving it a rosy glow. "I've got to shower real quick. Give me five minutes, and I'll be ready to roll."

True to his word, he emerges from the bathroom five minutes later with a blue bath towel slung around his waist. His dark wet hair clings to the sides of his face, and there are water droplets on his skin. If I look at his bare torso much longer, I'm going to start having some serious self-esteem issues. In less than an hour, I'll be performing alongside this freak of nature, and Christina is going to be comparing us. She's told me I have the hottest body of any guy she's ever seen in person, but once she get a look at Corey, I'm sure she'll forget all about me.

While I'm pondering the intimidating perfection of his body, he inches past me and picks up his clothes from where he has them folded on the sofa. I've forgotten he has no bedroom, or more accurately that I'm standing in it, so when he turns his back to me and drops his towel, I nearly choke on my own saliva.

"Sorry, Ben" He looks calmly over his shoulder as he pulls on a pair of gray boxer briefs. "I hope you're not shy."

I try to sound nonchalant. "Nah… I guess I'd better get used to it, anyway. We're about to be naked together at Christina's house, right?"

"That's the plan," he says. "Do you mind if I ask you a nosy question?"

"Go ahead."

"Your place is much nicer, and roomier. And you've got that amazing walk-in shower in your room, which I have to admit I'd love to take a spin in. So why didn't you invite Chris over here for our little love party?"

"*Love party…*" I can't help laughing at his choice of words. "I don't know, I guess I'm just kind of protective of my space."

"I'm here in your space." He pulls on his green scrub pants and ties the string.

"Um, that's different. You're not a woman."

He abruptly stops what he's doing and stares at me with an confused expression. "What exactly do you mean by that?"

"Women have certain expectations, especially if they think you have money or that you're what some would consider a good catch. You know what I mean? I'm afraid that if I invite one over here, within a week she'll have her little pink toothbrush in my bathroom, then her millions of shoes in my closet, then her diet food in my fridge, then she'll want to redecorate in pastels and florals... Next thing you know I'll be married."

"Wow," he breathes, slipping his scrub shirt over his wet head. "When you put it that way, it sounds terrifying. So I guess I can assume you don't want to get married?"

"Oh, I do..." We both laugh at my ironic choice of words. "I mean, in theory I'd like to get married one day. I guess I just haven't met the right woman yet. But I do like the idea of meeting a soul mate, and having a family, and not growing old alone."

"Hmmm..." Corey muses, but he doesn't speak.

"Have I ruined your dreams with my bleak take on relationships?"

"No, Doc. My dreams are still very much intact. But when I first met you and Christina, I figured you were about to move in together or something. That's just the first impression I got from the way she was talking. You might want to say something to her, because I think she's got the wrong idea."

"I doubt that. I've never—"

"She called you her fiancé."

"Oh. That's news to me. I had never even spent the night at Christina's until you were there with us the other night, and that was only because we'd been drinking. If I could have driven, I would have come home."

"And look at me," he says with a grin. "I've already slept at her house, your pool house, a motel, and some biker chick's trailer. I'm just a regular vagabond, huh?"

"Sounds pretty cool to me, actually. Sometimes I think I've gotten too settled. I don't know how my mother would feel about that. She was always sort of carefree and loving. I know she wouldn't like it that I spend so much time alone."

"Well, now you can tell her you have a roommate of sorts. So you're not alone."

I give a little wistful smile, realizing there's no way I could tell my mother such a thing. Or anything ever again, for that matter. "She's gone," I tell him. "Died when I was in college, so I just have to try to imagine what she might think, you know?"

"Oh, I'm so sorry, man. I didn't know."

"No way you could have known."

The atmosphere has turned a bit gloomier than I'd planned. I need to liven things up, but I don't know how. Before I can come up with anything, Corey has decided to take gloomy all the way to desolate.

"My grandmother is dead, too. She raised me, but she passed away when I was fifteen. Left me on my own, so I had to live on the streets."

Shit, I thought my story was sad, but he's just one-upped me. Not in competitive way, of course. Neither of us wants to be the victor in this conversation.

"I'm sorry to hear that, Corey. I guess we've both lost our anchors."

"Let's get going." His tone changes abruptly, and he claps his hands together and heads for the door. "We've got a love party to get to."

He's more eager to do this thing than I am, and I can't really blame him. He's got nothing at stake. Any guy would probably jump at the chance he's been given, to be the new guy in town and have free, no-strings pussy dropped right into his lap. But it's different from my point of view, because I'm not a stranger. Even though Christina and I aren't exactly serious, and I'm seriously considering breaking up with her, I can't help but feel that this is a little like cheating. Maybe a lot like cheating.

Christina is waiting for us in nothing but the expensive red baby doll nightie I bought her and the red heels from the Christmas party. Ever since I told her the shoes give me an instant erection, she wears them all the time. Of course I'm not complaining. Truth be known, I couldn't give two shits about the nightie. I bought it to compliment the shoes, to encourage her to wear them when I'm visiting.

The gown is sheer lace, and it leaves nothing to the

imagination. Since this is the first time Corey is seeing her body, I can't help but try to read his reaction, but he masks his feelings well.

"Hi," she says, looking through her lashes from one to the other us and back again, her eyes dancing with mischief. She wraps her arms around my neck before I even get through the door and presses her soft lips against mine.

I lick her lips with the tip of my tongue. "Mmmm… cherry lip gloss."

"Do you approve?" she asks.

"I don't know, let me get a better taste." I suck her bottom lip into my mouth and worry it with my tongue and teeth, smacking my lips as I pull away. "It'll do."

Up to this point, I've been more than a little apprehensive, but she's doing a good job of driving any negative thoughts from my head. I could definitely get used to this style of greeting.

I skim my hand over her lace-clad backside and squeeze. It's round and feminine, and my cock stirs behind my scrub pants. I'm already picturing her on her knees, ass in the air, taking every inch of my cock.

When she breaks the kiss, she's breathing hard, her lips pink and swollen. I'm surprised to discover I've got her ass cheek in a punishing grip, and I instantly let go. Guess I'm a little edgy.

From beside me, Corey watches with a mixture of fascination and amusement. "Why don't you two get a room?"

"Hi, Corey," she whispers, and suddenly she's shy. He looks at her like a tiger sizing up his meal, and I'm mystified by my own reaction to it. Somehow, I find it incredibly sexy.

"Aren't you going to invite us in?" he asks, his tone and

expression so dark I barely recognize him as the same guy I've been hanging out with for the last forty-eight hours.

"Oh, sorry," she apologizes with a breathy laugh and steps aside and to let us in.

Candles flicker on every flat surface in the room, and she's got the place scented differently, with an exotic aroma that reminds me of Morocco.

I take a deep, calming breath. "Smells great, Chris. The candles are a nice touch."

"I'm glad you like it. I was worried it would be too over the top, you know?"

Corey pushes roughly past us and sits on the sofa, his sprawl taking up almost half of it. "I could really use some sweet tea, Christina."

"Oh, I'm being a poor hostess, aren't I?" she asks with a coy twist of her hips. "Unfortunately, I haven't poured the tea up yet. I can do it if you really want, but it'll take a few minutes."

"We've got time," he says without even looking our way. He grabs the remote and flips the TV on to a rerun of *Criminal Minds,* kicking back like he's in a man cave rather than the home of the woman we're about to sleep with.

Christina frowns, and I offer an apologetic smile. But that doesn't stop me from agreeing with him. "Uh... tea would be good."

I join Corey on the sofa while Christina bustles off to pour up the tea in her lingerie. I assume from his attitude that he's asserting his dominance over her, which is fine. I can play that role, too. Seems better than letting her orchestrate everything. Besides, he's already proved himself to be quite the pickup artist, so who am I to question his methods?

"I love this show," he says. "Those BAU people are geniuses the way they figure that shit out."

"Or at least the writers are geniuses. I wonder if they work the plot backwards. Seems like it would be easier to write a mystery if you figure out the ending first and then fill in the clues."

Corey stares at me for a moment and then grins. "Thanks, Ben. You just ruined the show for me."

We fall into an easy silence as we watch the investigative team work their magic. I guess we can both relate to being part of a team that solves life-and-death problems for a living.

During the first commercial break, Corey surprises me by taking off his shirt. "You don't think she'll mind if I get comfortable, do you?" The question is rhetorical now that he's naked from the waist up.

"Um… No, I suppose that's what we're here for. She was already comfortable when she met us at the door."

"Yeah, she looks good, man. That outfit is hot. And the tits on her… You scored big time there, my friend. But I'm not surprised. You could have anybody you want."

I feel my face turning red. "Thanks, but—"

"Take your clothes off, Ben." It's that same dark, authoritative tone he used with Christina.

He pulls off his shoes and socks, stands up and unties his scrub pants, and lets them drop to the floor before sitting back down. Thankfully, he leaves his boxer briefs on. My posture stiffens as I make a conscious effort not to look in his direction. I can't possibly concentrate on what's happening on the television now with him sitting beside me in his underwear.

When I haven't moved in over a minute, he prods me. "Come on, man. You've seen me in all my glory already. It's only fair."

I take off my shoes and socks first, then pull my shirt over my head. Corey lets out a low catcall that makes me feel self-conscious, but he's smiling playfully, and I know he's just trying to loosen me up. "Nice bod, Doc. Let's see the rest of it. Don't be shy."

I never would have imagined I could feel so naked with pants on, but sitting beside Corey, who reeks of testosterone and male beauty, I feel laid bare in every way. What am I doing? I'm taking off my clothes at the behest of a guy. There's not even a woman in sight at the moment, and suddenly I realize I'm already semi-hard, and he's going to see. *Shit.*

"Do you need help?" he asks ominously, and I jump up.

"Hell, no." I pull my pants down quickly like it doesn't bother me in the least. "But you need to lay off the gym, Corey, so an average guy has a chance to compete."

I'm standing before him in nothing but a pair of boxer briefs, with an obvious quarter-mast erection in them. *Is that okay?* His eyes sweep my body, blatantly appraising me. My insides have gone hot and tingly, and I want to shrivel up and skulk away to somewhere dark and safe, away from his shrewd blue eyes.

"Nothing average about you, Dr. Hardy. You're hot as fuck."

If I didn't feel awkward before, I do now. But there's also a little pride mixed in there. Getting a compliment from a guy like Corey... *What the hell am I even thinking?* It is dawning on me belatedly that two heterosexual males should probably not be naked in the same room when sex is involved. Some wires are bound to get crossed somewhere, no pun intended.

Just as I'm considering the possibility of backing out, Christina shows up with a tray of iced tea, and I've never been more pleased to see her. With her pale skin and white blond hair that curls around her shoulders, she is the picture of feminine glamour. I need to get my dick buried deep inside her. Right now.

"Forget the tea, Chris." I slide my boxer briefs off and sit down on the sofa. "Get on your knees."

I grasp my cock in one hand and pat my inner thigh with the other. She and Corey both look shocked as hell at the sudden change in my demeanor, but she drops in front of me, no questions asked. She runs her red painted nails up and down my thighs, eying my growing erection, and licks her lips unconsciously.

When she bends to take my cock into her mouth, her hair tickles the tops of my thighs. I grunt in response and raise up slightly to push deeper into her warm mouth. She wraps her fingers low on the shaft and moves them gently up and down along with her lips. Corey makes a strangled sound in the back of his throat, and when I look over at him, he catches my eye. He smiles wickedly and reaches down to palm his own erection through the fabric of his boxers.

"Our guest is feeling a bit left out, honey," I tell Christina. "Reach a hand over there and make him feel welcome."

Before her hand can even make it to him, he's shucked his shorts and leaned back into a reclined position. His long, thick cock springs straight up and comes to rest against his belly. Enormous and ever so slightly curved, it lies in wait, putting me in mind of an anaconda. At the sight of it, my dick jumps so hard in Christina's hand that she takes her mouth off of it and stares up at me with a look of naked horror. I just pray Corey didn't notice.

"Keep going," I tell her, and I have to clear my throat to get the squeak out of it.

I groan when she wraps her lips back around my cock and sucks, and she tentatively reaches over and takes Corey's monster dick in her hand and starts to move it up and down the shaft. After a moment he covers her hand with his own, brazenly guiding her movements as he watches what she's doing to me, and he might as well be pleasuring himself for all the control she has.

He knows what the beast likes.

I have to contain the sudden urge to laugh hysterically at my increasingly inappropriate thoughts. This was not a good idea. I've stepped right off into something I am not equipped to handle. *Damn you, Christina.* But I can't blame her. I agreed to this insane shit, and here we are. End of story. Might as well make the best of it.

That's when it occurs to me that I'm watching what she doing to him, and he's watching what she's doing to me, and I don't know if that's normal. Are we supposed to be looking at the other guy's junk, or our own, or does it even matter?

Fuck, fuck, fuck, fuck. Think, Ben. What did they do on the movie?

I can't remember the movie. All I know is what's going on here.

"That's enough," I tell Christina. "Stand up and take your clothes off."

She does, pulling the negligee slowly down her shoulders, letting it puddle onto the floor along with her panties. She kicks them away and bends to remove her shoes.

"Leave the shoes on, and sit on the couch between us."

She sinks into the leather seat, and we descend on her as one. I attack her mouth with mine, squeezing her breast mercilessly until she cries out. Corey follows my lead, slipping a hand between her legs and rubbing gently, making her squirm. We don't even give her time to breathe. If she wants to be taken by two men, she's about to get her money's worth.

"She's wet as hell," Corey announces, palming her clit. I watch him push his middle finger up inside her as far as it will go. "Soaking wet. She definitely wants us."

I dip my tongue into her mouth, find hers, and we suck at each other ravenously. I don't know when our kisses have ever been so unbridled, and she sighs and moans and gasps so much I know it won't take her long to climax today. She's getting more charged up by the second, liking the roughness, rocking shamelessly on Corey's finger as I tongue fuck her mouth.

"Are you ready, Corey?" I pull away from her and wait for his call.

He nods. "Let's double tap this bitch."

Christina tenses. She's not used to being talked about like that, but I like it. A lot. His words give me a hard ache in my groin. The kind that usually makes me have to touch myself. As far as I'm concerned, Corey and I are the baddest motherfuckers in the world right now. We're a team, and Christina is an object to use however we like.

I want to bind her, but the wrist cuffs are in a hat box under her bed. No time for that. I stand up and flip her around to where she's lying on her stomach, half on and half off the sofa. Grabbing her panties off the floor, I use them as a makeshift restraint to tie her hands behind her back. She cries out, and I run my finger between the fabric and her skin to make sure it's not hurting her or cutting off circulation. Then I stand her up in front of Corey like a slave on the auction block. There's heat in his gaze as her admires her and shoots me a look of undisguised approval.

"Her safe word is *velvet*, Corey. If she says it, we immediately stop what we're doing."

"Got it," he says. I push Christina down onto her knees in front of him, and the smile on his face is nothing like nice.

She looks apprehensive, almost fearful, but I think she's just edgy with desire and the unknown. Anyway, she has her safe word, and she knows how to use it, though she's never had to before.

"Fuck her mouth," I tell him. "I want to see how much of that fat cock she can take."

He immediately squeezes his dick and guides it into her mouth. She has to stretch her lips wider than usual, and then he's stuffed it in about half way. She whimpers around it, her breathing labored through her nose. He's really taxing her, and I have to admit I'm getting off on it.

"Give her more," I coax, and he pushes harder, meeting resistance against the back of her throat and triggering her gag reflex. Her breathing stops for a few seconds. He backs off slightly, unblocking her airway, and her breathing starts noisily back up.

Now that he's found her limit, he starts to move slowly in and out, working against the suction she's trying to apply. Normally, she gives a pretty mean blow job, but I can see this is difficult for her.

I'm standing behind her, facing him. He smiles at me while he does my girl's mouth, and I smile back. "Feel good?" I ask.

"Oh, yeah. But I know something that will feel even better." I dare not ask, for fear of what he might come up with.

"Come up here, darlin'," he tells Christina, reclining against the back of the couch and pulling her along with him. She's shaky and unbalanced with her hands bound behind her back, and she's got mascara rivulets down her cheeks. If she had any idea how used she looks, she would die of shame, but I think it's sexy.

Corey grabs a condom off the end table, tosses it to me, and I put it on. Then he grabs another, rips it open, and rolls it onto himself. He's got Christina straddling him, and he lifts her up, poising her petite body over the tip of his ungodly erection. "Do you mind, Ben? I don't want to be impolite." He leans sideways to look around her shoulder at me, waiting for my response.

"Be my guest." Truth is, I'm dying to see it.

He looks at her face for a long moment, and when she shows no sign of protest, he pushes her down onto his cock. She throws her head back and bites her bottom lip hard as he slowly sheaths himself in her all the way to the hilt. When she's all the way on, he starts rolling his hips, his expression dark and intense. Now she starts to moan, and I can only imagine what that huge member feels like inside her, stretching her.

"No *velvet?*" He smiles knowingly, and she shakes her head. "What a little trooper."

I can tell she's laboring on it, though. Her breathing is shallow, and tiny droplets of perspiration are glistening on her upper lip.

He leans around her again and beckons me to come and stand close behind her. "Put your foot here." He indicates the seat beside him, and I do as he directs. "Now put your knee here." I position my knee on the sofa on his other side. He pulls Christina in close to him so that I can lean over her back and place my hands on the back of the sofa on either side of his body, balancing myself and trapping her between my arms. You can't be a man and not see where he's going with this, and believe me, I know how to take it from here.

"Lube?" I ask, and he grabs it off the end table. I reach for it, but instead of handing it to me, he flips the top and leans around Christina, who is subtly gyrating against him. He turns the bottle upside down and drizzles it slowly and deliberately onto the head of my dick. I get harder just watching the liquid glisten and roll down the sides in twisting rivulets. I never knew getting lubed could be so erotic.

"Fuck," I groan, before I realize I'm even speaking, and I wish like hell I could call back the word. Corey's expression goes dark with perverse amusement, and Christina wrenches around to try to see what's going on. From my reaction, I can only imagine what she thinks he's doing to me behind her back. I make a mental note to control myself better, which I suspect I'm about to lose all ability to do. Well, at least I was able to amuse Corey, who now probably thinks I'm easily aroused.

"Turn around." I bark the order at Christina, annoyance encroaching on my desire. I should make her pay for the suspicion in her eyes when she just looked at me. She's the one who started this shit, after all.

"Is it going to hurt a lot?" She's asking two guys who have no clue, and I'm wondering why she waited until now to be concerned about pain.

"Let me pull out first," Corey suggests. "It's easier to get in the… uh… back door first." He pulls out, being careful to control where his member goes, holding it close to his own body, and I appreciate the consideration.

"I thought you'd never done this." I try to keep the accusation out of my voice, but it's there anyway.

He cocks his head to the side and smirks. "I did some reading online in the ambulance shack. I figured one of us ought to be prepared."

"Oh… Well, let's figure this out. It can't be too terribly difficult, can it? It's not ACLS or brain surgery."

Christina whines. "Could we cut the small talk, guys? This is so unsexy for me."

I slap her hard on the ass, and she cries out. I know how to get her focused.

Christina and I have done anal enough times that I know how to work into her. First I gather some lube onto my fingers and work them in slowly, so as not to tear her or make her muscles tighten more. Then I use the broad head of my dick. She cries out and then sucks in a sharp breath as I press slowly but firmly against the tight ring of muscle. She's more nervous than usual, so it's not easy. "Relax," I tell her. "Breathe out. You know how to do this."

She blows out a long breath, and then suddenly I'm in. I feel her body shudder, and I keep still for a moment to let her body stretch around me. I know my cock is big, and I always try to be mindful of a woman's comfort.

"Can I come in now?" Corey asks. "It's getting cold and lonely out here."

"Please," Christina whispers. "I can't wait to have you both inside me."

As he pushes in, the squeeze on my dick is magnified unbelievably. It feels so good I have to bite back a groan. Then I feel the distinct ridged shape of Corey's dick through the vaginal wall, and my eyes widen. I'm a doctor, but I have to admit I didn't see this coming. I glance over Christina's shoulder at Corey's perfectly angelic face.

"Surprise," he whispers, and raises his eyebrows just enough to let me know that he knows what I'm thinking.

He moves inside her, against me, and I am instantly lost. His movements are small, and mine are more pronounced. I can't help it. The feeling of tightness is overwhelming, and I have no idea how Christina is possibly handling this load. She drops her head onto Corey's chest. I can't see her face, but she is shuddering, her movements erratic, like she's experiencing sensory overload.

I try to focus on her pleasure, reminding myself that's why we're here, but it proves to be very difficult. The combination of Corey's height and her petite frame being crumpled against him puts me and him looking directly and awkwardly at each other. I try in vain to pull her body up between us, but she is limp and shaky, unable to control herself. I don't think any of us envisioned things going down quite like this. We don't look anything like porn. In fact, I'm sure if this *was* a porn, we'd be fired from the set for underacting. Christina is spineless, I'm trying not to make eye contact with Corey, and the cold blue intensity of his eyes is the only indication he's feeling anything at all. Thank goodness no one suggested filming this fiasco.

Corey is apparently also aware of the flagging of our scene, and I'm grateful when he takes control. "I'm going to start fucking her, Ben, but not hard. We need to stagger our movements. When I pull out, you go in, okay? This is going to be very intense for her."

I nod, feeling grounded again, but when he pulls out and I feel his hard length rub against me, I am undone. I concentrate on executing the move he's described, and soon we have a piston thing going on. In, out, in, out... Our rhythm steadies and intensifies, and that's when the magic happens. Christina stirs to action and begins to work with us, adjusting her bottom to give me perfect access. She's mewling and panting now, holding herself up off of Corey with one hand and dropping the other between her legs to rub her clit. I bury my face in her soft hair, inhaling the sweet honeysuckle scent of her shampoo. Her muscles quiver around me, and Corey's cock swells even bigger and harder, filling her up and up, and now I'm being gripped and massaged with a rippling ferocity that makes my dick feel like it's going to explode.

Christina's sounds become more desperate, more animal, and I know her climax is here. I've been with her enough to sense it coming, and I want Corey to know it, too. If we can pull off a simultaneous three-way orgasm our first time, that would be the most awesome trick ever.

While Christina shudders and moans her way to orgasm, I move my hand from the back of the sofa and wrap it around the back of Corey's neck, grabbing on and anchoring myself, squeezing hard to signal him of our impending climaxes. When I touch him, my fingers sliding across his warm skin and into his hair, our gazes lock and he intensifies his movements down below without messing up the driving rhythm we've got going. I feel the friction of his cock against mine, the frenzied twists and pulses of Christina's hot flesh around throbbing around us, encasing us, squeezing us both to climax. I have literally never been this turned on before. Never wanted an orgasm as much as I want this one.

Just as Christina starts the little rhythmic moan that signifies her climax, I feel Corey's cock swell up and jerk, and it sends me careening over the edge with them. All three of us tense and buck against each other for a long moment. I can't possibly pull away now. Our bodies are as one, bound together by our melded sex organs, driven by the undeniable instinct to mate.

There are sounds, words, exclamations, some of them even coming from me. But in my present state of exultation, I may as well be in a noisy airport in Moscow for all I'm understanding.

As the climax subsides, I feel myself sinking, deflating, becoming aware of my surroundings. I sense the other two stirring back to the present, as well. We have to extricate ourselves from each other, and it's almost painful, as if I'm leaving something behind. Like something has broken open inside me, and a profound melancholy is seeping in and hollowing me out. I don't know what it means, but I have the distinct feeling it's going to get worse, and there's not a damn thing I can do but hang on for the ride.

6

WORK is the last place I want to be right now. After leaving Christina lounging peacefully on her bed in a filmy bathrobe, I drop Corey at the ambulance shack and check in with the ER nurses. Julie gives me a funny look when she sees me.

"Is everything okay, Dr. Hardy?"

"Fine, fine." I dismiss her with a slight wave of my hand, wondering how different I must look to her after the afternoon's activities. I certainly feel different.

"I can help field calls and stuff for you tonight, if you like. Maybe help out a little more than usual?"

"Julie, are you asking me for more responsibility? I'm impressed." I'm only teasing her, of course.

She smiles. "I just want to be here for you is all. Isn't that what you trained me for?"

"Yes, and I appreciate your dedication." When I touch her on the arm, her smile brightens and she drops her lashes. I'm beginning to think she likes me. Or maybe I'm just shooting off a boatload of post-threesome pheromones that she can't resist.

"I'll be on the floor if you need me." I take my leave before she can press me for more conversation.

I check my patients on the floor and do my charting, hoping the activities will occupy my mind enough to drive out the demons that are frolicking in there, but no such luck. Concentration is not something I'm able to pull off right now.

I've made a mistake.

Something is different in me now, and I don't like it. There's an edge to my thoughts and feelings that I can't escape. The thing today with Christina and Corey has now become a part of my history, a piece of who I am from here on out, and the permanence of that fact is disturbing on a level I don't care to fathom right now.

Once I finish doing my half-assed rounds, I try to come up with an excuse to go out to the ambulance shack. Any legitimate reason will do. After brainstorming and coming up with nothing, I go anyway.

Fuck it.

The ambulance is there, and so are Corey and his partner. When she lets me into the gloomy back room, I spot him in the shadows of the bottom bunk, laid back watching TV.

"Busy night, huh?" I ask him.

"Ben…" He jumps to a sitting position and bumps his head on the metal bed frame. "Uh, I mean Dr. Hardy. What's up?"

"Nothing." I shrug. "I'm just bored as hell. Not much going on over there, either. But next time maybe I should call. If I keep surprising you, you're going to end up with a concussion."

He puts a hand to his head and smiles. "I'll live. Denise, have you officially met Dr. Hardy?"

Denise shakes her head. "Been working night shift with him for months, but we ain't never spoke a handful of words to each other as I'm aware."

She must be right, because I had no idea she was so country. I like her instantly. Local country folks, especially the old-timers, have a certain way of expressing themselves that leaves no doubt as to what they mean. An endearing quality if you're on their good side, otherwise not so endearing.

"Nice to finally meet you, Denise." I extend my hand, and she gives me a suspicious look before shaking it.

"Well, I'll be damned. A doctor in the ambulance shack." She laughs, and from the wet sound of it I know she smokes and that she probably has stage two COPD. I also know from experience that she probably won't acknowledge it for a while yet, and by then it might be too late. "What brings you to our humble neck of the woods, Dr. Hardy? You slumming it tonight?"

This is where I'm supposed to insert my great and logical excuse for coming here, but since I never came up with one, I stare at Denise like a complete moron, saying nothing.

Corey stands and walks over to us. "I'm renting Dr. Hardy's pool house, Denise. We need to discuss the terms. You know, business stuff."

"Ohhh," Denise says, her face easing. "That's nice, Corey. I'm so glad you're finally getting out of that old motel. It's a bad lot around there. Drug dealers, prostitutes, meth heads, you name it.

Honey, you know if I had the room, you'd be staying with me no questions asked." She looks pointedly at me. "Corey is very special to me. He's had enough misery. He don't need nobody making life hard for him, you know?"

I have to wonder what the heck she means by that when I'm just trying to help the guy. "Pardon my prying, but didn't you two just meet a few days ago?"

She laughs her crackling wet laugh again. "I could ask you the same, as buddy-buddy as you two are. But no. For your information we did not just meet. I'm Corey's aunt. I helped him get the job here." There's pride in her voice, as well as a healthy dose of defensiveness.

Corey moves closer to her side. "Denise was the only family I had, or at least claimed, after my grandmother died. But we didn't know each other all that well, so I ended up on the streets."

She wraps a protective hand around his arm and her eyes well up with unshed tears. "Corey, if I had known you had nowhere to go, I would have done more. If I could have, I'd have done more. You know that, baby."

"It's okay, Aunt Denise. No need to feel bad about it. I didn't want anyone to know."

"Told me he was going to live with his mother." She appeals to me with shrill voice and animated gestures. "She and I hadn't spoken in years, because we didn't get along at all. You have to understand, I had no way of knowing he was lying."

Corey laughs and puts a hand on her arm. "You came through when it mattered. Thanks to you, I had a job lined up before I even graduated." He turns to me. "I used to live on the streets in

77

Atlanta. There's a pretty serious homeless underground there, you know. Almost feels like you're living somewhere, especially if you're doing drugs." He trails off, as if he's lost in thought and has totally forgotten where he is. In his mind, he's probably back on the streets. "I haven't been homeless in a while, but my living conditions were… Well, let's just say they were less than desirable. I had to get out, so I borrowed five grand from Aunt Denise six months ago and took an online EMT course. Then I flew to Idaho for a five-day EMT boot camp. I didn't even sit for the test until the day before my training started here at the hospital."

Denise moves a stray lock of dark hair from Corey's forehead with her finger. "When he decided he was going to become an EMT, he planned everything down to the second and stuck to it. I'm so proud of him, and I don't want him to ever be in a bad situation again. I've been on him about getting somewhere better than that motel. I can't help him. I gave him almost all of my savings and that old Harley his uncle had out in the shed. He promised me he'd find a place as soon as he got his first paycheck. Looks like he found one sooner than expected, thanks to you."

"Yeah, Doc, I don't get paid for another two weeks. If you can wait till then for rent…"

"Corey, I haven't even mentioned rent."

"I know," he says. "And I haven't asked how much. I'm trusting you wouldn't frisk an underpaid EMT." He flashes an obviously fake exaggerated smile, and I can't help but laugh at him.

"Hmmm…" I pretend to think. "How does six thousand a month sound to you?"

The smile drops from his face, and for a second he looks

genuinely horrified.

I put my hands on my hips. "If I had expected you to pay rent, we would have agreed on an amount up front. That's typically how real estate deals are done. I don't need a renter. I'm trying to help you save your money to afford a place of your own. Hell, if you save a thousand dollars a week, you could buy a small house after a year, and a pretty darn nice house after two. Fix your credit during that time, and you can finance your dream house with a hefty down payment. This ain't Atlanta. Real estate is dirt cheap around these parts."

"A thousand a week?" Corey laughs. "Ben, I think you're spoiled on your doctor's salary. I don't even bring home a thousand dollars a week after taxes. But I do appreciate the opportunity you're giving me, very much. I keep wondering if I'm going to wake up any minute in my motel bed and realize this was all a dream."

Denise starts cackling and breaks into a rattling cough. "You guys are quite the pair. A doctor with a heart of gold, and a derelict-turned-EMT. Y'all would make a great book."

"You think?" Corey asks, throwing an arm casually across my shoulders.

"I'd read it," she says. "But then I read romance novels like they're going out of style, especially when I'm stuck in this hell hole with nothing to do." She gestures to the corner beside the bunk bed, where a huge pile of paperback novels looks ready to topple at any second.

Corey's arm across my shoulders is uncomfortably heavy. I use the books as an excuse to shrug out from under it, walking over to get a closer look, as if I give a damn about romance novels. When I return, I can't seem to look him in the eye, so I direct my focus onto his aunt. "Nice meeting you, Denise. I'd better get back before someone misses me."

Corey retreats to his spot on the bed, grabs the remote and starts flipping channels. "See ya," he mumbles.

"Alright." I wave awkwardly. "If I'm not here when you get ready to leave in the morning, just come wait in the doctor's lounge, okay?"

"Oh, the doctor's lounge." Denise wags her eyebrows. "Moving up in the world, ain't ya Corey?"

He grabs one of the novels and throws it at her, and I get out quickly before I'm tempted to say longer. It's much more entertaining over here than in the hospital.

After an eternity, seven a.m. finally rolls around. It's fifteen minutes until the end of the shift, and I'm inside the big glass-encased nurses' station charting a couple of patients. I'm pissed because I fell asleep in the on-call room for about an hour when I should have been finishing up my shift. Now I'm tucked into my usual corner at the charting desk, scrambling to get out on time. Two nurses stand at the front counter keeping watch over our three hospital hallways, which are all visible through the glass on the front and sides of the station.

"Oh lord have mercy," one of the nurses says in an excited voice. "Look coming here. That's the new guy I was telling you about, Fran. The one who was at the Christmas party."

I don't usually listen to their annoying chatter, but that comment catches my attention. I don't even have to look up to know who they're talking about. Corey seems to have turned our small town hospital on its head.

"Jesus, Tabitha. I believe that is the best looking thing I've ever seen in my life. I think I just had a—" Fran shuts up when she realizes I'm still here.

For some reason, it really irritates the shit out of me that they're talking about him that way. I hate jealousy, but I can't deny I'm feeling it right now. I guess it's a natural reaction, since I've always been the top dog around here, and now I'm being nosed out by the new guy. But it's even more than that, because he's my friend, and I have the unsettling impression that he's being exploited.

Why should that even bother me?

Corey saunters up to the door of the nurses' station, grabbing the top of the doorway easily with both hands and leaning in like he owns the place. Everything he does is so effortless, so laid back, those sharp blue eyes the only indication of the intensity beneath the cool facade.

"Hi, ladies." From his mouth, the simple greeting sounds like flirting. In fact, most everything that Corey does or says is like flirting. He's a walking flirt factory.

"Hey." The skinny brunette nurse holds a hand for him to shake. "I'm Fran, and this is Tabitha."

Tabitha, a buxom redhead with freckles, takes her turn to shake his hand.

"Nice meeting both of you," Corey says. "Have either of you

seen Dr. Hardy around? He was supposed to meet me in the ambulance shack or the doctor's lounge, and I can't seem to find him."

Tabitha hooks a thumb in my direction. "He's charting around the corner there. Come in and make yourself at home."

"Anytime," Fran adds suggestively, and Tabitha jams an elbow into her side.

Corey spots me and smiles. "There you are. I've been looking all over for you." He comes to sit beside me, and I find myself feeling a little agitated that he didn't wait in the doctor's lounge like I asked.

"I'll be ready in about two seconds. This is my last patient."

"No problem, Doc." He kicks back on his stool, hanging onto the edge of the desk for balance. "I was beginning to think you'd forgotten about me."

I fix him with a stern look. "How could I forget about you with all these goddamn nurses drooling over you like dogs in heat? Any minute, I'm expecting them to start backing their asses up on you and whining."

Corey bursts out laughing. "I think somebody's jealous..." He lets front legs of his stool back down and grabs that absurdly ticklish spot just above my knee, clamping down hard with his fingertips in a move my mom always called a *nervous breakdown*. I drop my pen and instinctively struggle against him, trying in vain to push his hand away, but he's too damn strong. It takes a total of about ten seconds for both of our stools to topple, spilling us onto the floor. Corey narrowly manages to keep his footing, but I end up flat on my ass with a hard thud, and I can attest to the fact that the commercial grade carpet in this place does nothing to cushion a fall.

Corey quickly pulls me to my feet, and I clutch desperately at his scrub top, trying to regain my balance. For the second time since we met, we're both laughing so hard we can't even stand up straight.

"What the fuck just happened?" I howl through peals of laughter.

Then it occurs to me that we're not alone. Fran and Tabitha are standing on the other side of the charting table staring at us with their mouths hanging open. When we make eye contact with the two of them, we stifle our laughter and attempt to look respectable again. It's difficult to straighten up with the belly cramp I've got from laughing so hard.

"Sorry, girls," I say. "I lost my balance."

Corey snorts and nearly loses it again. "Ben and I have been bad boys, acting up at your nurses' station. I think I got a scratch on my hand. Can one of you nurses look at it? Maybe put a band-aid on it?"

He leans his big body across the desk and holds his hand out toward them, looking adorable and contrite. They both scramble to have a look. Fran takes his hand in both of hers. "Where is it, hon?"

"Right… there." He points to a barely visible spot on the top of his hand.

"Get a band-aid, Tab," she tells her friend, who hustles to the closet and returns promptly with a box of band-aids with pictures of dinosaurs on them.

"Really?" I roll my eyes, and Corey looks over his shoulder and winks at me.

Tabitha shoots me a withering look as she unwraps the bandage and smooths it onto his hand. "Don't be insensitive, Dr.

83

Hardy. Do you have a boo-boo? I can bandage yours, too."

"I may have one on my ass. I don't suppose you'd like to put a band-aid there."

She gasps, and for a moment I think she's considering it until Corey bursts out laughing again. "He's only teasing you, Tabitha. Dr. Hardy's not about to let you anywhere near his ass."

The day shift nurses file in, and all four of them crowd around Fran and Tabitha, blatantly admiring Corey. I guess I shouldn't feel so competitive with him. He's fresh meat, and I've been around for years. It makes sense for them to be fascinated.

"Thanks, ladies, but we have to go." He stands and turns toward me. "Are you done charting, Ben?"

"Yeah, I finished just before you threw me down in the floor." I shove my pen into my shirt pocket, and lead the way from the nurses' station before he can make any more scenes. The laugh fest was fun while it lasted, but now I'm irritable again, and I don't know why. I keep feeling threatened when he's around, and I realize I'm lashing out blindly, but I can't seem to stop myself.

"Corey," I say under my breath as we make our way down the hall, "don't take this personally, but you're acting a bit childish, and you're pulling me down with you. I'm Chief of Staff at this hospital, and I have a reputation to worry about. I can't afford to be seen as unprofessional. The minute I show any weakness, one of these other prick doctors will jump up and challenge me for my job. They're already yapping at my heels, just looking for any little thing."

He looks humbled. "I didn't mean to upset you. I was just having a little fun, that's all. I would never do anything to jeopardize your job. I guess I'm not really used to working in a professional place like this." He shrugs. "I doubt the nurses will complain, though. They seemed to like it."

"I don't give a damn what they like," I snap. He doesn't deserve this kind of treatment, and yet the compulsion to be mean to him is very strong in me.

We're in the parking lot now, approaching the reserved space that used to mean so much to me. It's got my name on it, but I don't care. It's just another thing, and as my mama always said, things don't make you happy. Corey starts to hang back, as if he's changed his mind about coming with me. Or maybe he wants to fight me in the parking lot. I couldn't blame him either way.

"Dr. Hardy, are you having second thoughts about me staying with you? If that's what this is, you can be honest with me. I'm man enough to take it." He's come to a complete stop now, waiting for my answer. "Maybe I should have taken the hint when you stood me up this morning, and I had to go looking for you."

I run my hand through my hair and let off a huge sigh. "No, that's not it. Not at all." I bend over and brace my hand on my knees, feeling like I might be sick if it weren't so damn cold. "It's just... I'm confused after yesterday afternoon. After what we did. It's... changed things. Changed *me*."

Corey is motionless, his expression wary. "In what way, Ben?" He looks like he's not sure if he wants to hear my answer.

"It's hard to explain. Nothing feels the same. I guess I just don't want to be in a relationship anymore."

He looks relieved. "I thought you were going to say you hated me now, or I grossed you out or something." He pauses, comes closer. "Do you not want to be in a relationship at all, or just not with her?"

"Just her, I think. Now let's get in the car. I'm freezing."

We both laugh, though the situation hardly warrants it. Once we get on the road, we're solemn again.

"Isn't there supposed to be some sort of sanctity in a real relationship?" I ask suddenly, squeezing the steering wheel so hard it hurts. "I mean, Christina was hell bent on bringing someone else— no offense— into our bed, and I didn't really want that. All that menage stuff is fine if you're not looking for anything permanent, but I've reached a point in my life where I'm leaning toward forever. I don't want to share my forever person with anyone else. Does that make sense?"

Corey takes his time answering. "It definitely makes sense, and I think a lot of people feel that way. When you have two people trying to make a go of it, and then one invites a stranger in, it's bound to get confusing. But I think you're forgetting something."

I look at him and nod for him to continue.

He bites his bottom lip. "Please don't get mad at me for saying this, but you've never even invited her to your house. You're talking about forever, but I think it's clear that she was never that person to start with. Even before I came along."

I sigh loudly. "Jesus, I know that. Don't you think I know that?"

"From the outside looking in, it doesn't seem like either one of you were ever serious. She was pushing a threesome on you when it clearly made you uncomfortable, and you wouldn't even let her into your house for fear she might want to stay."

I bang my hands on the steering wheel. He's right, and I

know it. But now I'm in the awkward position of having to break up with her, and I wish I could just skip over it.

"Of course you're preaching the gospel, man," I tell him. "I'm not even sad. Just mad as fire. See, this is exactly why you don't get some bitch's clothes in your closet and things in your house. Imagine how much more complicated this would be if I had to return her stuff, or let her come get it."

"You don't have any of your stuff at her house?" he asks.

"Nope. Not a thing."

"I'll help you out however I can," he says quietly. "I know we don't know each other that well, but I feel like we can be friends, you know?"

"Yeah." I think about the hazy old days when I used to have friends. Corey doesn't have many, either. "What happened to your friends in Atlanta? I know you had some, as charismatic as you are."

"Oh, now I'm charismatic?" he asks with a wry smile. "A few minutes ago, I was *childish*."

I notice he hasn't answered my question about his friends, but I don't press him.

"Don't mind what I said before. If my position as Chief of Staff can be threatened by a little horsing around at the nurses' station, then I'm not doing my job well enough. The truth is, I'm just irritable about this stuff with Christina, and I was taking it out on you. It's not your fault. I had already decided to break up with her even before she brought you over to meet me at the Christmas party." I pick up my cell phone from the center console and dial her number. "Speaking of Christina, I might as well get this over with."

"Might as well get what over with?" Christina asks through

the phone.

Shit.

"Uh…" I can't help but stammer. I wanted to tell her in person, not over the phone. "We need to meet somewhere, Chris."

"You don't want to see me anymore." It's a statement rather than a question, and she imbues it with all the emotion of a piece of plywood.

"Uh…" I stammer again. Why the hell couldn't she just meet me? I had the whole damn speech planned out in my head, and now she's stealing my thunder.

"It's fine, Ben. I got that feeling already, even while we were doing it yesterday. And when you didn't call me after, it was pretty obvious."

Wow. It hadn't even crossed my mind to call her. How fucked up is that?

"Chris, this is not going like I'd planned. I wanted to meet you somewhere in person. Over the phone is not the way—"

"Don't sweat it, doctor. There are plenty of men out there who would kill to have me. Manly men, strong men who know what they want and aren't afraid to go after it. I'm just too much woman for you, Ben. That's the problem. You don't deserve me."

She hangs up, and I smirk at Corey, who is watching me closely.

"Good news," I say. "We don't have to meet Christina. But the bad news is, I'm single again. Or maybe that's good news, too. I'm not sure yet."

"I know how to make it good news." Corey points to a road that shoots off of Main Street, on the other side of the tracks.

"There's a little club down there called The Bottom. Ever been there?"

"No I haven't, and it's that whole area of town that's called The Bottom, not just the bar."

"Oh." He's genuinely surprised. "Well, whatever it's called, I say we go tonight."

"There's only two of us. Who's gonna be the designated driver?"

"We'll walk," he says with a flourish. "It's only a few blocks from your house. Come on. I'd like to buy you a drink. Or ten."

"You really think I should get drunk?"

"Ben, everyone should get drunk when they break up with someone. In fact, I think it's a rule."

7

THE Bottom is scary as hell, I won't lie. Corey and I both have on jeans, t-shirts, and leather jackets, so you'd think we look similar, but we don't. My jacket is a Dolce and Gabbana hoodie, and his is a battered throwback to the seventies. My black Converse high tops are like cartoon versions of his lace-up military jump boots. While I'd fit in perfectly at an L.A. nightclub, Corey is clearly the style victor here in the Bottom.

The walk isn't bad at all, though by the time we're halfway there, the cold has set in and we've both abandoned talking in favor of blowing warm air into our hands. Even in this weather, the streets and sidewalks of The Bottom are populated with rough looking guys of all ages, and I don't even want to know what they're up to.

"Don't make eye contact with anyone," Corey mumbles under his breath without looking at me. He doesn't even have to tell me that. My instincts won't let me look anywhere but straight ahead. By the time we get to the run-down shack of a bar, I'm glad, though it looks like it could fall down if a good gust of wind came by.

Shortly after we sit across from each other at a table for four in the dimly lit one-room bar, a tired looking woman approaches us. "Can I get you boys a beer or somethin'?" she asks in a bored monotone. Her frizzy bottle blond hair is tied back in a low ponytail, her makeup all but gone. She doesn't have a tray or a uniform, but I'm pretty sure she's the waitress and not just some random woman offering to buy us drinks.

"Bring us two Vodka Red Bulls." He smiles at me from across the table. "For a pick-me-up. You can choose what we have next, but I'm buying all night."

"You haven't even gotten paid yet, Corey. Don't hurt yourself financially just to impress me. I have more than enough."

"Chill out, Doc. I had a few dollars put back for living expenses, but thanks to this awesome, wonderful, amazing man, I don't have any living expenses now." He puts a hand on my forearm and squeezes. "Please let me say thank you. I don't have much to offer a guy like you, but I can at least buy you a few drinks on the day you break up with your girl."

I snatch my arm away before I realize what I'm doing, and for a split second his face registers pain. I don't mean to be rude or hurt his feelings. He's just a touchy-feely person, and I'm not, that's all.

"I appreciate it, Corey, and I'm glad to have you staying with me. It'll be nice to have someone around for a change. Big houses aren't that much fun when you're just wandering around inside by yourself all the time."

"Well, technically I won't be in the house with you. I'll be out back in the pool house."

"Yeah, technically," I agree.

"How do you feel about throwing parties?"

His question catches me off guard. "What do you mean? What kind of parties?"

"Don't worry. I'm not planning on turning your pool house into a stoner's hangout or nightly rager or anything. I mean like both of us hosting a party and inviting the people from the hospital, so you can show off your gorgeous house. I know you want to. You were beaming with pride when you were showing me around, like a kid showing off his new toy. It was so damn adorable."

My face heats with embarrassment. "Yeah, when I was remodeling, I always imagined having parties. Incredible music, exotic food, good wine, dancing in the ballroom... I even had a whole house sound system installed, plus the one at the pool house. Sometimes I hear a song and think about putting it on my party playlist. The party just never happens."

"You should let me help you plan one. I'm fairly good with people."

"What do you mean *fairly* good? People fall all over themselves to get to know you. Work has turned into a freaking Corey Butler fan club. The nurses are probably out right now getting t-shirts with your face screen printed on them."

He looks down at the table with a shy smile, then lifts only his eyes, looking at me from beneath his lashes like girls do when they're smitten. It coils my stomach up into a double knot and flips it upside-down. No wonder the nurses are melting into puddles at his feet. I think he's just accidentally zapped me with his flirt laser, and while I know he didn't mean anything by it, I'm mortified by my own reaction.

"You okay, Ben?"

Thankfully, the waitress chooses that moment to return with our drinks, and I practically swallow mine whole while Corey is counting out cash to her. "Bring another round, and hurry," I tell her before she can leave the table. I don't want to be able to think at all right now.

It's around nine p.m., and the room is slowly filling with people. All types and ages are here, men and women. Some look like they could be underage, but I'm a doctor, not a cop. If one of them chokes on an olive or overdoses on drugs or gets stabbed, I'll be here to help. Otherwise, I guess it's none of my business. It's a different culture, anyway, in this tiny little section of our tiny little town, and I don't know the rules yet.

"I'm going to have to carry you out of here if you keep downing drinks like that," Corey says with a smile.

"I'm just a little nervous about being in this part of town." It's not exactly a lie, but I'm more nervous about him than our surroundings. "You aren't worried at all?"

"You have no idea where I've been, Ben. I've slept under bridges and squatted in crack houses before. It wasn't always that bad, but sometimes it got that bad. The past few years have been much better. Getting my equivalency diploma and going to EMT school completely changed my life. I'm legit now. But that doesn't change the fact that I know my way around the ghetto, or that I can survive any-fucking-where. So to answer your question... no, I'm not worried." He flashes a big grin, and I have to admit I'm fascinated.

"You sure are a gritty son of a bitch, I'll give you that. Not sheltered like me. I meet all kinds of people in the hospital, and I get close to them on a certain level. But I always manage to stay in my little world, you know? The grocery store is as close as I get to the real world. I just work all the damn time. Even talking about working makes me tired these days. Don't tell anyone, but I think I'm burning out."

"You definitely work too much. Even I can see that, and I just got here. You need to get your mind off of work, and anything else that stresses you out." He scans the room with his keen eyes. "Which lady would you like to have tonight, Doc? Pick one."

I laugh. "I just broke up with one, now you're wanting me to choose another?"

"Nothing serious, just a little fun. Some dancing, flirting… Pick one."

"Uh… that one." I point to a natural-looking redhead at a table near the sparsely populated dance floor.

"Pretty, but she's taken."

"How do you know? She's sitting alone."

"I'm more observant than you can even imagine. A side effect of living on the streets. That woman's husband is at the bar getting drinks, but you knew that, which is exactly why you chose her. I'm not letting you off the hook that easily. Choose another."

He's right. I did know the woman was taken, but I'll be damned if I can guess how he read me so easily. This time I choose a woman with long, dark hair and colorful knit cap who's selecting music at the jukebox.

"That's more like it. I'll be back in two shakes."

He leaves me alone and vulnerable at the table. My drink is

gone, and I have nothing to do to occupy myself. I'm sure I look just like what I am, a socially awkward geek who's going to implode if his cool friend doesn't hurry back.

Corey approaches the girl as easily as he seems to do everything. His hands are shoved in his pockets, and he's taken on the posture of a shy but charming schoolboy. I wonder if it's all affectation, because it's hard to believe someone can be that artless and that deft at the same time. He's either a master manipulator, or sex incarnate. Either way, it's some scary shit.

Of course the woman takes the bait. She follows him to the table, and he deposits her into the chair to my left before taking his seat opposite me. "Allie, this is Dr. Ben Hardy. Ben, this is Allie. She's a waitress at the seafood restaurant out on Highway 280."

"Nice to meet you, Allie." I shake her hand.

"I'm going to get drinks," Corey announces. "What are we having this round, Ben?"

"Manhattans. And a glass of ice water. A glass of ice water per alcoholic drink helps with a hangover. Doctor's orders."

"Good lord, we'll be in the restroom all night."

While Corey trots off to the bar to order our drinks, Allie looks as embarrassed as I feel. "You're *the* Dr. Hardy? I have friends and relatives who are your patients. You're my mother's doctor, for crying out loud. Are you sure you're really Dr. Hardy?"

"What, do you think I'm an impostor using a doctor's identity to pick up chicks?" I immediately regret my rudeness, but she only laughs.

"You wouldn't need to use anyone's identity to pick up chicks. I just wasn't expecting someone so young and good looking.

Also, it seems a little odd to see a doctor in this hole-in-the-wall."

"Yeah, I've never been here before. It was Corey's idea."

"Well, I'm glad you decided to take his advice. He said you broke up with your girlfriend today." She lowers her lashes and shoots me a look similar to the one Corey gave me earlier, but hers is a pale facsimile and has absolutely no effect on me.

"Yeah. I figure if the Stud Muffin of the Year over there is giving love life advice, I ought to take it." I gesture toward the bar, where Corey's already got three young women hanging on him. Two on one side, one on the other like a scene out of a movie. I never thought things like that happened in real life, but her it is right in front of me.

Allie laughs. "He's really popular, that's for sure. But don't sell yourself short. I came over here was because I thought you were the cutest guy in the room." She settles her hand indiscreetly on the table near my arm, and I choose to ignore it.

Corey shows up with the tray loaded with a round of Manhattans and three high balls of ice water. "I can't believe you made it all the way across the room balancing all that and didn't spill anything. With three martini glasses, no less. I can't even manage to hold one without spilling it."

"Hey, man," he says in what he thinks is a Manhattan accent but is unfortunately more Midwestern. "If I can intubate a four-hundred-pound man with vocal cord nodules, I can carry a few stinkin' drinks. I do expect a nice tip, though."

I laugh like hell, and so does Allie though I'm sure she doesn't understand the medical terminology.

"You tubed an opera singer?" I ask.

"No. It was a scenario in our textbook. But you're a fucking genius to figure that out. I'll bet your IQ is 160 or better."

I give a tiny mock bow before tasting my drink and coughing. "Uh... as far as Manhattans go, this is worse than awful. But then this isn't the Waldorf-Astoria."

"Maybe you should take us to the Waldorf-Astoria for Manhattans sometime," Allie says.

This girl's daddy must have been a glass maker, because she's transparent as hell.

Corey's expression is arcane as he regards me from across the table. The dark gleam in his eyes and the slight curl of his lips give the eerie impression that he's just looked straight into my soul and picked up on my thoughts.

Is he laughing at me?

Suddenly I can't focus on anything else. I don't give a shit about the pretty waitress sitting beside me babbling about Cozumel and needing a new passport. I just want to know what's going on in Corey's mind to make him look at me that way. And I want to know what he thinks of me. Does he think I'm a repressed bore? A workaholic asshole? Does he like me?

Shit. I'm drunk.

I slam the rest of my horrible drink, setting the empty glass down carefully, because as an emergency doctor I happen to know that a large percentage of nerve and tendon damage to the hand is caused by stemware punctures. Then I stand and make my way silently to the restroom. I need to get out of the smoky room and clear my head. The Red Bull has got my heart thumping and my thoughts racing.

Unexpectedly, Corey follows me in. "You okay, Doc?"

"Yeah, I'm fine. Just needed to get out of that smoke. I'm not really used to it."

"I feel you there. I can't stand it, either. It burns my eyes, gives me a headache, and makes my clothes smell horrible."

"Same here." I lean over the sink and splash cold water on my face, feeling my senses come alive from the temperature shock.

"Why don't you come dance with this lovely young lady I've procured for you this evening? She is so hot for you, I can feel the waves coming off of her."

"I don't care about her, Corey. She's a digger." My voice is harsher than I intend it to be.

"Ben, I'm only trying to show you a good time and help you take your mind off the negative stuff, but I certainly don't want to make things worse. I just want you to be happy. You tell me what I can do to make you happy, and I'll do it. Whatever it is."

I regard my image in the mirror. My eyes are slightly hollowed from stress, but my hair is damp and curling at the temples after splashing my face. I'm feeling refreshed, but also a touch manic, which is never good. "I want to play a drinking game."

A plan is developing in my mind, but I don't even want to elaborate on it to myself yet. It's going to be hard to pull it off with a hyper-observant guy like Corey, but I'm thinking it will be amusing for me.

When we return to the table, Allie is looking pretty uncomfortable. If I had to guess, I'd say she was about two minutes from bolting.

"Sorry about that, Allie." I take her hand delicately in mine and playing with her fingers one at a time. "The smoke in this room was really getting to me. I'm not used to being around smoke."

"I hate it, too," she says emphatically, wrinkling her pert nose. "It burns my eyes and makes my clothes stink. And it gives me a terrible headache."

Corey shrugs. "Apparently those are the official symptoms of cigarette smoke exposure. You should write a paper on it, Doc."

"I think that one's already been done. But I'd love to do one on the mating behavior of humans when there are three parties involved. What do you think?"

"Sounds brilliant, but won't that take a lot of research?"

"Definitely. I'll need an assistant, preferably one with medical training. Are you up for the task?"

Corey frowns and shakes his head slowly. "I don't know, Ben. I don't have much experience in that area. You know I just started."

"Trust me, you're a natural." I'm assaulted by an uncomfortably lucid memory of the feel of his cock rubbing against mine through a thin wall of flesh, and I have to take a deep breath to keep from hyperventilating.

Jesus, don't let me have any more thoughts like that.

Allie is smiling vacuously, and I'm positive this is all sailing right over her pretty little head. That's okay, though. Corey understands where this is going, and that's all that matters.

Our waitress returns after what feels like an eternal absence, and she has three Mojitos on her tray. "These are for you, from the guy over there." She points at a man who looks to be in his late thirties, very fit, and very good-looking with blond hair and wire-rimmed glasses. He's sitting alone, and when we glance at him, he raises his own Mojito in an understated toast.

He looks even more out of place than I do in his suit coat and crisp white button-down shirt. Probably a traveling businessman who discovered that the one decent hotel in town has no lounge.

"Don't drink them," Corey says quietly, and Allie and I both stare at him.

"Why not?" she asks. "It's just a free drink. He looks like he's got plenty of money to afford it."

Corey sets his drink back on the tray. "We don't know what he wants."

"Maybe he likes me," she says. "Guys buy me drinks all the time."

Corey shoots me a hard look that makes me set my glass on the tray and put my hands in my lap.

Then he takes Allie's drink and puts it on the tray and pushes it toward the waitress. "Send these back to him. Tell him thanks, but we can't accept. And bring us six shots of tequila."

"Whatever you say." She picks the tray up and heads back over to the businessman's table.

Allie pokes her lips out and crosses her arms like a child about to throw a tantrum. "There goes my free drink."

"Corey is right, Allie. We shouldn't accept drinks from a total stranger. What if he's some serial killer? We can buy you drinks until you drink yourself into a coma if that's what you want, so calm down."

I glance toward our mysterious benefactor to see how he's taking the brush-off, but he's gone. The drinks are sitting untouched on his empty table, a stack of bills pinned beneath one of them.

For a while, we fall into light conversation, covering such topics as favorite pizza toppings, worst accidents we've ever rubbernecked on the highway, how many pairs of shoes we each have, best concert we've ever been to, and the importance of protein shakes after a workout. The drinks are going down way too easily, especially the tequila shots. After three, I'm pretty much toast.

"Ben wants to play a game," Corey tells Allie. "I'm not sure what it is, though. Why don't you tell us, Ben?"

"Oh yeah, I almost forgot. I thought we might play a few rounds of Spin the Bottle."

Both Corey's and Allie's brows shoot up in surprise. Allie starts laughing and clapping, obviously thrilled at the idea. Corey just looks stunned.

"Dr. Hardy," Allie says, "I'm sure everyone in this bar would pay good money to see the three of us play a game of Spin the Bottle. I'd especially like to see it."

"We can't very well be spinning a glass bottle in this fine establishment and risk it smashing into a million pieces on the floor, so I have an alternative method. I call it Flip the Quarter. We used to play it in college." I fish a quarter out of my pocket and hold it in the air. "I'll be the coin flipper, and turns will move counter-clockwise. Heads means you kiss the person to your right, and tails means you kiss the person to your left. So Allie, say it's your turn, and I flip the coin. If it lands on tails, you kiss Corey. If it lands on heads, you kiss me."

"I have a question, Doc," Corey says, raising his hand like a school kid. "What happens if it's my turn, and you flip heads?"

"Then you have to kiss me." I smile innocently. "Are you

okay with that?"

He swallows hard. I can see his Adam's apple working, and his jaw is tight. He looks almost angry, and I wonder if I've already gone too far with my game.

I move on before he can answer. "How about you, Allie? Are you okay with it?"

"Hell, yes," she cries loudly. "I told you I'd pay good money."

I push forward, gauging both of their reactions. "It wouldn't make you uncomfortable seeing two guys kissing?" I lean back in my seat, and I'm beginning to realize I've had way the fuck too much to drink.

"Dr. Hardy, I would love to kiss either one of you. A lot." She smiles, and her tongue darts out to touch her bottom lip seductively. "But if two guys as hot as you and Corey were to kiss each other right in front of me, like a real kiss with tongues and everything… I think I'd probably pass out. You'd have to do CPR on me."

I don't bother to correct her on the purpose of CPR. Instead, I turn my attention to Corey. "I never got your answer."

"Sure, I'll kiss you, Ben." He smiles and winks at Allie. "With tongue."

Allie looks like she might combust on the spot, but I'm sure the tightening I get in the pit of my stomach when he says that… when he winks… is much stronger than anything she's feeling.

I cover my face with my hands. "I've had way to much to drink."

"Yeah, I know you have," Corey says, and I swear he's reprimanding me with his voice, and with his eyes. "Maybe we should call it a night." He starts to push back from the table, but I halt him with my hand.

"Just a few rounds of the game, okay?" I'm definitely slurring. "Why aren't you as drunk as I am?"

"I quit drinking a while back. Someone has to make sure we get home in one piece."

"How very responsible of you." I flip the coin for Allie's turn and display it on the back of my hand for her to inspect.

"Tails," she says. "But this is an old quarter, with an eagle on the back. Shouldn't we say heads or wings?"

I laugh, wondering if she thinks newer coins have a picture of a tail on the back side. "Okay, I'm just drunk enough for that to make sense. Wings it is. Which means… you kiss Corey."

He glares at me through slotted eyelids. Either his signals are screwed up, or my sensor is, because I don't have a clue why he would be cross with me for getting him some make-out time with an attractive woman.

Allie leans over, and Corey bends down, and their lips come together in a lukewarm kiss. Hell, they don't even use any tongue, which disappoints me. "Boo…" I say. "Can't you two do any better than that? I'd like to see a little tongue action, too."

Allie blushes and smiles. Corey leans against the back of his chair. "Your turn," he says to me, and it sounds like a dare.

I flip the coin and slap it onto the back of my hand, never looking at it, but feeling the ridges with my fingers. I show them the coin, already knowing what it will be. I never lose a coin toss as long as I'm the one doing the flipping.

"It's wings," Allie cries, clapping and bouncing in her seat.

"Wait till I tell my mama I kissed her doctor! She's going to lose it!"

I lean toward her and let her lay one on me. Only I'm determined to put on a better show than Corey did, so I snake my tongue out and slide it between Allie's soft lips. She sighs against me, obviously surprised and pleased. I wrap my arm around her shoulders and pull her close, crushing her to my chest and invading her mouth with an aggression that is fifty percent liquor, fifty percent bravado. There is no passion involved, because to be honest, I'm just not interested in her.

When I release her and sit back, I think she's going to topple. Her eyes are still half closed, and her lips are slightly swollen and smeared. She glances at Corey as if to gloat, and I almost laugh.

He's leaned back in his chair, looking intently at me with those arresting blue eyes. The look on his face almost has me ready to back down.

"Are you mad?"

"My turn." He ignores the question, but his expression eases.

"You sure you want to chance it?" I don't know why I'm goading him, and taking such perverse pleasure in this game. I already know the outcome, so there's no risk for me, but I seem to have an uncontrollable urge to mess with his head.

"Oh, yeah," he says. "Bring it on."

"I don't know. I think we should bet on it. Allie, do you think Corey will go through with it, if it happens to land on tails?"

"Tails," Corey mutters. "How appropriate."

Allie slaps a ten dollar bill on the table. "I think he'll do it."

I fish a twenty out of my pocket. "I don't have a ten, but I've got twenty that says he won't."

Corey smiles evilly and pulls a twenty out of his own pocket. "I'm doing it, Ben. You can bet your sweet ass on that."

The way Allie's gaze swings from one to the other of us, you'd think she was watching a tennis match.

My eyes are glued to his as I flip the coin, feeling for the familiar roughness of the eagle, manipulating the coin with a quick sleight of hand that puts it right where I want it. Heads.

I reveal the head of the coin to him with a dramatic flourish, but he doesn't even look down at it. Instead he leans over and gives Allie a chaste peck on the lips. "It's been nice, Allie," he says in a quiet voice. "Maybe we'll see you again sometime."

He gets up from his chair and stalks around to mine with a murderous look on his face. He's always so good-natured. I've never seen him like this. He leans low over my chair, puts his big hands on my shoulders, and kisses me. On the lips. With his mouth slanted over mine, he forces his tongue roughly between my lips and kisses me repeatedly, devouring me with his bruising lips and deep licks of his tongue. With every invasive plunge, I feel completely taken by him. He sucks my bottom lip so hard it aches as he pulls away, and in that moment he has owned me.

I'm breathless and bewildered, my mouth hanging open. The kiss I gave Allie was nothing compared to the mouth raping he just laid on me. He took every thought I had left in my head, and now I'm nothing but a drunken shell wobbling on my seat.

"That's for cheating on the coin toss, asshole." He looks at Allie, and his face softens. "And the young lady wanted a show. Was that entertaining enough for you, darlin'?"

She nods, her mouth hanging open just like mine. I don't

think she's any more capable of speech than I am.

He grabs me roughly by the arm and pulls me to my feet, then he slides the bet money over to Allie. "Dr. Hardy isn't usually like this. He doesn't drink often, and he's totally blitzed tonight. Please don't tell anyone, okay?"

"I won't. But I might tell my mom he kissed me." She shrugs apologetically. "She'll get a kick out of it."

He laughs mildly. "Okay. See you around. Tell your mom he said hi."

When we pass through the front door, the night air shocks me. It's a different world out here now. There are still guys hanging around on the sidewalks and on the corners. I don't know how to act in this world, so I just try to keep steady on my feet and let Corey lead. Even though he's pissed at me right now, I feel safe with him. I know he'd never let anything happen to me.

I pull my jacket close, trying in vain to get warmer. "Jeez, it's freezing out here." Corey doesn't reply.

At the corner just before we cross the tracks, a man approaches us. He leans in close to Corey and says something near his ear, but I can't hear what it is.

Corey shakes his head. "Nah, man. Maybe later."

"What did he want?" I ask when the man has rejoined his friends on the corner.

"Wanted to know if we needed anything. You know, drugs."

We continue on across the tracks and up a low grade hill three blocks to my house. For the first time, it strikes me how close my world is to the strange, dark world across the tracks, yet they might as well be on separate planets.

"You're so worldly," I slur. "And I'm so sheltered. I wish I could be more like you. You can handle anything."

He laughs, but it's a bitter sound. "I think you've got that backwards, Ben. And if you don't quit fucking with me…"

"Fucking with you?" My brain isn't working properly. I can't remember now if we've been arguing, but it seems maybe we have. Even the kiss is some vague memory that doesn't seem real. I'm beginning to wonder if it even happened, or if my drunken brain is fabricating a memory. "What are you talking about?"

"Nothing. Let's just get you home."

8

(COREY)

AFTER the gods of irony test me with an awkward moment of fishing the house key out of his pants pocket, Ben and I are able to make it into his house and to his bedroom. He's not really seeing now. His body has succumbed to the alcohol, and he's leaning against me like he's boneless. If I had known what a lightweight he was, I never would have encouraged him to drink those tequila shots. The Red Bull served to keep him going long past the time he should have stopped.

I feel terrible. All I wanted was to make him forget about that bitch Christina, but he ended up getting way too drunk and doing things he's going to regret tomorrow. Things he'll probably hate me for.

And then there's what I did.

There was no excuse for kissing him when his defenses were

down, but he was pushing my buttons. I wasn't exactly sober, either. Thank goodness I hadn't even drunk my last couple of shots or I may have jumped him in the bar.

By the time I've got him standing in front of his bathroom sink, he's regained control of his muscles and seems more coherent. For a fleeting moment, it occurs to me that he may still be yanking my chain, pretending to be more wasted than he actually is.

"Can you brush your teeth and wash your face?"

He nods and pulls an unopened toothbrush from a drawer. "Here's a toothbrush for you."

"Are we having a sleepover, Doc?"

He laughs, and we both brush our teeth and splash cold water on our faces. Afterward I feel refreshed, like I've gotten my second wind, which is not necessarily a good thing. I was kind of hoping to pass out and not have to think tonight.

"There's some acetaminophen in the cabinet," he says, picking up a glass from the counter and filling it with water. He swallows the two pills I hand him, and I take two as well.

"Ben, you're a doctor even when you're drunk. Now let me help you get comfortable for bed, okay?" I get him up onto the bed, and as I start to unlace his shoes I have to smile. Freaking Converse high tops. He's such an adorable geek, I just want to eat him with a spoon.

When I get to his jeans, he starts laughing with his eyes closed. "First you kiss me, now you're trying to get in my pants. Better watch out or I might start to think you like me."

Yep, still yanking my chain.

"Go to sleep, Ben. Before you say something you'll regret."

"I won't regret anything with you, Corey. I love you, man. You're so... cool." He yawns like a little boy who's played too hard. "Maybe we can find some more women to share. We can do all the nurses at the hospital together. Can you imagine? A different woman between us every day. And I hope we can come at the same time every time like we did with Christina. Did you notice that? God, that was awesome... Felt so good..."

"Really, Ben. Go to sleep and quit babbling. You're gonna hate yourself in the morning."

I lean him back and unfasten his jeans. When I slip them down his legs, he wiggles a little to help me out. I try not to notice the way his thigh muscles bunch when he moves, or the perfect curve of his calves. I'm sure it will irritate the hell out of him that I toss the jeans onto the rug, but at the moment I don't care.

Sitting him back up, I pull his t-shirt over his head. He holds his arms up for me, and it's like undressing a child, only there's nothing childlike under his shirt. His muscles are finely sculpted across his chest and abs, his skin a creamy color that has rarely seen the sun. At Christina's house when we were doing the deed, I couldn't really get a good long look at his body without risking the two of them noticing. But now that he's nearly passed out and laid back on his bed, I can look at him all I want.

My belly clenches with longing as I take in the sight of him. He's so strong, so manly, and yet so vulnerable. His face is relaxed as if in sleep, but his long, sooty lashes flutter restlessly against his pale cheeks. I'm dying to run my hand over that defined chest, that ridged six pack, that flat stomach.

Pale blue silk boxers hide what's down below, but I've already seen it. Already felt it rubbing against me, though unfortunately there was a barrier between us at the time. God how I'd love to grip his trim hips firmly in my hands and slide those boxers off…

"You like my underwear?" Ben asks, and I look up to discover him watching me with narrowed eyes.

I panic, swallowing a big gulp of air and struggling to come up with a good excuse for why I'm so blatantly checking him out. Fortunately, he doesn't seem offended. He probably won't remember any of this tomorrow, anyway.

"Yes, very nice. I had a pair of silk boxers once, but I wore them completely out. They were hanging apart at the seams by the time I had to throw them away."

He laughs drunkenly and uses his elbows to scoot up onto his pillow.

"Are you all set, then?" I tuck him under the covers and make sure his head is straight on the pillow. I don't really want to leave him alone in his condition, but I also don't want to overstep my boundaries and get kicked out of my new home. "I'll leave the door open and lie down on the couch so I can hear you if you need anything. I moved the trash can to your side of the bed as a make-do emesis basin, just in case. Thank goodness we don't have work tomorrow, or we'd both be in trouble. Not to mention any unlucky patients we might have had."

I start across the room, but I only make it as far as the door.

"Stay," he says.

"Um, I don't know if I should…"

He pats the empty spot beside him on the bed. "Please. I don't want to be alone tonight. You know what happened to Jimi

Hendricks, Janis Joplin, and Mama Cass. Could you stand that on your conscience?"

"Mama Cass wasn't drunk when she died, and I really don't think you're in any danger of asphyxiation. But I'll stay if you really want me to."

"Pretty please."

It's a terrible idea, but I do it anyway. I can't stop myself. Not when he's begging. "Alright. You must really be desperate for company if you're using dead rock stars to coerce me to stay."

He's on his side, and I climb onto the bed behind him, not sure if I should take off any of my clothes. At first I try keeping them on and sleeping on top of the covers, but in the end, comfort and temptation win out. Ever since I've been sleeping indoors in decent places, I can't stand to sleep in my clothes. It feels too much like having no place to go.

At least that's what I tell myself while I'm stripping, trying not to disturb Ben with my movements. First my pants come off, then my shirt, and I'm feeling very exposed in nothing but my boxer briefs. A little thrill trips through my body at the thought of being here with him in his bed, almost naked.

"This is a bad fucking idea, Corey," I whisper to myself as I slip under the covers. "Like the worst idea ever in the history of the universe."

"Huh?" Ben stirs but keeps his back to me.

"Nothing, Ben. Go back to sleep."

I realize I've forgotten to turn off the light, so I reach across him to flip the switch on his bedside lamp. My bare chest grazes his back, and I'm done for. My dick shoots up instantly.

Ben sighs, as if his drunken, half sleeping self enjoys the contact. *Fuck.* He's going to be the death of me. I lie there stiffly, unsure of what to do, and finally I give in to the temptation to slide against his back and wrap my arm around his waist, spooning him like a lover would. Even worse, he snuggles back against me, seemingly oblivious to the fact that I'm a guy and his ass is cradling my rock hard cock. I believe he would literally murder me if he had enough wits about him to know what is going on... and still I let it happen.

I reason that I'm not doing anything to hurt him, and that he won't even remember enough to be upset. On the other hand, if he is sober enough to remember, then maybe he doesn't mind. Maybe it will be just the thing to make him realize he wants me.

"Ben..." I whisper.

"What?" Still conscious. So far, so good.

"How drunk are you?" I'm going to hell for even asking. I should just get up and walk out of here right now.

"I'm not that drunk," he slurs, wiggling backward, getting impossibly close to me and sighing again.

"So you're totally fucked up, huh?" It is unethical of me to even be having the thoughts I'm having right now when he's in this condition.

"Don't worry about it."

I'm shocked at the way he's acting, even if he is drunk, because when he's awake he can barely stand for me to touch him. I've been toying with the idea that he has a hint of Asperger's Syndrome, but now I'm not so sure. Maybe I just make him feel things he's not comfortable with yet.

Wishful thinking, asshole. He's going to kill you tomorrow.

"Let's just go to sleep," I whisper, tightening my grip around his waist. My cock is wedged firmly between my abdomen and his ass, and I can't believe he doesn't feel it. It's all I can do to keep from sliding it between his thighs just to get some relief. Or worse, snatching his shorts down and straight up fucking him. My insides are in knots trying to control my urges when every instinct in my body is telling me to go for it.

I close my eyes and rest my lips against his dark hair, which smells like shampoo, bar smoke, and Ben. His body feels so good in my arms, pressed up against me right here, ready for the taking if I have the courage. Or rather the audacity. A strangled squeak comes out around the lump in my throat. I don't mean to make a noise, it just happens because I feel so desperate.

"You wanna kiss me again?" he asks in a husky voice, and my heart jumps up into my throat.

"Fucking go to sleep, Ben. You don't know what you're saying." I'm pleading with him now.

I want so badly to overlook the fact that he's drunk. I want to ignore it and give him what we both want, but I can't, because I don't know how he'll feel about it tomorrow. And I can't trust that he really wants it anyway. People do some crazy things when they're drunk.

I want to, but I don't. Instead, I do what I should have done in the first place. I roll quietly out of the bed and go lie on the couch, where I can still hear him if he needs me, but I won't have the temptation of his body being so close to mine.

9

(BEN)

THE buzzing of my cell phone is the only reason I claw my way up to consciousness before noon. For some reason, my curtains are open, letting the cruel sun have its way with me. As a night shift worker with blackout shades and strong habits, I am not at all used to this. In fact, I'm in total empathy with vampires at this moment.

I hiss and hold my hand in front of my face, scrambling off the bed onto the floor to find my phone, since it's not on my bedside table. "What the hell?" It looks I invited a natural disaster home with me last night. My clothes are heaped in a pile beside my bed, and that's where I find my phone, still in the pocket of my jeans. "Hello," I gasp, lying on the rug and trying to catch my breath.

"Dr. Hardy, where are you?"

"Julie, is that you? Why are you calling me before noon?"

"Yes, it's me. Why aren't you here yet? It's almost time for class to start."

I search my brain, which is difficult though the haze and headache. "Class?"

"You're teaching the CPR class this time, remember? Class starts at noon. You've got fifteen minutes to get here."

"Shit. I forgot. Can't we reschedule?"

"No! We've got fifteen people sitting here waiting to get re-certified, including me. If I don't get this done within a couple of days, I won't be able to work, which is what I get for putting it off until you were the one teaching it. Stupid, stupid…"

"Why the heck would you do that?"

"Dr. Hardy." She's practically screaming into the phone. "We don't have time to discuss it. This is serious. If administration finds out you didn't show, it won't look good. What do you want me to do?"

I struggle to straighten out my brain and come up with a solution. "Okay, Julie, listen carefully. I want you to look in the closet of the classroom. There's a list of things we need, along with all of the equipment. Get the list and set everything up. Ask someone to help you if you need to. Announce that I'll be there at a quarter after, then send everyone to the cafeteria for coffee or something."

"Alright, Dr. Hardy. Just please hurry."

"Oh. My. Lord." I talk aloud to no one, tossing my cell onto the bed and pulling myself up off the floor.

I run to the kitchen for ice water, lots of it, and coffee. Once I get cup brewing on my single serve machine and down an entire bottle of water, I head to the shower. I've got twenty-five minutes to get there.

As I pass the living room, I stop short. Corey is lying on the couch in nothing but his underwear, curled up like a baby with no cover to keep him warm. My mouth goes dry, and my heart skips a beat.

When I get my bearings and am able to stop staring at him like a jackass, I rush over and shake him awake. He jumps up so fast we nearly crack heads.

"What is it, Ben?" When he sees me, his eyes go dark for a moment, and his face colors. He looks embarrassed to be discovered passed out half naked on my couch. We must have had a wild night, but I don't have time to think about that right.

"Do you feel like helping me teach a CPR class in twenty-five minutes?"

He rubs his eyes and runs his hands through his hair. "Sure. Sign me up."

"Alright, I'm getting a quick shower and brushing my teeth. Run get ready and meet me back here in ten minutes. I'm putting you on a cup of coffee now. And drink some water." I feel like a master coordinator right now; I'm on fire.

He jogs to the pool house in his skivvies, and I grab my coffee and start his brewing. Then I hop into the shower. Five minutes of vigorous scrubbing, brushing the alcohol and heaven knows what out of my mouth from the night before, and I'm fresh as a daisy. Well, fresh as a daisy with a slight hangover.

When I return to the living room, Corey is drinking his coffee, looking unfairly attractive in his scrubs and damp hair.

"You look good for a hung-over guy," he says to me.

"Funny, that's exactly what I was just thinking about you.

And I feel surprisingly good. How about you?"

"I'm fine after that speed shower. Adrenaline's pumping, got some caffeine in my system…"

"Let's go, then." I lead the way to the car and drive the short distance to the hospital. We're only one minute later than I promised, so I consider it a victory. It could've been so much worse.

"Sorry to keep you all waiting." I bluster purposefully into the room. "We'll make sure you get your money's worth, though." Most everyone nods or laughs. All but three of the students are female, so that's a good sign. Between the two of us, we should be able to charm our way back into their good graces.

Five seats at one end of the long table are free. Corey takes a seat next to Julie, and I sit on the corner of the table. Julie pokes Corey in the shoulder, whispers something in his ear, and giggles quietly. "Kids…" I clear my throat and shoot them a hard look until they stop talking.

Class goes very well, considering it almost wasn't. Somehow I'm only marginally hung over. Corey proves to be a great assistant, especially since he has such a natural adroitness where CPR is concerned. He's doing the physical demonstrations for me, and all the women are panting as he performs chest compressions and mouth-to-mouth with a barrier device on our CPR dummy, Annie.

A group of four women approach me and request personal instruction. "Since you're a doctor," their leader explains.

Julie looks like she's going to die laughing. "Not only is he handsome, he's also an excellent doctor, ladies." She puts her hand on my shoulder. "He's Chief of Staff here, you know. You girls are so lucky you signed up for today. He rarely teaches this class."

The women all widen their eyes and nod. Julie knows exactly what she's doing, and judging from the look she's giving me, she also knows I hate it.

"I'll get you for this," I whisper in her ear, and she laughs.

I look toward the other side of the room where Corey is working his magic on Annie, and he's looking at me, watching me interact with the growing group of women around me. He smiles, but it's only half-hearted, and I wonder if he's more hung over than I thought. I don't remember how much he drank last night, or much of anything else for that matter. With the drama this morning, I haven't had much of a chance to think about it. I'm only glad I don't feel worse than I do, and that I was able to make it to teach this class.

I was bitching at Corey yesterday about jeopardizing my job, and I almost did it myself by forgetting I'd promised to do this. I make a mental note to thank Julie for saving my ass.

"What is your number one tip for CPR, Dr. Hardy?" one of the women asks.

"I'd have to say the most important thing is that when you're doing chest compressions, you want to get the full compression and full recoil. Remember, you're physically pumping the blood for the heart. If you're not pumping, it ain't moving."

"What if we're not strong enough, being women and all?" another asks.

"Just give it your best effort. You're stronger than you think, especially in times of stress. But please use correct hand placement and don't break the xiphoid process. You could lacerate or puncture the diaphragm, or worse, the liver. You don't want your patient to bleed out from a liver puncture."

"Huh? Xiphoid what?" Most of the women look confused.

"Let's show them," Julie says, and there's a bit of mischief in her eyes that I'm not so sure I like.

Before I know what's going on, she's hopped up onto the table, reclined onto her back, and pulled her scrub top up to just below her bra.

I'm shocked, and I look around like I'm going to get in trouble. The other males in the room must have a sixth sense or eyes in the back of their heads, because suddenly it seems like they're all watching. Corey's eyebrows shoot up, and he almost knocks his dummy onto the floor.

I look back down at Julie and clear my throat. Her belly is slightly rounded, soft and feminine. It looks like she gets in the tanning bed on occasion, because she's got a golden glow even beneath her shirt. A pale yellow belly ring twinkles above her navel. She's a very attractive girl, but to me she just looks like a sexual harassment lawsuit waiting to happen.

"Um… this is the xiphoid process, ladies, as seen on a real person rather than a dummy." I touch her skin just below the sternum and press down lightly to highlight the location of the sternal notch. "I'm going to let you feel one by one, but press gently. You will notice that the bottom of the sternum extends slightly beyond the spot where the bottom ribs meet."

The ladies take turns feeling Julie's sternum and nodding, and I notice the three young men have now joined our group and copped their feels.

"It's even more of a danger when you're performing the Heimlich Maneuver," I explain, "since the correct hand placement is just below the sternal notch. Just be sure when you do chest compressions that you place the heel of your hand higher on the sternum between the nipples." I glance at Julie's face, and she looks content, not shy at all. "Do you mind if I demonstrate proper hand placement on you, Julie?"

She shakes her head, her eyes soft and compliant. "Be my guest, Doctor. I'm yours to command."

I clear my throat and place my hands on her sternum in the proper spot. "It can seem different when you're looking at a real person rather than a dummy. And truthfully, a person's weight and build can affect your perception as well."

I pull Julie's shirt down and take her hand to help her up. When she stands, she lifts onto her tiptoes and speaks quietly, close to my ear. "That was fun. Would you like to demonstrate mouth-to-mouth on me? I'll bet everyone in here would pay good money to see that."

And just like that, my world comes crashing down.

I'm sure everyone in this bar would pay good money to see the three of us play a game of spin the bottle.

Allie's words reverberate through my head, and suddenly I'm remembering the bar, the drinks, the game, the kiss… I'm in a trance, staring at the wall, images from the night before superimposed on it like a movie screen.

The kiss. Jesus Christ on a cracker, Corey kissed me in that bar last night, right in front of everyone. In front of the daughter of one of my patients, for heaven's sake. And it wasn't just a little token kiss, either. It was the hottest, raunchiest, most sexual kiss I've ever received in my entire life. I think he licked my soul with that kiss.

The worst part is that I started it. I was being an asshole with my stupid magic trick, and he was just calling my bluff. Why would I even have done such a thing to him? Shame grips me tightly, squeezing the air from my lungs.

He was angry with me, I think. But he helped me home. How did I get to bed?

My face heats as I half remember asking Corey to stay with me in my bed. *Did I really do that?* Had he crawled into my bed with me when I was wearing nothing but my underwear?

He was sleeping on the sofa this morning. Maybe I'm imagining things. My brain is so damn foggy I can't remember any details of what happened, but I do know one thing for sure. Something doesn't feel right. There's a memory lurking just beyond my mind's grasp, taunting me, and it's not pretty. It makes me feel like I want to run away, and I don't even know what it is.

I physically shake the images from my head and look around. The ladies are talking among themselves, and Julie is talking too, but she keeps glancing at me with a concerned expression. I probably look like I've seen a ghost.

When I dare to glance in Corey's direction, he's looking at me again, and now I realize why he keeps watching me. He's been waiting for me to remember, checking for a reaction. Suddenly I can't breathe in here anymore, and I think I'm going to pass out.

"Excuse me," I mumble, rushing to the door as fast as I can without alarming the students.

The hallway is empty, and I lean against the wall and slide down into a deep squat, resting my head in my hands. Julie follows immediately, with Corey on her heels.

"Dr. Hardy, are you okay?" She touches my forehead as if checking for a fever. "I hope I didn't offend you about the mouth-to-mouth. I was just joking around, that's all."

"It's fine, Julie." I wave her away without looking up. "It's not you."

"Dr. Hardy is just a little under the weather today," Corey tells her. "We've covered everything in there, anyway. Can you please excuse the class so I can take him home? We'll do something to repay you for helping out."

"Sure." Her voice is shaky with worry. "Feel better, Dr. Hardy, okay?"

I hear the classroom door swing closed as she goes back in, and Corey kneels down beside me. He's so big and so close, I can feel the heat coming off of his body. His nearness comforts me even when I know he's the reason I'm feeling so bad.

"Come on, Ben." He pulls me to my feet with little effort. "Let's get out of here before that mob comes through the door." He leads me down the hall and into the parking lot. "Mind if I drive?"

Without a word, I toss him the keys and drop into the passenger seat, wishing I could just fall asleep and get away from the way I'm feeling. It's a lot like mourning, this emotion that's weighing me down. It's so deep I can't even fathom it, like loss and regret and shame all rolled into one. After the fact as always, I realize I've been manic for days, but I can never see it until I crash.

We ride all the way home in silence, and thankfully he doesn't try to turn on the radio like so many people would. For me silence can be cathartic, as if the negative space can pull off some of what's bothering me. When the space around me is full of noise, there's nowhere for it to go, so it just stays inside, roiling and festering and making me miserable.

Once we're inside my garage, Corey moves quickly to the passenger side and opens the door before I can bring myself to do it. He follows me all the way inside the house and to my bedroom.

"You need more sleep," he says. "Hangovers are a bitch, and there's nothing like sleep to cure one."

"I'm not hung over." I unconsciously straighten the covers of my unmade bed. "Not much, anyway."

"Oh." Corey lurks in the doorway, fiddling with the drawstring on his scrub pants and not looking at me.

I sit down on the bed. "Would you like to come in?"

Why do I feel so sad?

He sits on the opposite edge of the bed, still not looking at me. "How much do you remember, Ben?"

The fact that he feels the need to ask me that question fills me with dread.

"I remember you… kissing me in the bar, that's all. But I feel like there's more… as if that's not enough." There's a perpetual sinking feeling in my stomach that, like a Shepard scale or an old-fashioned barber pole, keeps going down and down but never hits bottom. "It's like something bad has happened, and I can't remember. Don't want to remember."

Corey keeps quiet, his dark brows drawn low and lips thinned to nothing.

"Your silence is making this worse for me, you know. I think you remember more than I do, and you're keeping something from me."

He taps his thumb rhythmically against his thigh and takes a deep, wavering breath. "What do you want from me, man? There's nothing, okay? What could there possibly be? You got wasted. You acted like an asshole at the bar with your goddamn rigged coin toss, and I called you on it. Yeah, I kissed you. Big fucking deal. It's nothing you weren't asking for."

He stands up, looking impossibly tall and oddly calm. His hand twitches slightly, and I realize that there are some powerful emotions behind his cool facade, and he's barely got them reined in. God help the person who's on the receiving end when he can no longer contain them. At the moment, that person is potentially me, and I'm a little bit scared. But just when I think he's about to cut loose on me, his shoulders slump, and he walks out of the room, closing the door gently behind him.

I have the urge to scramble across the bed and run after him, but instead I lie down on top of the covers and use the remote to close the blackouts. Sleep is where I need to escape to right now, into the cool black nothingness where time doesn't exist.

The faint sound of the garage door opening startles me, and I hear the erratic rumbling of Corey's motorcycle as it comes to life and begins to move away from the house. He's left the garage door up, but I don't have the heart to care. Let the whole neighborhood loot my house, or a serial killer cut me to ribbons where I lie. My stomach is still sinking, and my brain is humming a high-pitched note I recognize well. It means the sadness will take me over if I let it... if I stay alone too long and don't fight back.

I'm straining now to hear Corey's engine, hoping it gets louder again because he's changed his mind and decided to come back, but the rumble only moves farther and farther away into space until there's nothing left of it. That's when I know that I'm truly alone, and I let the blackness swallow me whole.

10

(COREY)

THERE'S not much to do in Blackwood, but I'll be damned if I'm going back to Ben's house. I can't face him after what happened between us this afternoon. Instead I rip along Highway 280 on my Harley, feeling the icy wind tearing at my hair and my face, wishing I was fourteen again and could curl up like a cat at the bottom of Granny's bed and tell her what's bothering me.

I keep going over everything in my mind, trying to make sense of it all. And I keep picturing Ben like he was the first time I saw him, his dark hair a spiky mess, murky gray eyes hollowed out underneath... He looked like he was about to drop from fatigue, but that didn't diminish his beauty at all.

When the admin introduced us, and Ben looked up from his charting and flashed that cute-as-a-button boyish smile of his, I was a goner. I don't even believe in love at first sight or any of that romantic bullshit, but something in him touched something in me. That's the only way I can describe it. I fell hard for him right there in front of everyone at the nurses's station, and I swear it was as obvious as one of those Looney Tunes cartoon hearts beating out of my chest. I've never felt anything like that before, and right now I'm wishing I'd never felt it at all.

...It's like something bad has happened, and I can't remember. Don't want to remember.

His words were a knife in my gut, and I realized for the first time that I'm fooling myself in the worst way. I don't know what ever made me think I'd have a chance with an arrow-straight guy like Ben. He's miles outside of my dating pool, and just as far out of my league.

Still, I could have sworn there were signs. His offhand comments about my looks, the way he acted when he was drunk and his defenses were down, the fact that he's letting me stay in his pool house free of charge... He's a very private person, so to me that seems like a big deal.

What really rocked my world was the way he latched onto my neck when we were having sex with Christina, when we were all about to come. I don't think that it was just my imagination that in that moment, it was just me and him in that room. Instead of grabbing his girlfriend like anyone would have expected, he wrapped his fingers around *my* neck, looked me dead in the eye, and rode the most explosive climax of my life all the way down with me.

And where was *she* during all of that? His oh-so-perfect girlfriend...

She really screwed the pooch when she decided to orchestrate that debaucherous triple tryst. Thought she could sample the new guy and keep her precious doctor, too. Sometimes I think of telling Ben the things she said to me when he wasn't around. I want so badly to expose her for the low-rent gold digger she is, but I don't want to hurt him. He got rid of her for his own reasons, and that's exactly how it should be.

Now if he'd only choose me instead.

Thirty miles outside of Blackwood, I pull a U-turn on the highway and head back toward town. Just past the city limits sign, I pull into the crunchy gravel parking lot of the Seafood Barn, the place where Allie waitresses. I didn't plan on stopping here, but I need to get some shelter and a cup of coffee before I end up in the hospital with hypothermia.

Besides, there are few places that feel friendly to me in this strange new town. I tend to gravitate toward people I know or places I've been, especially when I'm feeling so low. A familiar face would be nice right about now.

"Corey," Allie squeals from the podium near the door where she's chatting with the hostess when I enter. "Oh my gosh, I didn't expect to see you again today." She runs a hand self-consciously through her long brown hair.

"Yeah, I was just out riding my bike and… Well, it's freaking cold out there. Do you serve coffee?"

"Of course. Come on, I'll show you to a table."

I follow her to a corner booth in the back of the dining room, shivering all the way. There are only two booths with people in them, so I don't have to worry about a crowd. I can drink my coffee and mope in private.

"So last night was pretty crazy, huh?" Allie asks with an embarrassed smile. "I'm afraid I made a fool out of myself with Ben."

"You and me both, honey." I give her what I hope passes for a smile. "I think he feels like he made a fool of himself, too, so don't be hard on yourself."

"We were all drunk."

"No doubt."

"I'll get your coffee." She hurries off, stopping for a moment to talk animatedly with the hostess, who tries to steal a glance without me noticing. I sigh and slip further into the shadows, because I'm not in the mood to be seen right now.

When she returns with a tray of coffee and a tiny silver pitcher of cream, she surprises me by taking a seat across from me and pouring me a cup. "The Saturday night supper crowd won't start coming in for another hour or so. Believe it or not, we're the fanciest restaurant in town, so it will get packed. But until then I'm all yours."

I nod, drizzling cream into my coffee until it's the caramel color I like. Bringing the mug to my lips, I blow gently into it, enjoying the warmth of the steam on my frozen face. It makes me think of how Granny used to make me hot cocoa after the high school football games, and we'd talk late into the night. Even after she was so tired she was falling asleep mid-sentence, she'd still tough it out until I was ready to go to bed.

Why do I think of her so much more during bad times?

"Something's wrong," Allie says. "You're sad today. What is it?"

"Aren't you going to lose your job for sitting with me?"

"Nope. I own the place."

"No shit? A restaurant owner? I'm impressed. Why did you tell us you were a waitress?"

She shrugs. "I always do that when I first meet a guy. Weeds out the deadbeats. I don't want a man who's interested in my money or job title. I just want him to lust after my hot body. Now quit trying to weasel out of telling me what's wrong with you."

"Nothing you'd understand or even care to hear about. I didn't come here to whine. I just needed a warm place to sit for a while and think."

"Then why come to my restaurant in particular? You could have gone anywhere for coffee."

Now it's my turn to shrug. "You've got me there. I guess I just needed to see a friendly face."

"You can't go home?"

"Uh… Not right now." I look away, hoping she's done with the questions, but judging from the determined look on her face, she's not finished by a long shot.

"You live with Ben?"

"Sort of. I'm staying in his pool house."

"Oh, did he kick you out or something?"

"No, I just left because we were arguing. What the hell is this, twenty questions?" I'm getting irritated, but Allie is undaunted.

"Does he know you're in love with him?"

"What the fuck!" I set my coffee down so hard it sloshes onto the table, and she moves quickly to wipe it up. "No, Allie. I am not in love with him. Jesus Christ, is everyone in this town so damn nosy?"

Instead of getting offended by my outburst, she leans in and puts a hand on mine. I don't like it, because it makes me feel weak, but I don't pull away.

"I don't know you and Ben well at all," she says quietly. "But I can read people, you know? I can tell if someone's not enjoying their meal, even if they say everything is fine. I can tell if someone's going to leave a good tip, or if they're going to try to beat the check. I can tell if a guy likes me or not. I may not be the smartest chick in town, but I've got pretty good instincts."

I sit back and sip on what's left of my coffee, wondering if I can trust Allie. She seems genuine enough, and I'm desperate for someone to talk to. In the end, I decide to confide in her.

"Ben is straight. He's not interested in me. I told you last night, he just broke up with his girlfriend. That's why I took him out drinking."

"Hmmm…" She tops off my coffee absently, as if it's just a habit for her. "Why did he break up with his girlfriend?"

"It's complicated. Can you keep your damn mouth shut, or are you one of these gossip mongers everyone around here keeps warning me about?"

She laughs. "I enjoy good gossip as much as anyone, and most people in a little town like this don't really mind being talked about. Not deep down. It's part of the life, you know? But when I say I'll keep a secret, I'll keep a fucking secret."

I clear my throat. "Um… You didn't actually say you would keep *my* secret."

She regards me with narrowed eyes, then grins. "You are a shrewd dude, Corey. Let me be clear. I will keep your secret, okay? I will never breathe it to a soul. The National Guard could waterboard my ass, and I would still not tell them your secret. So spill it."

I take a deep breath, squeeze my eyes shut, and blurt it out. "Ben's girlfriend asked me and Ben to do a threesome with her."

"Oh my gosh!" Allie nearly flies off her seat with excitement. "That is so hot. Did you do it? If you tell me you did it, I'll have fantasy masturbation material for a year."

"Allie, have you ever heard the expression *TMI*?" I plug my ears with my fingers, and she slaps me on the elbow.

"Quit it. I don't believe you can ever have too much information, especially about sex. So please give me details, okay? I promise it will never go beyond this table."

I roll my eyes. "Okay, but if anyone finds out about this, I'll know who to kill. And I will kill you, woman. I'm highly trained in the assassinatory arts."

"*Assassinatory* isn't even a word, jackass." She leans against the back of her seat and crosses her arms. "So you all had sex together. Was it awesome? What was it like?"

"First of all, let me tell you that neither Ben nor I wanted to do it. It was all her idea, and we were sort of coerced into it. Ben was only doing it to make her happy, and I did it for him."

"And…" she prods.

"And it was amazing."

"So you recommend threesomes."

"Actually, no. Threesomes can be awkward, and a lot of extra work. But after a bit, I hardly knew she was there."

"Ohhh… I see." Allie's eyes are bugging out of her head, and she's leaned forward again. "Is that why he broke up with her?

Because he felt the same way you did?"

"I wish that was the reason, but not even close. I mean, there were a few times when it seemed like we were on the same wavelength. Especially when he grabbed onto my neck when we were… um… finishing."

Allie opens her mouth wide in delighted shock. "Scandalous," she breathes, and I feel a blush creep over my face.

"I have a biased view of the whole thing, though. I think a more realistic explanation is that it made him realize how selfish she is. Or how shallow. He really didn't seem to like her that much to begin with."

"Well, it's pretty obvious *you* don't like her." She gives me a pointed look.

"I know what you're thinking, but it's not just jealousy. She came onto me. Not like threesome style, either. I tried to ignore her flirting at first, especially when I found out who she was dating. But then the morning after she proposed the three-way idea, she drove me home. She told me no matter what Ben decided, she wanted to sleep with me anyway. On the side, of course. She wasn't about to break up with her doctor fiancé— that's what she called him. Told me they were getting married, which was total bullshit." I run my fingers through my hair and slump against the back of my seat. "She tried to come into my fucking hotel room, Allie. I had to physically push her out. How could a woman have an amazing guy like Ben and try to cheat on him with *me*? I'm… nothing. Less than nothing. How could she do him like that? How could she?"

Allie shakes her head and takes both my hands in hers. "Calm down, honey. It's not your fault. Just because you happened to be the target at that moment does not make you to blame."

"Maybe if I hadn't come along—"

"Stop it." She squeezes my hands hard. "Yes, you are extremely good looking, Corey. You're a serious temptation, that's for sure. But the best looking guy in the world can't turn a good woman bad. Please don't blame yourself. Ben made a poor choice in the girlfriend department, that's all." I stare out the window, and she leans around to catch my eye. "Imagine if you hadn't come along and sexed both of them up... Ben might have ended up marrying that witch, right?"

I smile in spite of my misery. "I guess you do have a point there."

"I know I do," she says. "And I think there's more to that breakup than him just realizing she was selfish. Ben's no dummy; he's probably known all along. As far as I'm concerned, it boils down to three questions you need to ask yourself. Number One, if he was upset enough about the threesome business to break up with her, why is he still hanging around with you instead of distancing himself from everyone involved? Number Two, why did he start that crazy game in the bar last night?"

"Um... to kiss you?" That explanation sounds a little thin, even to me.

"Yeah, right. He barely even spoke to me, Corey. There was only one person he was interested in at that table last night, and it wasn't me. I tried my best to get his attention, believe me, but he hardly even knew I was there."

"Okay, what's the third question?"

"I've already told you that one... Does he know you're in

love with him?" She leans back in her seat, a smug smile playing at her lips. "Hell, does he even know you're gay? That's some pretty pertinent information."

My head spins with the obviousness and utter brilliance of what she's just said. "Allie, you're a freaking genius. How could I not see that?"

She's doing a little victory dance in her seat, and I laugh so loudly the hostess and several patrons glance over.

"Sweet, naïve Corey," Allie says. "There's no way a straight guy like Ben is going to be able to admit he's into you if he doesn't even know you're gay. He's probably going out of his mind right now thinking he's got a forbidden crush on his new friend. Meanwhile, you're waiting for him to give you a sign, which ain't gonna happen as long as he thinks you're straight."

"Shit. I've been waiting for him to show me the exact thing he's been trying to hide."

"Bingo, sweetness. I guaran-damn-tee you that's what's going on. What I want to know is why I had to point this out to you? You're supposed to be the Stud Muffin of the Year, according to Ben."

"He called me that?" I grin and take a sip of coffee. "That's got to mean something, right?"

"You really are clueless where he's concerned, aren't you? Don't tell me you've never gone after a straight guy before."

"I've never really gone after *anyone* before."

She looks at me like I'm some sort of alien. "What do you mean, you've never gone after anyone?"

Before I can answer, we're interrupted by a waitress who

136

brings over two huge platters of food. There's shrimp, oysters, fish, deviled crab, and a two skewers of grilled vegetables. "My treat," Allie says at my confused expression. "One of the perks of owning a restaurant is being able to feed my friends."

"It looks delicious, Allie. I don't know how to thank you."

"Well, for starters you could finish your story. Tell me why you've never gone after anybody… which I don't believe for a minute."

"It's true," I insist, popping a savory shrimp into my mouth and making a show of enjoying it even though it's burning out the lining of my mouth. "There's always been plenty of action if I wanted it. I guess I just never wanted anyone who didn't come onto me first."

"Of course. Because everyone you meet comes onto you. Jeez, you are a spoiled rotten, sexy son of a bitch, you know that? You really have no idea what we mortals go through for love."

I dig into one of the deviled crabs with my fork. "I think I have some idea. Remember why I'm here? Ben, the hot doctor who treats me like I have bubonic plague…"

Allie laughs. "You mean he wears a creepy gas mask when he's around you? Some folks get off on that kind of thing."

We sit and talk while I eat, and I can't stop complimenting her on the food. After a while, she winks and picks up the coffee pot. "I've got to go, darlin'. This place is starting to fill up. You sit here as long as you want and enjoy your meal. Order whatever you want." She starts to walk away, then turns back. "Why don't you stay with me tonight, since you say you can't go home?"

"That's very nice of you, Allie. I'll definitely take you up on your offer if I can't work up the courage to go home."

If I still have a home.

"Okay, sweetie. Enjoy." She bustles off to tend to her customers. The place is getting packed just as she promised, and I'm starting to feel a little guilty about taking up space and eating for free.

I continue picking at my food, wishing I had some sweet tea. Outside of this small section of Georgia, there's not another place in the world that serves such delicious tea. Before I moved to Blackwood, I could never figure out why anyone liked the bland, watery mess. Then the waitress at the Huddle House near the hospital accidentally brought me a glass instead of soda, and I was hooked. The stuff is like liquid crack.

When a waitress comes by, I flag her down. "Could you please bring me a sweet tea in a to-go cup?"

"Sure, honey. Be right back."

I scan the room while I wait. There are all sorts of people in here tonight. Some are scrubbed and sparkling like they're on a date, while a few look like they came straight from the gym.

In a far alcove of the dining room, a flash of white-blond hair catches my eye, and I know who it is instantly. Christina sits across from a lanky red-haired man in a nice suit, and I think I recognize him as one of the doctors from the hospital. She reaches across the table with those thin, grasping fingers and touches him intimately on the arm. I've been around her enough to know what that means. She's gaming him like she does everyone else.

I turn sideways in the booth and sink back into the corner, because the last thing I want is for her to see me. When I change positions, I'm looking straight at the podium at the entrance, and what I see there makes my heart leap into my throat.

Ben...

He stands in the doorway, his hair a sexy mess, eyes searching. He's got his leather hoodie on, and a green sweater that intensifies the green in his eyes even at this distance. I've found plenty of guys attractive in my lifetime, but there's never been one who affected me like he does. It's not just looks, either. There are these little mannerisms he has, facial expressions, things I can't even pinpoint. Every time I see him, there's this strange weakness that washes over my whole body, and I get such a buzz of excitement I can hardly control myself. It's getting worse every day. If I can't tell him how I feel soon, I'm going to explode.

Allie comes out to the podium and hugs Ben warmly. I feel a twinge of jealousy when he doesn't pull away like he does when I touch him.

She points in my direction, and when he turns and his eyes meet mine, there's a hardness in them that freezes the blood in my veins. How can a man look so boyish and so intimidating at the same time?

Everything drops into slow motion as he crosses the room toward me. I stand to greet him, fighting the urge to wrap my arms around him like Allie did. Instead, I touch his shoulder with one hand, but he shrugs it off.

"What the hell do you mean riding off like that and staying gone so long? You don't even have a damn phone. How am I supposed to know if you're coming back, or even if you're okay?"

"Ben—"

"I've called the hospital, the sheriff, and the coroner."

"Jesus, I'm sorry. I had no idea you'd be worried about me."

"If you're going to live with me, we need some rules, or some boundaries or something, dammit." He's not yelling, but he's obviously agitated, and some of the diners have begun to look our way. I chance a glance at Christina, who is watching with interest.

"Ben, let's go home, okay? Let's at least get out of here so that we don't have an audience." I jerk my head in her direction, and he turns to look. She waves demurely. *Bitch.*

Ben smirks. "She didn't waste any time, did she?"

"That's what I thought, too. Do you know that guy? Isn't he a doctor?"

"Yeah, Dr. Frank Hannigan. That snake is living out half of his wet dream right now sitting there with my ex."

"What's the other half?"

"Getting my job. Come on, let's go before they come over here."

The waitress shows up with my tea just in the nick of time, and I grab the cup off the tray as I hurry to keep up with Ben.

He drives like a maniac all the way home, which is fine with me. I love driving fast. It makes me feel so damn alive, which is ironic because speeding is essentially begging for death. All you have to do is watch the news to know that.

When we hit an open stretch of highway with a dotted line, I pull around him, smiling and giving him a friendly finger as I move past his window. He's going to have to do some fancy driving if he's going to outrun me.

We race along the highway at almost a hundred miles per hour. Not as fast as they drive in the movies or on the race track, but it's a nice clip for a curvy country road on Saturday evening. At the beginning of a short straightaway, Ben's Porsche pulls past me to take the lead again, narrowly making it back into our lane before a pickup truck pops around the next corner, blaring its horn.

Jesus, that was close.

After a few seconds, my breathing starts up again, and I relax my butt cheeks. I can't help but think it's awfully irresponsible for a doctor and a medic to behave this way. We've dedicated our lives to saving people, and right now we're about one swerve away from ending lives.

He doesn't show any signs of slowing down, and I'm not about to let him get away from me. I'm gearing up to overtake him on the next straightaway, which I think is coming up in less than a quarter of a mile, when I see flashing blue lights reflecting off the Porsche's shiny black finish.

Great... This is all I need.

For about two seconds, I consider making a run for it, but that would be stupid. And besides, Ben would never run, and I can't leave him hanging to take the blame.

But he probably doesn't have a record like you do, idiot.

I wonder what Ben will do when he finds out I have a police record. No doubt I'm about to be cuffed and chauffeured off to jail. I might as well move back to Atlanta if I can make bail. Either way, my life is over.

"Sit right here," the cop orders as he walks past me on the way to Ben's car. I'm not about to disobey, because he's holding my future in his hands. If only he would speak privately with me about my record and whatever consequences I may be facing. Ben doesn't need to know all that crap. No felonies, but enough misdemeanors to paint a nasty picture. If he does find out, especially this way, I think I'll die of embarrassment. And he'll hate me.

Ben has his window rolled down when the officer approaches. I can hear their voices, but I can't make out what they're saying. At least the cop isn't yelling or snatching Ben out of the car.

After a moment, he heads back in my direction, and I steel myself for what's to come.

"Slow it down, son," he says as he passes me. I watch in my mirror as he gets in his car and drives away.

What the hell...

Ben sticks a hand out the car window and gives a quick thumbs up before pulling back onto the highway. I follow, though my head is reeling and I can't wait to get home to ask him what just happened.

When I pull into his garage, he's already inside the house, so I ring the doorbell. After a few minutes, the door swings open, and he's standing there in nothing but a pristine white towel wrapped precariously low around his waist. I feel the heat rising in my face at the sight, and suddenly my imagination has me slamming his perfect body against the wall and violating him in several interesting ways.

Maybe I should have just gone to the pool house, because now I'm going to have to figure out how to hide my growing erection.

"Why are you ringing the bell?" He steps aside to let me enter. "The door was unlocked. You could've just come in."

"Uh... last I checked, I don't live here, Ben. I live in the pool house."

He waves a hand dismissively. "Just come in. I was about to take a steam shower. After being out in the cold, I really need one."

"Okay, but first tell me what happened with that cop back there. We were going over 100 when he clocked us. So why aren't we both in jail with our vehicles impounded?"

Ben laughs. "Possum is a friend of mine. He didn't realize it was me until he got close to the car, so he apologized. That's all."

"Wait. I can't believe what I'm hearing. Did you just say that a cop apologized for pulling you over for racing on the highway?"

"Corey, I told you everybody knows everybody in a small town. Sometimes that can be bad, and sometimes it can be very good. Especially if you're a doctor." He winks and strolls back to his bathroom. "Make yourself at home."

I hear the shower come on, and that's when I realize he's left the bathroom door open. My breathing stalls as I stare at the open door. Ben unwinds the towel from around his waist, tosses it onto the counter, and steps naked into the enormous glass-and-stone shower. The only opening is the vent at the top of the door, and the shower quickly fills with thick, white steam, obscuring my view of his body. I'm sure it's for the best, because I feel awkward playing Peeping Tom out here.

Why did he leave the door open?

I'm tempted to just go to the bathroom and join him. Then I'd find out very quickly if he's interested or not. Only thing is, I don't have the courage. I'm a coward. There's too much on the line with Ben, and I'm not sure I can handle the rejection.

"God, Ben…" I whisper to myself. "Do you want me or not? I'm tearing my hair out over here. Please just give me a sign."

Wait. Maybe that's why he left the door open.

Suddenly I know I have to just go for it, because I can't feel like this anymore. I pull my jacket off, then my t-shirt, and I'm naked from the waist up. I slip out of my shoes and socks, and then my jeans, piling all of my clothes on the couch.

"Grow some huevos, Corey," I say out loud. "It's now or never."

I get my boxers down to mid-thigh and nearly jump out of my skin when the doorbell rings.

"Fuck!" *Screwed by the universe again.*

"Can you get that?" Ben calls from the shower.

I pick up my jeans to get dressed, but whoever is at the door is impatient, and the bell chimes loudly again.

"Corey?" Ben calls. "Are you still here?"

"Uh… yeah, Ben. I've got it. Finish your shower." I throw my jeans back onto the sofa. No time for dressing. I have to get rid of the asshole at the door before Ben comes out and sees me like this.

I open the front door halfway and peer around it, trying to hide the fact that I'm nearly naked. Julie is standing on the porch with a large fruit basket in her hands.

"Oh, Corey." She's obviously surprised to see me. "Um… Is Ben here?"

"Yeah." I rub the back of my neck, looking at the floor, wondering what the hell I'm going to do. "Come on in."

I take the fruit basket from her and set it on the kitchen counter. "It was nice of you to get him this, Julie. I'm sure he'll love it. Unfortunately, he just got in the shower."

"Oh." Her brows come together, and I can almost see her

brain working as she takes in my state of undress. "Are you—"

"I'm staying in Ben's pool house," I interrupt before she can speculate any further. "Come on out. I'll show it to you while he's in the shower."

I grab my clothes and carry them under my arm, hoping she doesn't think too hard about why I was getting undressed in his living room. It's freezing outside in my underwear, but I sprint, and Julie sprints along behind me, laughing.

Once we're inside the pool house, I turn the lights on low and open the curtains.

"This is my place. What do you think?"

"Wow, Corey. It's like a vacation in here."

"Yeah, I love it. Have a seat. Ben will be out in a few."

"Alright," she says, sitting on the sofa and folding her hands primly into her lap.

I've got a bad feeling about this. She came here looking for Ben for a reason, and I'd bet money it's the same reason she pulled her shirt up and let him use her as a human Annie doll at the CPR class this morning. Ben is newly single, and she's trying to stake her claim, same as me. Only I'm at a great disadvantage, because he's straight, and I haven't had a chance to let him know how I feel. It would be far too easy for him to fall into a relationship with a girl, especially one he already likes and respects.

Think, Corey. Think.

And then, miraculously, Julie solves my dilemma. She looks at me. But it's not just any look. She stares slack-jawed at my chest, my stomach, my cock outlined behind the fabric of my underwear. Suddenly I know beyond a doubt that Julie wants to fuck me, and that is my saving grace.

I follow her gaze brazenly down to look at my own dick. Then I look her directly in the eyes and give my most salacious smile. Realization dawns on her face, and she blushes and looks away.

Too late, little girl. I've already caught you looking.

I flip the stereo on. My MP3 player is still hooked in, and Kid Cudi's dark rap anthem *King Wizard* starts up. I could not have chosen a better song to defile Ben's little nurse to. I reach over and flip the outside speakers on, sending the music out across the pool and toward the house, because I don't just want to seduce Julie. I want an audience.

11

I'VE got Julie smashed naked up against the pool house window when I notice Ben standing like a statue beside the pool in a pair of plaid pajama pants and a t-shirt, his hair still damp from the shower.

Julie and I have barely gotten started, but she's on fire already. She's panting harshly in my ear, and when I push her ass even harder into the glass, she brings her legs up and wraps them tightly around my waist. I can tell this is going to be a good show.

"That's it, sweetie," I whisper in her ear. "You want me to fuck you?"

"Uh-huh," she moans.

"You like me?"

She nods. "Yes, Corey." She trails little kisses along my jaw and wraps her fingers in my hair. "I like you a lot."

"You like Ben, too, don't you?" She stills for a second as if she's unsure whether to answer or not, but I slap her ass just hard enough to make it sting. "Don't think, Julie. Just tell me how you feel."

"Y-Yes. I like Ben. I like you both."

"Hmmmm…" I kiss her deeply, dragging my tongue across hers and biting her lip. "Would you like to make love to both of us at the same time?"

"Are you serious?" She snatches her head back and stares wide-eyed into my face.

"As a heart attack."

She nods slowly, and I kiss her again and run my hand up between her legs to find her sweet spot, playing in the moisture there, making her keen with pleasure. She's past the point of refusal now. I know the symptoms well.

I look directly at Ben as I pull Julie's hair back, exposing the side of her throat to him. Then I tilt my head the other way and put my mouth to the other side of her throat, trailing kisses down onto the soft spot between her neck and shoulder, low enough so my mark won't show when she's wearing scrubs. Honestly, I've never been into hickeys, but it seemed the cool thing to do in Christina's case, and right now it's the only discreet way I can think of to get my point across to Ben.

It works like gangbusters.

Ben enters the pool house quietly, stopping briefly to turn off the outside speakers, and then moves close to us. I tip Julie's head a little more, giving him complete access, and before she even realizes he's in the room, he latches onto her other shoulder.

Julie gasps but doesn't protest. On the contrary, as soon as

Ben joins in, I feel a surge of wetness between her legs. Of course I don't really give a shit about that. I want Ben, and if the only way I can get him is with a woman between us, so be it.

After we've both put discreet marks on her, I spin her away from the window, kissing her with a passion that's not meant for her, but for Ben. It's all a show for him. I'm going to fuck this nurse of his like my life depends on it, because in a way it does. In a matter of days, my life has gotten so tightly wrapped up in his that I fear I'll have to leave a huge chunk of it behind when I go, and it's tearing me up inside.

Don't even think about that. Don't think about leaving.

I drop to my knees with Julie riding my hips and lower her to the floor onto her back. She keeps her legs wound tightly around me, writhing for my cock. I'm going to give it to her, but I want Ben to see it. I want him to watch every inch of it penetrate his special little night shift nurse. If I can't have him, then she won't either.

I meet Ben's hungry gaze, trying to will him to join in without saying anything. He drops to the floor at Julie's head and wraps his fingers in her hair, runs his palm along her cheek. She shudders and moans at the simple contact, and it's obvious that she's craved his touch for some time. When her eyes flutter open, Ben lowers his head to hers and claims her lips in a tentative kiss.

"See, I knew you wanted to give me mouth-to-mouth," she sighs when he pulls back. He laughs and dives back into the kiss.

Watching him kiss her has got me vibrating with jealousy, and with something else, too. A desperate need to get inside this woman, to claim her away from Ben, to possess her just so he can't. It doesn't make much sense, but I can't help it. My id is in charge now, and he's not known for his rationality.

I jerk Julie's hips roughly, getting both their attention, and Ben breaks the kiss. When he looks at me, his eyes are hooded with lust. I'm about to do my dead level best to push him over the edge, to make him lose that control he values so much.

"Ben," I say, my voice hoarse with a hostile sort of lust I've never felt before. "Do you want to watch me fuck your little nurse?" I grab a condom off the sofa and roll it on. Then I position myself between Julie's legs, nudging the opening of her vagina, threatening to penetrate her.

She's squirming on the floor, panting and thrashing about. The feel of the head of my dick pushing between the slick lips of her pussy has got her crazy. At this point, she doesn't care what I do to her, or what I'm saying. She's in that needful place that women sometimes get, when you could slap them around if you wanted and they'd still beg for you.

Ben is hovering over her, speechless, his eyes tortured. He's thinking again, and that's not good.

"Ben," I rasp again, louder this time. "What do you want? Tell me what to do, baby."

Shit. Why did I say that?

He looks startled, but then he licks his lips and watches my cock strain against Julie's opening, ready to go as soon as he gives the go-ahead, and his eyes go dark.

"Fuck her," he whispers. "I want to watch you do it."

That's all I need to hear. I buck hard into her cunt, not caring if I'm hurting her or not. She's slick enough, and I easily bury my thick cock to the hilt. I don't take my eyes off of Ben, though. I need to see his face.

Julie screams and grunts in pain, but I withdraw almost all the way, and she gasps loudly.

"Oh, God," she groans and bites her bottom lip.

"Do you think she likes it, Ben?" I ask, a sardonic smile twisting my lips.

"She's loving it." Ben lowers his lips to a pink tipped breast, and sucks the tight nipple into his mouth, making Julie moan and toss her head from side to side.

"Dr. Hardy… I've wanted this. Wanted you so— "

I grab her hips and slam her onto my cock full force, purposely cutting off her words and making her cry out. This time, I don't let up. I drag her body roughly back and forth on the carpet, impaling her over and over, until she's a mindless mass of female flesh, and I can tell she's about to come. A sheen of sweat is starting to glisten on her skin.

Ben, who is watching the action with increasing agitation, suddenly wraps his fist in Julie's hair and snatches back, immobilizing her head and making her yelp.

Her back is arched now, and he bends and touches his tongue to her heaving sternum, tracing slow circles there, then drags it all the way down to rim her tiny bejeweled belly button. He turns his head to the side and watches, his face only inches from where my cock is pounding in and out of Julie's pussy. He is breathing heavily, and his eyes are wide. Even through his clothes, I can see his muscles are tightly bunched. He's definitely aroused, but he doesn't try to touch himself or join the action in any significant way.

He looks up and sees me studying him closely, and we hold

eye contact for one eternal moment.

"Put your mouth on her," I tell him. "Down there."

I know she's ready to come, and Ben going down on her will put her over the edge. What I don't know is if he will do it or not, because putting his mouth on her will be almost like putting his mouth on me.

For one weighted moment, Ben hovers contemplating, and then he leans in and clamps his mouth over her swollen clit. She lets out a soft moan that seems to crescendo forever.

"My... God..." Her body bucks, but I tighten my grip on her hips and pin her to the tops of my thighs, and Ben's still got her hair in a death grip. She's not going anywhere now.

I gyrate my hips in a languorous rhythm, my cock moving inside her in tiny increments, so that both she and I can focus on what Ben is doing. I can feel his soft lips down there, sucking and licking at her quivering little nub, working with lustful enthusiasm. I savor the subtle feel of his lips barely touching me, the soft little twitches and rubs nearly making me come out of my skin. The brush of his cheek, the tickle of his hair against my belly. This is so close to what I want from him.

If this little bitch doesn't come soon, I'm afraid I'll explode all in her, and I don't want to come. Not for her. There's only one person in the room I want to spill my load for, and I'll hold off if it kills me. I want to show Ben that it's not this silly girl who's got my cock ready to blow. It's him.

Finally, not a moment too soon, Julie is shuddering to a tumultuous orgasm, making little bleating noises as she goes. "Dr. Hardy... Corey..." she gasps, as Ben licks her gently through her final breathy spasms.

Stoic Ben, who has remained completely clothed the whole time.

I pull my dick out and squeeze it hard, fighting the overwhelming sensations as I watch Ben's head move between Julie's quaking thighs.

I. Will. Not. Come.

My heart jumps when Ben rests the side of his face on her belly and stares unflinchingly at me. In that moment, I'm certain the connection I feel with him is not completely one-sided.

He drags the back of his hand across his lips to wipe away the nurse's juices, and I jump up and toss the condom into the trash. I quickly pull on my jeans and stuff my erection in, not bothering with the underwear lying on the floor beside them.

I feel like there are bugs crawling on me I'm so agitated. My cock is aching, pushing painfully against my zipper, but the pain is the only thing that's keeping me sane.

Ben helps Julie up onto shaky legs, holding her quietly, being all proper and gentlemanly. I don't have anything against the woman, and I hate to be cold, but I just want her out of here now. I didn't intend to feel this way, but I need to be alone with Ben before I lose my shit.

Julie is probably going to think I'm the biggest prick on the planet, and she'd probably be right. What the hell was I thinking dragging her between me and Ben? Granted, she was down for anything I suggested, which makes me feel a little less guilty. But that doesn't excuse my actions.

"Jesus, I'm an asshole," I shout out loud. "Always have been."

I stalk off to the bathroom, slamming the door behind me,

feeling claustrophobic in the tiny space. Ben is tending to Julie, and forever couldn't even take so long. I try to think of any excuse to get rid of her without hurting her feelings too badly or pissing Ben off. What if he hates me now? What if the girl talks at work and makes things difficult? The twisted logic that I'd used earlier to justify seducing her has abandoned me now, and I wonder how I ever thought this could work out.

I punch the wall. Not enough to do any damage, but the whole place seems to shake with the force of it.

No way they didn't hear that.

I wonder what they're doing out there. Now that some of the blood is returning to my brain, I realize I need to go back out there and face the problem I created. I have to put things right. It's not Ben's responsibility to clean up my mess.

When I emerge, I see the front door closing, and Ben is escorting Julie around the pool and toward the garage. She's smiling, and Ben touches her gently on the arm. I don't know which I feel more of, jealousy or relief. He's smoothing things over with her. I cross my fingers that there are no professional repercussions from what I've done tonight.

Why do I have to screw up everything I touch?

Since I've been in town, I've broken up Ben and his girlfriend, kissed him in public, groped him when he was drunk, gotten him so upset he called the morgue looking for me, and now fucked his best nurse. I'm nothing but a human wrecking ball.

I sulk on the couch, still dressed only in jeans, fidgeting with the cross necklace Granny gave me. My dick is still semi-hard. Ben does that to me. I know I'm obsessed with him. Nothing has consumed my thoughts this much since before I got off drugs, and unfortunately I don't think rehab would cure an addiction to Dr. Ben Hardy.

One thing's for sure. When Ben returns to the pool house, he's angry, and I feel ashamed that I'm the cause of it.

"What the fuck was that?" he demands, his hands shaking slightly at his sides.

I sit back on the couch and let my legs fall open slightly, not bothering to try to hide the fact that my cock is stiffening again just from his presence. Can he hear my heart beating out of my ribcage from across the room? I want to drop to my knees at his feet, wrap my arms around him, and tell him how much I fucking *need* him. Instead, I slump against the back of the sofa, stretch my arms along the top of it, and shrug. "What's the matter? You didn't like the present I got you?"

"She was an innocent, and you had no right to bring her into this. This is between me and you."

"What do you mean?" I pretend I don't know what he's talking about.

He purses his lips, and I can tell he's biting something back. "You used that poor girl to get back at me, didn't you?"

"Get back at you? For what?"

"I don't know." He runs his hands through his hair and paces a short path in front of the window. "Goddammit, I don't know."

"Calm down, Ben." I soften my voice, deciding to drop the macho act. "You're right about not bringing Julie into this. I was wrong, and I'm sorry. I'd take it back if I could. But this is not about revenge— not even close. Getting back at you is the last thing I want to do."

He doesn't respond, but I'm not surprised. I've come very close to telling the truth, and he's not quite ready to hear it yet.

"What did you tell Julie?" I ask.

"That you're a sex addict. That when I saw the two of you together, she looked sexy and I got carried away. I also told her it won't happen again. That our relationship has to be strictly professional." He glares at me. "It *won't* happen again, will it?"

"No. I promise I will not try to seduce Julie again. Although there wasn't much trying to it, if you want to know the truth."

"Oh, I have no doubt she was worshiping at your feet." He twirls his wrist and bends slightly at the waist in a perfectly executed mock bow, his lips curving into a cruel half smile.

He hates me. I've ruined everything.

Ben turns to go, but instead of leaving, he pauses beside the door and leans his head against the glass for several excruciating minutes. I'm too much of a coward to break the silence. Eventually, he clears his throat and speaks without turning to look at me.

"You can't keep doing this shit." Another silence follows. "Why didn't you come, Corey?"

"I didn't want to." I stare defiantly at his back, but he won't turn around.

"Why not?"

I sigh and fiddle with my necklace again. "I do want to come— need to come. But not in *her*."

"Jesus, Corey." He's still leaning against the glass, and now he bumps his head against it several times.

"You didn't come, either," I point out, walking quietly across the carpet on my bare feet and coming to a stop directly behind him. My heart is a runaway train, but I have to be strong or we're both lost.

"I didn't want to," he says, echoing my words.

My stomach does a double flip. I'm terrified that I've misread his signals, but there's only one way to find out for sure. I move up behind him, close enough for him to feel my breath on the back of his neck. He doesn't move a muscle, and that gives me the courage to do what I have to do.

I reach around him with one arm and slide my hand slowly, deliberately down his abdomen and onto his dick. "My God, Ben…" I gasp against his ear when I feel his straining erection. "You're as hard as I am."

As proof, I press my own rigid cock against him from behind and feel every muscle in his body tense and release. He lets out the breath he's been holding, and it's like a huge burden is expelled from his body.

I lower my head and press my mouth into the hollow at his throat, nuzzling in under the edge of his t-shirt and biting down. Since we met, we've ritualistically marked two women as our own. Now I'm going to claim the only person I've ever truly desired in my entire life.

There's no mistaking what it means, and he lets me do it.

12

(BEN)

WHEN I feel Corey's warm mouth moving in that sensitive spot between my throat and my shoulder, I can't help but shiver. It's so incredibly erotic I feel it in every part of my body, all the way to my toes.

What the hell am I doing?

My body tenses suddenly, and my instincts almost make me pull away.

"What is it?" He asks against my neck, and I get chills all over again from the tickle of his lips.

"I'm not supposed to feel this way... not with another man. I'm straight, Corey. I like women, right?"

He laughs under his breath, grabs my hand, and pulls me out the door and toward the house. The air is frigid, but I barely notice. I'm numb to everything but his touch now.

"Let's go in the house, Doc. I think you'll be more comfortable there." He pulls me silently along until we reach the kitchen. It's my own kitchen, and yet it seems strange to me tonight. Everything does. All I can do is stare as Corey grabs a couple of bottles of beer from the fridge, opens them, and sets mine on the counter.

He takes several long swallows of his beer, and I'm fascinated with the movement of his throat, and the contours of his ripped chest and abs. His faded jeans hang low around his hips, exposing his perfectly defined Adonis belt muscles and the thin trail of dark hair that extends down into his waist band, hinting at what's below. He must have been wearing these particular jeans for years, because they're worn to threads in spots. He's barefoot, and the too-long, tattered pant legs curve under his heels when he walks.

It's got to be a sin to be looking at him this way, and thinking what I'm thinking.

"I'm straight, right?" I ask him.

He seems to consider for a moment. "Do you like women?"

I nod. "Or I always have so far."

"Do you like me?"

I have to clear my throat to speak. "Yes. Am I… gay?"

"I don't know." He sets his beer on the counter. "Let me check."

Before I know what's happening, he grabs me by the shoulders and throws me roughly against the wall, slamming his mouth down onto mine. His big body has me tightly pinned, and he's licking into my mouth like he's after the last bit of ice cream in the bottom of the cone. I love the taste of him, the feel of him, the

159

way he's mastering me. He's in charge, and he knows just how to use his lips and his tongue to make me clamor for more. I latch onto his lip and suck it hard, moaning against him, wrapping my arms around his neck and trying to pull him closer even though he's already flat against me. When he snakes a hand around to grab my ass, and it's all I can do not to wrap my legs around him, too.

I want him so much I'm having freaking heart attack symptoms. Chest pain, shortness of breath, elevated temperature… Except the chest pain actually hurts in my heart, and it's more of an ache. I've never had this feeling before. Not with Christina, not with anyone.

Suddenly, he lets go of me and pulls away, grabbing his beer off the counter and taking a swig. "I don't know, Ben. That felt pretty gay to me."

"Nice. You're making jokes, and I'm having a heart attack."

"Hey, calm down. This kind of thing happens between men all the time. It's not like we're breaking new ground here."

"I know. It just feels a lot different when it's happening first hand."

Corey laughs. "It feels *better*. Now drink your beer. Want to watch some TV?"

I grab my beer and follow him on unsteady legs to the sofa. Maybe some television will clear my head, give me something to think about other than sleeping with Corey. Because I have to admit, I'm pretty well consumed with it right now.

I turn on the TV and put it on an old rerun of Happy Days. Fonzie is slow dancing with Richie, who's dressed in drag for some kind of initiation. I've seen the episode before, but the irony of it airing during my first official gay experience is too much. And besides, Fonzie is making me think of Corey, with his leather jacket and his motorcycle, and his magical way with the ladies.

"Heeyyy…" Corey does a really poor imitation of the Fonz.

"I think you need to stick to CPR."

The seat caves under him when he sits beside me, so that my body slides closer to him. I instinctively lean away, but he puts his arm around my shoulders. "Please don't pull away. You let other people touch you, but you always pull away from me."

"Other people don't make me feel the way you do."

Did I really just say that?

"Oh?" he asks. "How do I make you feel?"

"Jeez, Corey. You know."

He raises his eyebrows. "No, I don't. You've never told me. And quite frankly, a lot of the time you act like you can't stand me."

"What have you been smoking? I act like I can't stand you? Look where you are, for heaven's sake. I asked you to move in with me like two minutes after we met."

"You didn't ask; you ordered. And staying in the pool house is not exactly moving in with you."

"Are you in the pool house now? And where did you sleep last night?"

"I guess I haven't spent much time out there," he admits. "But you were telling me how I made you feel, remember?"

"I can't believe I'm telling you this. You make me nervous, okay? I can't think of how to act normal when you're around. The way you are, the way you look… I keep telling myself I just look up to you, like the popular guy everyone wants to hang around with in school. But that's not exactly true, is it?" I bury my hands in my face. "Jesus, I'm fucked."

Corey is smiling like a jackass. I wish I could tell him how I feel in a more manly, respectable fashion rather than gushing like some lovesick geek, but he doesn't seem to mind.

"And when I touch you…" He runs his index finger along the inside of my thigh, stopping just shy of the swell in my pajama pants, and I jump.

"It's wrong. I'm not supposed to feel the way you make me feel. I have to stay away from you, because if you touch me I might like it too much. I might want you to touch me more, and to never stop touching me. Then what will I do?" The words tumble out, and as I'm talking it's becoming clear to me for the first time.

I *need* him to touch me, and I'm terrified of that need.

Corey seems to sense exactly how I'm feeling, and he pulls me close, squeezing me tightly to his naked chest so that the warmth of his body begins to penetrate me. With his free hand, he rubs along the length of my thigh, my arm, my side, sending chill bumps dancing all over me.

"Everything is going to be okay, Doc," he whispers against my hair. "Whatever this is, we're in it together. You are not alone."

We sit that way for a long while, watching TV, laughing, drinking beer.

At around nine, I get up to go to the bedroom. My body is stiff from being in the same position for so long, because I was afraid if I moved too much, he'd let go.

"Stay with me?" I'm as nervous as a virgin on prom night, and I'm sure he can hear the quiver in my voice.

"Hell, yes." He jumps easily off the couch and follows me into my room. "I'd like to shower, though. I've got nurse all over me, you know?"

"Yeah, I think that's just an excuse to get into my amazing shower."

He chuckles as he strips out of his jeans and turns the water on, and I feel like I'm seeing him naked for the first time. It's a good thing I'm wearing pants, or he'd see my extreme reaction.

I try not to watch him through the glass as he showers. He is cut and contoured in all the right places, and the water traces sensual, sudsy white rivulets down his buttocks and thighs. When the glass fogs up too much to see any more than a tan blur, I busy myself with turning on the sound system and getting some good tunes playing. It feels like a classic rock kind of night, so I set it on my seventies playlist and kick back on the bed to a little Led Zeppelin until Corey pounces onto the bed in nothing but a towel.

I take a deep breath, inhaling the woodsy scent of the expensive body wash I have auto-shipped because I can't live without it. "Mmmm... My soap smells good on you."

"Yeah, I like smelling like you." He smiles self-consciously, training his amazing blue eyes on me from beneath his lashes. I'm coming to recognize that coy look, and every time he flashes it at me, I feel a tightening in my groin.

He pulls the covers up to his waist and slips the towel from beneath, dangling it from one finger before dropping it to the floor. "Does that make you crazy, Mr. Neat Freak?"

"Hmmm... Not for the reason you think." I reach beneath the covers and wiggle out of my underwear, dropping them to the rug on my side of the bed. The look on his face is definitely worth the clutter.

"Does that mean you like me, Doc?"

"Like?" I kick the covers off of both of us, sending them cascading off the bottom of the bed, and suddenly we're both completely exposed. I roll over and climb on top of him, straddling his belly, feeling the warmth of his freshly washed skin cradling my balls. "Like doesn't begin to cover it."

I'm wild with desire now, the cacophony of doubt that's been filling my head for days silenced by an urgent craving that will not be denied. I lean down and claim his lips in a searing kiss, trying to devour him, needing to have his taste on my tongue.

When I finally give him a chance to breathe, a slow smile spreads across his face and he folds his arms behind his head. "Surprise the hell out of me one time, why don't you?"

He bucks his hips, toppling me back down onto him, and we kiss for a long, lazy time. I let my hands explore his body, learning every hot inch of it, committing the feel of him to memory.

My cock is thick and stiff between our bodies, our frantic movements rubbing it almost to the point of finishing. I'm suddenly aware of the fact that he's got one, too. A really big one, and it's teasing up and down the crack of my ass. I reach behind me and grip it for the first time, loving the weight of it and the silky feel of the skin.

Corey gasps. "Ben… Be sure, okay? There's no turning back from this." I begin to stroke him gently behind my back, and he grits his teeth and squeezes his eyes shut.

"How much do you want me?" I ask, reaching back with my

other hand to cup his balls.

"From the first time we met, I haven't been able to think of anything else but you. Not for one second."

I bend and kiss his lips, trying to convey all of the passion I feel for him. "It's the same for me," I whisper just before I slide down his body, all the way to his cock. It's straining for me, and I can tell it won't take him long to climax. I've never had any part of a man's anatomy in my mouth, but I'm pretty sure I know what to do with it, considering I'm the proud owner of one myself.

I grip the thick shaft in my hand and wrap my lips tentatively around the head. His tortured moan gives me the courage I need to go for it. I snake my tongue out to tease the ridge, tighten my lips around the shaft and apply a light suction, moving my mouth up and down and following with my hand, using my mouth to lubricate the way. I work up to a nice rhythm, and before long Corey shudders beneath me, his dick swelling impossibly bigger.

"Suck it, baby. God, I'm not going to last… Held back too long. *Shit.*"

He comes in my mouth, a big, warm blast that jets down my throat and nearly chokes me. The taste is salty and strange, but I love it because it comes from him.

I hover over him in a cloud of ecstasy, watching him convulse and sigh in the aftermath of the orgasm I just gave him, and I'm vibrating with a feeling so new I can't describe it. I'm not the same man I was a few days ago, or even a few hours ago. I'm so alive and filled with warm light that I feel like I must be glowing.

"Was that okay?" I ask. "I've never done that before."

His eyes flutter open, and he smiles sweetly. "Come here." He pulls me into his arms and kisses me softly on the lips, trailing kisses along my jaw and down my neck.

Before I can even register what's happening, he flips me over and has me lying on my back with my legs hanging off the bed from the knees down. He stands looking down at me with a wicked gleam in his eyes that wasn't there a moment before as he languished spent on the bed. It's a look that tells me I've asked for something, and now I'm going to get it.

He grasps my cock firmly in his hand, and every muscle in my body tenses in reaction. He doesn't wait, but dives right into sucking me off with his hot mouth. He's aggressive, every move laser targeted to getting me to finish. He drags his tongue up my shaft, pumping me with his hand, and sucking me so perfectly I think he must be tapped into my brain. The sensations rippling up my cock with every pull of his mouth and hand are pure overwhelming pleasure, taking me over body and soul. I'm being physically *forced* to come, and almost before we've even gotten started, he snatches my dick out of his mouth and stands up, and I'm blowing my load all over his belly.

Fuck. My head is spinning so fast, everything goes black for a few seconds, and I wonder if I'm passing out.

"You okay?" he asks with a knowing smile, standing there all cocky with my semen running down his abdomen.

"Yeah." I'm so breathless and flooded with endorphins I can barely speak. "Is that all you've got?"

He laughs and retrieves his towel from the floor, using it to clean himself up. "Not by a long shot. Eventually, I'm going to fuck you, Ben. You can count on it."

"With that thing?" I eye the thick slab of meat between his legs with a mixture of desire and trepidation, and my heart rate picks up noticeably. "I don't know, Corey..."

"It's the only one I've got. What's the matter? You don't like it?" He puts one knee on the bed beside my hip and drops his heavy member onto my thigh.

"Sweet Jesus..." I blush and cover my face with my hands, squirming as the tingle of desire crawls across my skin and my dick twitches back to life. "What are you doing to me?"

"I'm trying to seduce you. Isn't it obvious?" He grabs the lube from the table drawer and climbs all the way onto the bed, straddling me, and sits on my thighs, inching his way up until his cock is even with mine. Then he takes both of them in one hand and begins stroking slowly, drizzling lube onto them as he goes. He sets a slow pace back and forth, and the feeling of his hand on one side of my dick, and his stiff cock slipping against it on the other side is exquisite. Just the idea that he's rubbing our most private parts against each other is taboo enough to make me painfully hard. Again.

Just when the stimulation is almost too much to bear, he stops, leaving me straining for an explosive orgasm that's just beyond my grasp.

I've already come once, and against all odds he's made me ready to do it again almost instantly. Multiple orgasms is something I've only been able to pull off a few times in my life, but apparently it's something Corey takes for granted. He's certainly not lacking in the readiness department, even after his own climax only minutes before.

"Get up on the pillow," he says, his voice rough with need,

and I immediately scramble to the top of the bed, still on my back. Still ready for whatever he wants to do to me.

He slides easily up over me, stretching his body straight out above mine in push-up position, and drops down to his elbows. When he angles his head to kiss me, I'm eager and hungry, nipping at his lips with my teeth until he growls and covers my mouth with his. His kisses are like a drug to me, potent and all-consuming. I can't remember a time when my conscious brain switched off so completely and gave way to instinct. That's what he does to me.

"Are you ready to come with me, Ben?"

I nod emphatically. "Are we going to have sex now?"

"You're not ready for that yet. But soon… Right now, we're going to share the hottest, raunchiest mutual orgasm either one of us has ever had, okay?"

Instead of answering, I lift my head and capture his lips in a kiss and moan against his mouth. I don't think I could possibly be any more turned on.

He grabs the lube again and squirts some onto my belly. The coolness of the gel hitting my skin makes me laugh, and Corey pauses to stare at me. "Hmmm… so ticklish. I'll have to remember that."

Still in the push-up position and leaning on his forearms with his elbows bent, he settles his cock right next to mine on my belly and lowers himself until our members are sandwiched tightly between us. My mouth falls open in shock when I realize what he's about to do, and he flashes a wicked little smile as he starts to move.

He slides his body smoothly up and down mine, the lube slicking the way nicely, both our dicks getting a full-body massage that has me making noises I never would have made if I'd been in my right mind. He kisses me rhythmically, latching onto my lips when he slides forward, letting go when he slides back. The concentrated onslaught of slippery sensation between our bellies is surreal. I've never felt anything even remotely like what he's doing to me— to us. At one point, it seems to transcend the physical world and morph into some new type of experience, and my brain becomes mush. Desire rises higher and higher in me, raw and untempered, until we both tense, and a delicious warmth spreads between our bodies. Then I'm shuddering down from a mind-numbingly juicy orgasm, and we're both soaked and clinging to each other like two non-swimmers trying to save ourselves from drowning.

My breath is coming in gasps, and his is even more ragged since he was doing most of the work. He collapses heavily onto me, and I'm surprised to find I don't care. The feel of his weight on me is comforting in a strange way, and I close my eyes and pant in shallow breaths until he grunts and rolls off onto the other side of the bed. We're both bathed in the evidence of our desire, and I'm thinking I don't ever want to wash it off, but he grabs his towel and wipes us both down before I can protest.

"Damn. Was that as good for you as it was for me?" he asks.

"Ask me later. I don't think I can speak English."

He laughs. "I'll take that as a yes."

"Shit." I moan and cup my worn out, deliriously sated cock and balls and curl into a fetal position. "What the hell are we doing? This can't be good. What's gonna happen to us now?"

He rolls up behind me and pulls my back to his front, wrapping an arm warmly around my midsection and cinching me up to him. "What do you mean? I don't understand. I thought... We like each other, right?"

"How can you be so naïve? You know what I'm talking about."

He's silent for a moment, and I'm sensing I've hurt him. In fact, I'm sure I have. He said he liked me, and I called him naive. "I'm sorry, Corey. I didn't mean to be insensitive. I—"

"No, it's okay. I guess we can just call this a mistake and try to forget it ever happened."

I twist in his embrace and stare at him. "I can't possibly forget this happened. I'm trying to tell you I'm totally fucked up now. Like screwed fully into the goddamn ground. Maybe this isn't that big a deal to you— "

"Not a big deal?" His voice is louder now, his eyes hard. "How can you say that? This is a huge deal for me. Probably even bigger than it is for you, because I'm not the one freaking out and trying to figure out how to keep it on the down low. I'm happy, Ben." He lets go of me and stands abruptly, stalking naked to the bathroom and slipping into his jeans.

I get out of bed and pull my underwear on, not wanting to be naked if he's not. "You don't look very happy."

He jams a hand through his hair and growls. "I am very happy about what happened between us. I just don't want you to be ashamed of it… of *me*."

He heads to the front door, and this time I follow him. I'm not letting him leave again like he did earlier. "Where are you going? It's late."

"I need some fresh air." He unlocks the door and swings it open, and goes suddenly still. "Who's there?" He runs out into the yard in nothing but his jeans.

Even worse, I run out after him in my boxers. If any neighbors are peeping out their windows tonight, they'll definitely get an eye-full. We may even see blurry cell phone photos of ourselves in the newspaper this week, knowing the nosy bastards in Blackwood.

"What is it, Corey?"

"Someone just ran out of the bushes."

We both run to the side of the house nearest the road just in time to see a man opening the door of his car and climbing inside.

"Was that the man from the bar?" I ask. "The one who bought us drinks?"

Corey shrugs, but he looks really worried. "Too dark to tell."

"I got his tag number." I hurry back inside to write it down before it escapes me. My adrenaline is really pumping, and I'm freezing to death. After I write the number on the dry erase board on the side of the fridge, I grab the remote and turn on the gas fireplace in the living room and lean over it rubbing my hands together.

Corey comes up behind me and wraps his strong arms around me, moving them up and down mine to create friction. "You're freezing. You shouldn't have followed me into the cold in your underwear, Ben. I was just being stupid."

"I didn't want you to leave again." I lean my head back against his chest and close my eyes.

"I'm not going anywhere unless you kick me out, okay?"

I nod, unable to speak around the lump rising in my throat.

"But I will stay in the pool house if you need your space."

"No," I whisper. "There's no point in that. I'll just be in here alone, thinking about you."

"So you do really like me? I'm getting a little confused."

"Corey, I'm not ashamed of you, alright? But the truth is, people in this podunk town won't understand. There are a lot of elderly people here who are set in their ways, and I'm their doctor. They expect me to be a certain way. If they find out our dicks have been anywhere near each other, they'll run us both out of town. If they don't fill us full of buckshot instead."

"Buckshot? Jeez, it's not that bad, is it?" His eyes widen in alarm.

"I'm exaggerating about the buckshot. I hope."

"Maybe I shouldn't have come here." He lets go of me and heads back to the bedroom. I turn off the fire and join him in the bed, where he's lying on top of the covers still dressed in his jeans.

"We'll figure something out. We're safe for now, I think. You're new in town, and everyone is bound to know by now that you're renting my pool house."

"Yeah, and there's at least one guy in town who knows more than that. The one who just saw us both come running out of the house half-dressed."

"That guy's ass is about to be grass, because I'm gonna have Possum run his tag. Where was he when you walked out the front door?"

"He was in the bushes in front of the porch."

"Peeping outside my house, buying us drinks at the Bottom... What could this asshole possibly want?"

"How should I know?" Corey turns over, putting his back to me. "Let's get some sleep. I'm pretty tired."

I pull the covers up over me, feeling really awkward. "Yeah,

172

we need to get up in the morning and make the most of our last day off."

I don't know how long it takes me to go to sleep. It couldn't be long, because the next thing I know, my alarm is blaring, and the sun is blinding me.

13

"GET up sleepy head." I cover Corey's belly with tiny kisses until he stirs. He's still on top of the covers, and still in his jeans, but he's sleeping so hard he's drooled a little on the pillow.

"Morning, Ben. Forgot where I was for a minute." He smiles and swings his long legs over the side of the bed.

"You're not disappointed, are you?"

"Hell, no." He stands and runs a hand through his disheveled black hair, looking just as sexy first thing in the morning as he does every other minute of the day. "In fact, I'd like to jump you as soon as I take a piss and brush my teeth. Why are you dressed?"

"Because I have other plans. Get your clothes on. I'm taking you shopping."

"Shopping? You don't like the way I dress?"

I laugh and grab him by the loose waistband of his jeans. "I'm not buying you clothes. As far as I'm concerned, you can wear these jeans and nothing else every second we're together— in private." I lower my head and nip his nipple lightly with my teeth, making him suck in a sharp breath and fist his hands in my hair.

"Keep doing that, and we're not going anywhere."

"Alright, get ready then." I push him toward the bathroom and rummage in my closet, emerging a moment later with a black Rush t-shirt I bought at a concert a few years back. "Here, this ought to fit you."

As he takes it from me, he smiles and runs a finger under the collar of my turtle neck. "Got something to hide?"

"Yeah, I burned myself with a curling iron." I knock his hand away point toward the bathroom. "Now hurry up. The day's a-wastin'."

While he gets ready, I make both of us coffee, feeling all warm and fuzzy because I already know exactly how he likes his. We're both living in a magical alternate reality right now, and I'm dreading going back to work tomorrow evening, because the spell will be broken. At least I can enjoy it while it lasts.

After we drink our coffee and wolf down a couple of whole grain bagels, we head to town.

"Hang on a minute." I swing the car into the parking lot of the police station. "I need to drop this tag number off so Possum can look it up for me."

"Why do they call him Possum?"

"Hell if I know. He's just always been called that. Might have something to do with staying out late, but I'm just guessing. Are you coming in?"

"Nah, I'll just wait out here." I have a suspicion that Corey is a tad shy of law enforcement, but then I probably would be too, if I'd been homeless at one time.

Possum, an enormous black man in his forties, stands to greet me when I enter his office. He can look extremely intimidating if you don't happen to know that he's really a big teddy bear at heart.

"Hey, Ben." He claps me forcefully on the back, nearly knocking the wind out of me. "Look man, I really am sorry about last night. I had that motorcycle in my sights, and I didn't really put two and two together until I was already pulling you guys over. However…" He gives me a stern look, and his black mustache twitches. "You know better than to be going that fast, don't you?"

I hang my head. "Yes, sir. I'll try to keep it down."

Possum has been policing this town since I was a teenager, and I still feel like one every time he chastises me.

"So how have you been, son? Your mama would roll over in her grave if she knew it's been almost a year since you and I sat down and had a talk. I promised her I'd look out for you."

"A lot of people promised her that. During her last months, I think she asked everyone she knew to look after me. I'm a thirty-three-year-old with a town full of babysitters."

"Well, I take my promise to her very seriously. She had a lot of friends, and we all care about you, boy. Are you doing well? I hear you're dating that blonde that works in the hospital office."

"Nope. We broke up."

His brow creases and his lips dip into a sympathetic frown. "I'm sorry to hear that, Ben."

"Don't be. I'm fine with it."

"Come to think of it, I guess you must be fine, tearing up the streets racing at over a hundred miles per hour. Who was that guy on the bike, anyway? That new EMT?"

"Yeah. I think he expected to go to jail."

Possum laughs his hearty rumble of a laugh. "I could tell by the look on his face. I thought about teasing him a little, but it was too damn cold. I hear that one is a real ladies man. Already plowed through half the women at the hospital."

I have to clear my throat, because I'm suddenly choking on my own saliva. I wonder if my face has betrayed anything.

"He's very popular." I will my voice to remain steady. "I think you'd like him."

"Hmmm… maybe. There's something shifty about him if you ask me, but then I never have trusted a man who rides a motorcycle. Always think they've got something to prove."

I laugh. "You'll probably be pleasantly surprised once you get to know him. But I'm not here to talk you into liking Corey. I actually have a favor to ask."

"Whatever you need, Ben."

I slide a piece of paper across his desk. "Can you run this tag number for me? I caught this guy lurking around my house late last night."

His eyebrows shoot up. "Really? What time was that?"

"I don't know, it was late. I'd already gone to bed."

"Where was he? Was he actually on your property?" He puts on his reading glasses and starts taking notes on my paper, biting his lip and worrying his mustache with his bottom teeth.

"By the time I got out there, he was already around the corner on the sidewalk and almost to his car. I couldn't exactly chase him down in my underwear, you know? That's when I took down his license plate. But Corey said he ran out of the bushes right up next to the front— "

Fuck. I think I just accidentally outed myself. *Fuck. Fuck. Fuck.*

Possum stops writing mid-sentence and looks at me for a long moment with narrowed eyes. My breathing stops cold, my heart slamming thickly against my ribcage as he assesses me for what feels like an eternity. Then he resumes questioning as if nothing is amiss, and I can breathe again. "He was in the bushes near the front door, you say?"

"Yeah. Front door. Bushes." *Corey. Underwear. I am so cold busted.*

"And you were already in bed? Any idea what he might have been trying to see in your house?"

A loaded question if I've ever heard one.

"No, sir. I have no idea. Not sure if he was trying to see anything. Oh yeah, and he bought us drinks at the bar the other night down in the Bottom."

Hey, if I'm going down, I might as well go down in flames.

"Alright, Ben." He waves me away one-handed, fiddling with some papers on his desk and failing to make eye contact. "I'll get this thing figured out. Call you later, bud."

That's definitely my cue to leave. I'm not at all sure what just happened, or if Possum even realizes the extent of what I've inadvertently admitted to. All I know is our exchange has turned awkward, and I'm just as ready to leave as he is to get rid of me.

Back in the car, Corey is listening to some rap song I've never heard. "How did it go?"

"Shitty." I put the car in reverse and tear out of the parking space as if I'm anywhere other than a police station.

"He's not gonna do it?"

"Oh yeah, he's gonna do it. I told you, he's an old friend. He'll do pretty much anything I ask. The problem is, I think I just outed myself to him, and I haven't even been gay for twenty-four hours." I slam my hand against the wheel before turning out into the lane of sparse Sunday traffic.

Corey's mouth drops open. "Really, Ben? What did you do that for?"

"Dammit, it wasn't on purpose. I told him what happened last night, which if you will remember involved you and me running around my yard in our underwear after hours."

"I was wearing jeans." He flashes a smile that makes it really hard for me to stay upset.

"Yeah, well, fuck it." I drive a little too fast to a small shopping center a few blocks away.

Corey stares at the salon directly in front of us. "Are we getting our hair cut?"

"No, we're going there." I point to the cell phone store next to the salon. "You're getting a cell phone. After yesterday's fiasco, I decided you needed one."

"Ben, I don't have the kind of credit it takes to get a cell phone. I'll have to pay a huge deposit, which I can't afford right now. You really don't have a clue what it's like to be poor, do you?"

I rest my hand on his thigh where no one outside of the car can see, especially through my dark tinted windows. Just the simple touch sends a current through my body all the way to my balls. "I'm getting you one on my plan, silly. I didn't mean for you to pay. It's a gift."

"I don't know, Ben. I feel strange accepting gifts from you. It's just—"

Sliding my hand up his thigh until I feel the bulge I'm looking for, I bend over and press my lips to either side of his dick through his jeans. It grows instantly, filling out his pants, making him have to shift to reposition it. When I pull back, a slight wet mark darkens the denim where my mouth was. I lift my gaze to meet his, and he stares back like he could eat me alive.

"Are you trying to use sex to manipulate me, Ben?"

I nod, unable to speak.

"Well, it's working. But I just don't want you to feel like I'm using you, or that you're... paying me." His expression is so sincere, so troubled.

"This is just what people do, Corey."

"What people?"

"Hell, I don't know." I remove my hand from his thigh and open the car door. "Think of it as a matter of practicality. You live in my pool house, I need to be able to get in touch with my freaking tenant. Okay? Why do you have to make this so difficult?"

I close the door a little too hard, and he follows me silently into the store, where a lone sales girl smiles brightly at us and twists a finger in her hair.

"What's the best phone on the market?" I ask her, not wanting to waste any time.

She holds up her own cell phone. "This is the one everybody is dying for. It's got everything." She leans across the counter, displaying far too much cleavage to be considered professional. "It's got the best camera ever." She flips through picture after picture of herself plumping her lips and showing her barely covered breasts.

"Oh, yeah… nice, very nice. The resolution is fantastic. I'll take two of these, and here's my number." I smile and hand her my business card, which she promptly slips into her bosom.

"Do you want my number, too?" At my confused look, her face turns bright red, and she pulls the business card back out of her top and holds it up between two fingers. "Oh, this is for your account. Most of the time if a guy gives me his card… Well, never mind." She turns awkwardly away and begins looking my account up on the computer and readying the phones.

I turn and raise my eyebrows at Corey, trying not to laugh at the sales girl's ridiculous faux pas, and Corey snickers and gives me a discreet thumbs up. I'm not sure what to make of his odd sign of encouragement. Maybe he's thinking she's a candidate for a threesome? I hate to tell him, but I'm not really all that into threesomes, and right now all I can think about is him, which is going to be the death of me one way or another.

We pace the store for fifteen minutes, aimlessly browsing the phones we're not going to be buying, not talking. When the girl finishes programming our phones, she clears her throat puts them on the counter with the boxes and paperwork in a bag.

"Come get yours, Corey."

He slides up beside me, brushing his fingers purposefully against mine as he takes the phone from my hand. My eyes dart instinctively to the sales girl, but I can't tell if she's noticed.

God, I'm so paranoid.

"Matching phones…" Corey muses. Then he snaps a picture of me with his.

"What are you doing?" I laugh and hold my hand in front of my face.

"Setting my phone background. I don't want to use the generic one that comes with it."

"Oh." I blush slightly. "You shouldn't—"

He leans in and kisses me softly on the mouth, darting his tongue in for one small but obvious lick. Right in front of the sales girl, whose eyes stretch so wide I'm afraid they're going to pop out. Even worse, I think my eyes are just as wide, and my whole body is vibrating with a potent mixture of arousal and shame.

"Thank you, baby," he whispers in the stunned silence. "I'll be in the car."

We both watch him leave, unable to tear our eyes away. He turns and pushes the door open with his back, biting his lip and giving that damn sexy look that destroys my mind every time I see it. And now I know for sure that he knows what it does to me. He fucking knows it, and he's using it against me. But why would he want to embarrass me publicly? He knows I'm not ready for anyone to know about us, if I ever will be. And then it dawns on me.

Corey is jealous. He thinks I was flirting with the sales girl.

Against my will, the knowledge makes my heart beat faster. I feel elated, my ego dancing a private jig. But at the same time, I'm mortified. What if someone finds out? I know that girl is going to run right out and tell at least five people before the day is over. It's just a matter of time before I have to leave the county.

Goodbye life. It was nice while it lasted.

I face the sales girl, having no other choice at the moment. "Cock-blocking bastard," I say. "He's just bluffing."

182

"That didn't look like a bluff. My knees got weak."

Yeah, mine too.

"Nah… he's just messing around. So how about your number? Can I have it?"

"You really want my number? Are you sure?"

"Of course."

She hands me a business card and writes her cell number on the back. "I'm off every night after six."

I smile and take my leave before anything else can happen. Now she expects me to call her, and there's no way in hell that's ever happening.

Back in the car, Corey is playing absently with his phone. "You got her number, didn't you?" he asks without looking up.

I sigh loudly and deliberately. "Yes."

"I knew you would. You couldn't possibly have stared any harder at those softcore porn pictures she was showing you."

"Corey, I was admiring the quality of the photos, not the subject matter. And the only reason I got her number was because you kissed me, and now she's gonna go run tell everyone in town. Thanks a lot, by the way. We might as well have just fucked on her counter. I had to reassert my manhood by getting her number, which I absolutely did not want, by the way." I pull out of the parking lot and into the road.

"Reassert your manhood?" Corey leans his forehead against the dashboard. "Liking me doesn't make you less of a man."

"You're right." I reach out and put my hand on his back. "You're absolutely right. This is just new territory for me, and I'm struggling, okay? I'm sorry. Please have patience with me. I may be freaking out and acting like an asshole, but one thing's for sure. I was not flirting with that woman in there, and I didn't want her number. I panicked."

He sits upright in the seat, looking calmer. "I know I'm just being stupid. This is as new for me as it is for you."

"Wow. I guess I just assumed you'd been with men before."

"I have, but I've never been jealous before."

"Really?" I can't stop a huge grin from overtaking my face. "Are you sure about that? You haven't been jealous of anyone else, even in high school?"

"No, Ben. Only you. And now you're buying me things. I'm getting really confused."

"What is it with you and the gifts thing? It was supposed to make you happy, not sad."

"Some men— usually older men— will give you gifts to be with them. Sometimes money." His face colors, and I'm getting the feeling he's talking more than hypotheticals and hearsay.

"Has that happened to you?"

He nods and looks down at his lap. "I didn't have anywhere to go," he whispers. "I didn't have anywhere to live. No food. I had a drug habit."

I park the car in the garage and go inside the house, so relieved not to be in public anymore. Corey sits on the couch looking uneasy, and I sit beside him. I want to be familiar with him, let him know I'm not judging him, so I kick off my sneakers and lean back on the cushy sofa arm, propping my feet casually on his lap.

"Tell me about it," I urge quietly.

He takes off his boots and leans his back against the opposite sofa arm, bracketing my legs with his longer ones, his bare feet nudging my hips. My feet are together in the vee between his legs, and I wiggle my toes down into the warm spot beneath his ass. In a way, our position feels even more intimate than sex, and we lounge like this for long moments in the quiet of my house. It's not a lonely quiet like usual, though. It's nice, and it gives me an unfamiliar squeeze in my chest.

Eventually, his voice breaks the silence, cracked and husky and laced with a darkness I haven't heard before. "When Granny first passed away, I was still in school. I was on the football team, so I had a lot of friends. No shortage of people I could spend the night with. I was kind of on a rotation, and the parents were oblivious to what was going on. There was one boy, Jamie… I liked to stay with him the most because I had a secret crush on him." He smiles, but there's sadness in his eyes. "I did something stupid one night. We were watching a movie in his room on his bed, and I kissed him. I could've sworn he liked me too, or I never would've had the courage to do it."

"I take it he didn't react favorably?"

"I thought so for a minute, but then he freaked out. Made me leave in the middle of the night. It was raining, and I had to sleep under a nearby overpass with a handful of bums. I don't mind telling you I was scared shitless, and me a big football player. I cried like a baby."

"My God, what happened?" I'm totally engrossed now, my body so tense with worry for that young, scared boy that my back is up off the sofa arm.

"A man named Harold took me under his wing. Said I didn't need those stinking riches— that's what he called them. He said to give him a week and he'd have me making a living in the streets and doing whatever I wanted, whenever I wanted. Sounded pretty cool at the time, as young as I was."

"So what did you do? Where did you stay?"

"I panhandled, pick-pocketed drunks as they were leaving bars…" At my shocked expression, he laughs. "Hey, I didn't say I was a good person, or that I led a glamorous life."

I roll my eyes at him. "You're not a bad person, Corey."

"Hold your judgment until you've heard it all," he warns. "I ended up doing drugs, pretty much anything I could get my hands on, and for money I would give blow jobs in club bathrooms or alleys near bars. It's amazing how many straight men will pay for a blow from a guy when they're drunk, especially if they've struck out in the bar and are leaving alone."

"How did you… you know, get them to do it?"

He chuckles and sways his legs playfully against mine. "Do you really want to know the gory details?"

I nod vigorously, unable to contain my curiosity.

"Tell you what," he says with a wicked gleam in his eyes. "We'll go down to the Bottom tonight, and I'll show you what I did. See if it works on you."

And with that, I'm instantly hard. I stare across the sofa at him with a mixture of awe and lust. No more pity for the little boy; the man sitting across from me is confident, strong, and sexier than any person I've ever laid eyes on. He exudes raw masculinity, so rough around the edges yet so perfect.

"Mmmm…" He bites his plump bottom lip hard and leans forward, speaking in that husky sex voice I could pick out blindfolded in a crowd. "If you fuck me any harder with your eyes, I'm going to make a mess all over your couch, Ben."

"Oh my God, you're killing me," I groan, leaning back onto the sofa arm and pressing a fisted hand firmly against my dick, as if by squeezing hard enough I can make the desire go away.

"No, baby. You're killing me." He flips his legs under him and crawls toward me, parting my legs smoothly and climbing between them, stalking me on all fours. "If I don't get in here soon…" He rubs my asshole through my jeans, sending a jolt of pure animal desire radiating through every nerve in my nether region. "I'm going to lose my mind. You have no idea how badly I want you."

"Stop it, Corey," I cry breathlessly before I know what the hell I'm saying. When I catch my breath, I've pushed him up off of me with my knees, and he's looking down at me with a confused, hurt look on his face.

Oh, shit.

It occurs to me too late that it seems like I'm rejecting him, possibly like the boy who sent him out helpless into the rain all those years ago.

He walks away toward the kitchen, running a hand through his hair in obvious exasperation. He looks so edible in those jeans, I want to run after him and throw myself on him. Tackle him to the ground and fuck him until neither one of us can move. But I can't. My feelings are so damn strong. And so unwanted.

"I don't want to feel this way, Corey," I plead with him as he cracks open a beer and downs half of it. "Please make it stop. It hurts. I don't think I can handle it."

"Oh, quit whining. Jesus, don't you think it's painful for me?

You just pushed me off of you like I was a rapist or something. What, do you think I'm forcing you to feel this way? Tricking you into it? I've got some voodoo doll stashed away in my duffel bag with your face on it? It's not about laying blame. You want me. They're feelings, Ben. They're real, and they're yours."

Just then, Corey's ring tone interrupts his tirade with an ironically jaunty tune. "Hello?" His voice is gruff enough to scare off whoever is calling, but they stay on the line.

"Yeah, this is my new cell number. Program it in." He covers the microphone and whispers to me. "My aunt. I texted her my number while you were flirting with the phone sales girl."

I roll my eyes and push past him to grab a beer for myself.

"No, I'm not spending up all of my money or spreading myself too thin... No... I'm at Ben's house... Doctor Hardy." He paces away, talking low into the phone where I can't hear him.

I follow him and tap him on the shoulder. "Invite them to a late lunch here. Her and your uncle. We'll cook."

"Really?" His voice goes up an octave, as if he can't believe what he's hearing. "Are you sure?"

"Yeah. Tell them two o'clock."

After he hangs up, he turns and gives me a hug. "That's awfully nice of you to invite them." He gives me a kiss on the lips that, despite its chasteness, makes my dick twitch.

"They're your only family. You need to get to know them better."

And so do I.

14

AFTER the tenseness of the scene only moments before, it's nice to be getting along. We set about planning and making lunch, and I'm so glad Corey is getting into it, since he doesn't seem like the cooking type.

As for me, I love cooking and make sure to keep a well-stocked kitchen most of the time. I rarely eat out, preferring instead to whip up healthy, interesting dishes at home.

"You like Mediterranean cuisine? Lighter stuff, less meat, more veggies, pasta…"

Corey smirks at me. "I know what Mediterranean is. And yes, I love it."

"I should have known with that amazing body you're not eating hamburgers, fries and pizza every day. No offense, just around here folks eat kind of heavy. Lots of casseroles and fried meat. And desserts."

"And don't forget sweet tea. It's my new addiction. Can we make some?"

"Sure." I pull out a white enamelware pot and fill it with water to boil.

Corey stares in fascination at the simple pot on the stove. "I figured you'd have some kind of tea machine like in the restaurants. Some big silver thing with a black nozzle and a metal plate that has *Property of Ben Hardy's Kitchen* engraved on it."

"This is old school, boy. Watch and learn."

We have a great time in the kitchen. I can tell that Corey is not accustomed to cooking, at least not beyond frying eggs or making sandwiches, but he's eager to learn and surprisingly good with a knife. When it's almost time for our guests to arrive, we've arranged a gorgeous dining table with a large bowl of Greek salad, one of angel hair pasta tossed in a homemade sauce I concocted on the spot, garlic toast, and for dessert a very ripe sliced cantaloupe. Just in case his aunt and uncle are like most Southerners, who feel it isn't a meal unless there is meat, I include a few pieces of grilled chicken breast.

The highlight of cooking is when I let Corey pour up the tea, steeping the bags for ten minutes in half a pitcher of lava hot sugar water, then filling it the rest of the way with ice. He looks so proud when he's done, like a grade-schooler showing off his macaroni art project. "I can't believe how easy that was. Will it taste good?"

"As good as any Southern grandmother's, I promise. Now all you need to do is learn to quilt and make peach cobbler, and you'll fit right in around here."

He's beaming with pride as he slips out to the pool house to take a shower and change into clean clothes. I do the same in my own bathroom, and we meet back in the living room fresh and damp just as the doorbell rings. Since it's his family, I let Corey answer the door while I hang back behind him.

"Aunt Denise, Uncle Daniel... Oh my gosh..."

I peer around him to see what's got him so surprised. His aunt is dressed in a blue Sunday dress, and his uncle is wearing a crisp, dark pair of overalls and carrying a large basket of locally made jellies and sauces. Behind them stands a skinny young man in a red ringer t-shirt, jeans, and vintage Adidas sneakers, his overly-long blond hair flopping over one eye.

Corey and the strange guy approach each other and execute what I imagine to be a secret gang handshake, bending their right knees and bumping their inner ankles together at the same time their hands clash in a sideways high five. "Allister, what a shock. What... What are you doing here?"

Denise stammers. "Um, Corey... Allister called and came by looking for you last night, and I told him you didn't live with us, and that you had only used our address on your hospital paperwork."

Allister interrupts with a high-pitched laugh. "Boy, you knew I wouldn't rest until I found you. I was just headed back to your aunt's house to beg her for your address, when I happened to pass her driving out of the neighborhood. I chased her down, and well, here I am. Surprise!"

"Yeah." Corey looks bewildered. "Surprise!"

I step around Corey to greet our guests. "Come on in, everyone. It's cold out, and we've got a nice fire going in the living room."

"Thank you, Dr. Hardy," Denise says, skirting Corey and following me into the house. "This is a lovely home you have, Dr. Hardy." She twirls in the foyer, gasping as she admires the chandelier.

"Denise, please call me Ben. I'm only Dr. Hardy at work."

She giggles, her demeanor much different than when she's at the hospital. "This is my husband Daniel. He runs the fruit stand on Highway 440."

"I thought I recognized you." I say, shaking the man's hand. "I shop there a good bit."

"Yeah, I seen you around, Dr. Hardy... Ben. I'll be sure to drop off some stuff to you now and again, when we get something especially good."

"That would be fantastic, Daniel. I appreciate it." I take their coats and hang them in the coat closet before showing them to the fire. Denise and Allister bend over it, warming their cold, red hands. Daniel sits on the sofa in what I can only describe as typical Southern working man fashion, legs sprawled, his large hands tucked under the bib of his overalls. There's an old-world formality about the way he and his ilk carry themselves that has always intrigued me.

Corey hasn't spoken a word, so I summon him to the kitchen to help me get wine glasses. Once we're out of earshot, I put a hand on his shoulder. "Are you shy with your family here?"

"A little, I guess." I hate to see him uptight, when he's usually so free-spirited.

"Well, lighten up. I need to get used to entertaining if we're going to host a New Year's party here this year."

His face lights up, and I'm thrilled to have caused it. "Really,

Ben? That will be kick ass."

"So let's get some practice. If you act all sour-faced at our party, people will run screaming to their church parties to get away from the gloom."

"Shut up." He nudges my arm playfully. "Alright, let's serve these people some wine."

Conversation is pleasant enough around the fire. Corey's crowd clearly isn't used to drinking wine from wine glasses. I feel like they're trying to put on airs, sticking their pinkies out and what-not. I've never seen Denise's posture so ram-rod straight. It's almost funny, but then I guess I'm putting on airs a bit myself. I don't know why I feel the need to impress everyone here.

Corey's friend Allister has some qualities that my inexperience wants to attribute to gang activity, but I'm probably just being ignorant. I've been pretty sheltered here in Blackwood. Most of the wild city problems never touch us here, though we do have our own eccentricities and vices, just of a different kind. Instead of liquor store robberies, drive-by shootings and raves, we have domestic disturbances, hunting accidents, and bonfire keggers on someone's back forty.

"So, what kind of trouble you been getting into, Corey?" Allister's got a shit-eating grin on his face, but Corey doesn't smile back.

"I haven't been in any trouble in a long time, Allis. I'm an EMT now, you know."

"Yeah, I'm just messing with you, man. Still, nurses are allowed to have fun, too. Why don't you come out to my hotel room tonight and I'll remind you what it feels like."

Okay, there's a very definite undercurrent that I don't like between Allister and Corey, and it's got my sixth sense standing on its head.

"I might. What hotel are you in?"

He's actually considering going to this guy's hotel room?

"Why don't you stay here?" I hear myself saying. "No sense paying for a lousy hotel when I have a nice pool house out back that no one is using."

My words travel out into the room, and it's as if I can see them floating there all ugly and destructive, and I want to call them back, but it's too late. Ever since I met Corey, I've been dropping about twenty IQ points a day, I think. By the time he's done with me, I'll be the village idiot.

And gay.

Denise frowns, a crease forming between her thick brows, and she looks from me to Corey and back to me. "Corey, I thought you said you were renting Dr. Hardy's pool house."

Allister's face splits into an evil grin, and he stomps his feet on the hearth in a short fit of silent laughter. He doesn't say anything, but he fixes me with a shrewd look that says he knows exactly what's going on here.

I feel my face color, and the only way I can try to salvage the situation is by lying. "Oh crap, I forgot. Silly me. I'm just not used to having a tenant." I face-palm and address Allister, though it chafes my ass to have to do it. "Allister, the pool house is taken, but you're welcome to stay in one of the upstairs bedrooms."

"I'd absolutely love to, Ben," he says, and his eyes glitter with mischief. "I won't be able to get back until around eleven tonight, though. Is that okay? I met some people I'm supposed to have drinks with up the road at someplace called the County Line."

I don't dare make eye contact with Corey. I wonder what he thinks of all of this, and why the hell he had to consider meeting Allister in his hotel room. If he'd just said no, none of this would be happening.

"Let's eat," Corey says loudly, waving us all toward the dining room. They all go in front of us, and he and I bring up the rear. He leans in close to my ear. "Good save." He runs a hand quickly down my back and grabs my ass before anyone is the wiser.

Lunch is a success, and the conversation is thankfully less dramatic than it was in the living room. There are no more slip-ups, and Allister behaves for the rest of the visit.

As she leaves, Denise turns and gives Corey a quick peck on the cheek. "Oh, honey, I almost forgot. Daniel and I are leaving for Ruby Falls tomorrow. We're spending our twentieth anniversary in the same place we spent our honeymoon."

"How romantic," Corey says with a smile. "You guys have fun."

"We will, but you're going to have to work with a sub all four nights this week."

"Who is it?"

"Not sure. The crew is short-handed with Amanda out on maternity leave, so they're sending over one of the first responders from the fire department. Hopefully he won't be as big of an asshole as most of them are. There's like a rivalry between the EMS and the fire department, which never made sense to me. We're all out there trying to save lives. Anyway, just giving you a heads up. Good luck."

Corey hugs her goodbye. "Enjoy your trip. Keep your fingers crossed for no codes."

"Yes. No codes," I agree.

"Bye," Denise calls over her shoulder as her husband drags her down the steps. Before turning around, she casts a worried glance in Allister's direction, which really sets me on edge. What is the deal with this guy?

When their car has disappeared around the corner, we all quit waving like idiots and go back into the house.

"Whew," Allister squeals, running a hand across his forehead in exaggerated relief. "Corey, honey, I thought your folks would never leave. Another half hour of acting straight, and I would have actually *turned* straight. Do you have a beer, or something with a kick besides wine?"

"In the fridge. Come on." He looks apologetically at me before getting a beer for his now very overtly gay friend.

"Corey, why have you not come out to those nice people? They won't care."

"Not really your business, Allis."

"Ha. I know everything about you, boy. Including the fact that you've got a very hot doctor on the chain." He appraises me from top to bottom and smiles evilly with half his mouth. "Are you sharing?"

"No," he roars, and the anger in his eyes is apparent. "Ben has been nice enough to offer you a place to stay, but if you don't shut the hell up, I'll kick you out myself."

Allister looks at me. "Does he have that kind of authority in your house, Ben?"

196

"Most definitely."

"Good. That means you're taking care of my boy." He taps Corey playfully on the butt and twirls away toward the foyer, and it's all I can do to keep from tossing him out on his bony haunches. He's Corey's friend, but I know I've made a mistake inviting him to stay.

"Mind if I get a look at that pool house?" he asks, and I shoo him away, glad for the privacy.

"Might not be a good idea to let him roam unattended." Corey moves to follow him, but I stay him with a hand on his elbow.

"He'll be fine." The truth is, I don't want Corey to be alone with him, especially in the pool house.

"He might steal something, Ben. For real."

"Let him." I'm not backing down on this. "Have you slept with him?"

Corey is clearly taken aback by my question. "No. Hell, no. He's a friend, and a shaky one at best. I'm telling you, he can't be trusted. Why did you invite him to stay here?"

"He's your friend. I was trying to be nice." I shove my hands in my pockets and look away. "And you were going to go to his hotel room."

Corey laughs quietly, hooks his fingers in my belt loops, and pulls me up against him. "Now who's jealous?"

My hands are trapped in my pockets between us, and he's got me firmly anchored by my belt loops, so there's no way I can push away when he covers my mouth with his. He moans against me, and I open my mouth to him, reluctantly at first. The feel of his hard body against mine coupled with my helplessness incites a hunger within me, and I show him in the only way I can at the moment—

with my mouth. I stand on my tiptoes and lean aggressively into his kiss, nipping and sucking at his lips, knocking him off kilter with my weight and making him stagger before gaining his footing again. He laughs against my mouth.

The abrupt sound of a throat clearing has us scattering apart, and I snatch my hands out of my pockets and straighten my shirt.

"Sure you won't share?" Allister rolls out his bottom lip in a dramatic pout. "He looks so yummy."

Corey is on Allister in a blink, fisting his t-shirt at the collar and backing him up against the nearest wall. "He's mine. Got that? Only mine." His voice is gravelly and deep, and frighteningly intense.

Allister stares him squarely in the eyes without flinching. "I see you still like the rough stuff, Cor. Better confine it to the bedroom, though, unless you want a replay of last New Year's." He twirls his finger, imitating the sound of a police siren, and then breaks into a fit of laughter. "You beat the shit out of that dignitary, dude. I thought you were going to kill him for sure."

"You're leaving, Allis," Corey grates, letting go of his collar. "Don't come looking for me again. We're finished."

Allister rolls his eyes and sighs. "Fine, Corey. No wonder you can't keep any friends, with that temper of yours." He turns his gaze on me. "You better watch out, Ben. I know he doesn't seem like it, but—"

"Get the fuck out," Corey rages, and Allister makes a gangling escape through the front door, slamming it behind him.

"What was he talking about? Dignitaries, fights, police…" It all sounds very mysterious, and difficult to reconcile with the Corey I am coming to know.

"Ben, there are things about my life that I'm not quite ready to talk about. All the stuff I've told you so far is old news. Things I came to terms with a long time ago." His eyes darken as he seems to mull something over in his mind. "The other stuff is too fresh, and to be honest, I can't quite believe I'm out of it yet. I promise I *will* tell you. Just not yet, okay?"

"Okay." I'd like to press him, just because of my own gnawing curiosity, but I don't. I figure a man's demons are his own until he's ready to share them with someone else.

15

"WE gonna get another show in here tonight?" The waitress at the Bottom is much more talkative with us this time. I guess now that we've been here twice, we're regulars.

"What do you mean?" I ask, and Corey squeezes his lips into a tight line, biting back a laugh.

"You know what I'm talking about, honey. I saw him lay one on you the last time y'all was here. Don't worry, though. The Bottom is a lot like Vegas. What goes on down here stays down here. I told my girlfriends about it, but I didn't mention names, Dr. Hardy. "

My eyes widen. "I didn't know you recognized me. What's your name?"

"Helen Fields. You doctored my little grand baby for the croup last winter."

"What did your girlfriends say when you told them, Helen?" Corey asks.

"They said to give them a call if you boys showed back up."

"Oh God." I bury my face in my hands. "This has gone way too far."

Helen pats me gently on the shoulder. "I haven't called anybody. But I wish I could. Those girls could always use a good thrill."

"No, Helen, please don't call your friends. We were just horsing around that night, playing a game that got out of control. I had just broken up with my girlfriend, and Corey was showing me a good time, that's all. You can rest assured that he and I are just friends, and there will be no more of... that kind of thing. I'm not gay."

Helen frowns and looks to Corey.

"Well, I *am*." He shrugs, taking me completely off guard with his surprise admission.

"Then I'll tell you what," she says, her eyes lighting up. "I know someone who's just perfect for you. He comes in here a good bit. Hang on, I think he's here right now."

Before he can answer, she bustles off into the back room, where I think I caught a glimpse of pool tables and video games. While she's gone, I search Corey's face, trying to divine how he's feeling about all of this, but I can't read him.

"Corey, I—"

He holds up a hand to silence me. "Don't say anything. It's not necessary to explain yourself. You're a prominent figure in the community, worried about your image, and I'm a monkey wrench. I get that. I need to accept the reality of how things are and quit hoping for more than what you can give. It's my fault for crushing on a straight guy, anyway."

"It's not your fault. But I'm glad you understand that I have a serious problem, and that I have no idea what to do about it. If I could give you more, I would."

"I know you would." He reaches out to put his hand on mine, but pulls back at the last second. "Oops. Gotta watch myself. Wouldn't want anyone to get the wrong idea."

I give him a wistful smile. I really don't want to hurt him, but I can't see any way to incorporate him into my life in any public way. It's tearing me up inside. I hope he knows that.

"Jesus *damn*," he exclaims, staring wide-eyed over my shoulder.

When I turn to see what he's gawking at, Helen is returning from the back room with a sandy-haired mountain of a man in tow. Substantially muscled and even taller than Corey, he is easily the largest man in the room. As he and Helen approach our table, I'm praying with every molecule of my being that he is *not* the someone she thinks is just perfect for Corey.

"You have got to be kidding me," the man says in a smooth, deep voice when he reaches our table. "The new EMT? This is like some cosmic joke."

Corey shoots him a puzzled look. "Have we met?"

"Nah, but I know who you are. It's a small town. Everybody knows the new guy."

Helen beams at Corey. "This is the one I was telling you about… Mike Tanner. He's a fireman."

Corey reaches out and takes his hand in a big macho handshake, and I can practically feel the testosterone firing. "Corey Butler. Nice to meet you, Mike. Why don't you sit down and join us? This is my friend Ben Hardy."

"I know who he is." He clasps my hand and shakes. I think

he's trying to crush my knuckles, but I'm not about to flinch. "Nice to meet you, Ben."

"Same here." That's not exactly the truth, but I can't tell him how I really feel.

"I'll bring you boys a round of beers on the house," Helen announces and scurries away.

Corey leans closer to Mike. "So it is pretty ironic that we've met here, huh? A fireman and an EMT."

Mike laughs, leaning back in his chair and smirking playfully. "More than you can imagine. Because I know something you don't know."

"What?"

"I don't know if I should tell you. Maybe I ought to wait until tomorrow and surprise you."

"Don't tease me. What is it?"

They're flirting right in front of me, and I'm about to be sick. Especially because I just pretty much told Corey that nothing is going to happen between him and me.

"Well…" Mike leans in close, licking his lips and eying Corey like he's his next meal. "I'm going to be your partner on the ambulance for the next four nights."

Oh. My. God.

"No shit. You're the sub? This is surreal, man. Absolutely unbelievable."

Mike winks and nods. "Fate is a funny thing, ain't it?"

Indeed.

Helen serves our beers and smiles at the other two, practically ignoring me. I guess if I'm not part of her Cupid operation, I'm

203

worthless. "Have fun, boys," she calls, crossing the room to wait on another table.

Mike looks directly at me. "Hey, I'm not stepping on any toes here, am I?"

"No," Corey blurts before I can reply. "Ben and I are just friends. He's straight."

A huge grin spreads across Mike's face, and he rubs his golden-stubbled chin. "Cool, cool, cool. You guys wanna play some pool? My table is reserved for almost another hour."

Corey pushes his chair back and stands. "Sounds like fun."

"No, thanks," I say. "You guys go ahead. I think I see a girl I went to school with over there."

"Really, Ben? Are you sure?" A hint of worry flashes across Corey's features, and then it's gone again.

I take a swig of beer and nod, and the two of them retire to the back room... where I can't see them anymore. I'm going to need more alcohol. I get two more beers, feeling like Dr. Hannigan clutching one in each hand, but I'm beyond giving a shit.

"Hey, Ann."

The woman looks up from her mixed drink, tossing her long auburn hair and smiling. "Ben Hardy, oh my gosh. What a surprise."

"Yeah, there are a lot of those tonight. Are you alone?"

"Well... I'm supposed to be meeting a girl from work, but she just called and said she'd be another half hour. Would you like to sit with me?"

"Love to."

We chat for a while, and just as I'm polishing off my first beer, my cell phone vibrates once in my pocket, alerting me that I have a text message. "What the hell…"

Corey: Are you okay? You're not going to do something stupid, are you?

Me: Talking to Ann about taking her virginity at prom. Better watch out. Your boyfriend is going to get jealous if you keep texting me.

Corey: Don't worry. He knows you're just a friend. Did you really take her virginity?

Ann gestures toward my phone. "Business or personal?"

"Business," I lie.

Me: Yes. Thinking about getting a replay tonight. Come get the house key so you can let yourself in. And don't wait up.

Corey: Screw you, Ben. Why are you doing this?

Me: Don't bring that skeevy fireman to my house. If you want to fuck him, do it at his place.

"Must be serious business," Ann says. "Is something going on at the hospital?"

"Nothing to worry about. Just dealing with a smart-ass employee."

"Well, I hope you're not too upset tonight. I thought you and I might do a little dancing, for old time's sake. Maybe I should request our prom theme song, what was it called—"

"I'm sorry, Ann. Will you please excuse me? I need to take care of something." I scoot my chair back, and she gives me a confused half-smile. "Maybe I'll see you around sometime."

"Sure, see you."

I make a beeline for the front door. I do feel bad about being rude, after all I am the one who approached her in the first place, but I'm far too agitated to pretend to be interested in her chatter. Hell, I'm not even interested in my own chatter. I just need to get out of here, away from Corey and his new fuck buddy in the back room, because I'm suffocating.

The air is brisk outside, just what I need to clear my head. Maybe I'll be sane by the time I get home.

"Hey man, wait up. You got a light?" Corey runs up behind me with a cigarette shoved between his fingers.

"I don't smoke. And I didn't think you did, either."

"Yeah, I quit. But I'm so stressed out right now, I gotta have one. I bummed this one off of some guy inside, but I forgot I had no light."

"Guess you're shit out of luck, then." I pause at the corner, shivering from the cold and from emotional overload. My nerves are jangled right now, and I just need to get home and go to bed.

Corey laughs, cupping his hands together and blowing warm air through them, still clutching the cigarette between his fingers. "You seem stressed. Didn't work out with your lady this evening?"

I sigh and run a hand through my hair. "I don't care anymore. Don't need anyone. I do just fine on my own."

"Yeah, but I bet you thought you had a piece of ass lined up for tonight, and now it's just you and the hand, huh?"

I stare at him, particularly at his pupils, wondering if he's been doing drugs or something. He seems... off.

"Sorry, man," he continues. "Guess I've got sex on the brain.

See, my girlfriend and I were dancing in the club, and I asked her to come to the john and suck my dick, and she got all offended. Then she drives off in *my* fucking car, with my wallet in her purse. No way to go, no money, no place to even sleep tonight. So I know how you feel. I'm screwed, too."

I'm gaping at him now. "What the hell are you talking about?"

He stretches and runs his hand not so subtly across his dick, and my heart jumps up into my throat. When he speaks again, his voice is low, conspiratorial. "I'm so desperate for money, I'm thinking about going in that bar and finding a guy who's got fifty bucks and offering to suck him off. I mean, I'm not gay or anything, but there's nothing wrong with two straight guys helping each other out, right?"

I swallow hard, my head spinning as I realize what's going on. This is what Corey used to do to scam guys for money. This was his game. It makes me sad and a little sick to my stomach, but my dick stiffens just the same.

Even though I know it's an illusion, I want him. I can almost see the mechanisms of his seduction, subtle little hand motions, the way he cocks his head… Like my coin toss trick, he's choreographed a seamless performance meant to guide and manipulate. Only he's way better at this than I'll ever be at sleight of hand. He hasn't propositioned me directly, but he's worked the thought so scrupulously into my mind that I almost feel like it's my idea.

"So what do you think? Should I do it? Give it to me straight, man. I don't want to get punched in the nose if someone gets the wrong idea. Do you think there's a guy in there with a little bit of money in his pocket who wouldn't mind sliding his cock into my hot, wet mouth and letting me suck on it for a few minutes, maybe let him come all over my face? Or am I just wasting my time?"

I want to say something, but the words are stuck in my throat. He's got my brain so addled, all I can think about is him sucking cock. There's a moving picture of what he's just described looping in my brain... my cock sliding in and out of his hot wet mouth, me shooting a load all over his eager face. That one short scene plays over and over, like a sexy animated GIF, crowding out any other thoughts.

He toes the sidewalk with the tip of his boot and gives an embarrassed little smile that melts my heart. "Sorry, man. You're right, that was a stupid idea. Guess I'll just sit out here and hope that bitch comes back to get me sometime tonight."

"Wait," I blurt as he turns to go back to the club. "You can't freeze. I guess I could spare the money, since it's for a good cause. Um... How do we do this?"

"Well, there's an alley right over there. You give me the money, and then we can slip into the shadows in the alley. No one will ever know."

I dig in my pocket with a shaky hand and pull out a hundred dollar bill. "Do you have change?"

He shakes his head slowly and nails me with a sexy look that drops my balls straight into my toes.

"Fuck it. You need the money." I hand him the bill, and he slips it into his pocket, heading straight to the alley at a brisk pace. I follow along, looking around to make sure we're not followed. I look like the guiltiest sonofabitch on earth. I could probably get arrested for just looking around all nervous like that, especially in this neighborhood. And I know for a fact I could get arrested for what I'm about to do in the alley. It feels so damn real, I wonder for one delirious second if Corey might possibly be an undercover cop.

"What are you chuckling about back there?" he asks.

"Nothing. Just losing my mind, that's all."

When we get halfway down the brick lined corridor, Corey slips into a recessed doorway and drops to his knees. It's a side door to the club, and I can hear the music pulsing from within.

"Open your pants." He waits patiently for me to comply, his arms hanging at his sides.

I unzip my jeans and pull them down to mid-thigh, bracing against the shock of the cold. He looks up at me, eyes glistening, and I can just make out his striking features in the glow from the streetlights. Soft, haunted eyes, plush lips that would feel so good wrapped around my cock…

"What do you want me to do, baby? Anything."

"Lick my balls." My voice is hoarse with need and a hefty dose of fear.

I feel his tongue working my balls, flicking them lightly, nipping playfully at them with his lips until they tighten. He sucks one gently into his mouth and releases it, moving to the other side and doing the same to its twin. Then he works his way slowly and expertly up the shaft, using both his lips, his tongue, and his hand, drawing the sensations out exquisitely until I'm aching for him to take me inside his mouth. When he reaches the head, he sucks it hungrily into his mouth and slurps at it while he jerks me off with an economical grace that only another man could achieve.

I grab his head in my hands and move it exactly how I want, feeling the silky strands of his hair between my fingers. He varies the suction and tongue action until I'm in a frenzy, ready to blow any second for him. Wanting him to take it, take it all, swallow it, let me fuck him, be *mine*. Then he pulls it out of his mouth with a hollow popping sound, over and over, working against his own suction until it's all I can do to keep from crying out, begging him to never, ever, ever stop.

"Shit, here I go." I grind out a low, raspy growl as he purposely aims my dick and lets me defile his face with four full jets of hot cum.

Still reeling and spasming from my orgasm, I run a quivering hand along his cheek, and he peers affectionately up at me. "You're so beautiful, Corey. So damn beautiful."

He smiles and wipes his face clean with the tail of his shirt. "So it was worth a hundred dollars?"

"It was worth a hundred *thousand*." I pull him to his feet, stuff my still-sensitive member into my pants, and zip my fly. For a moment, I imagine paying him a hundred thousand dollars, just for shits and giggles, because I could easily do it. But that's taking the fantasy a little too far, and he'd probably think I was a nut job. Plus, he has no idea that I have that kind of money, and I'm not ready to tell him.

We don't say much on the way home, but we walk so close together that our arms keep bumping together. I don't care if anyone sees us at the moment. I have my hood up. And besides, it's damn cold, so we have an excuse for taking advantage of body heat.

I don't know what the hell I'm doing anymore. As we make

our way up my front walk, it strikes me that this isn't just my home anymore. It's *our* home. Against all reason, I'm living with a man and trying to deny that it means anything to me. And tonight, everything is just raw. I'm jealous of a fireman, and I'm disturbed by the bittersweet blow job I just paid for in an alley on the wrong side of the tracks.

Suddenly, tears well up in my eyes, and I can barely see to get up the steps.

"Ben…" Corey reaches out to steady me. "Are you okay? What's wrong? Why are you crying?"

"I'm not crying." A couple of tears escape and slide down my cheeks.

"Yes you are. What is it?" He takes the key from me and unlocks the door before leading me to the bedroom.

I swipe at my eyes with the back of my arm, which does little good since my leather jacket isn't absorbent. "I can't believe you had to do that, Corey. It breaks my heart that you had to do—" I'm so choked up, I can't finish my sentence.

"It's okay, Ben. All of that stuff was behind me a very long time ago."

"Yeah, but what kind of world is this that a teenage boy has to sell his body just to keep from freezing or starving to death? They should have just given you the money out of kindness. It makes me angry, Corey. I want to go beat the fuck out of every man who ever took advantage of you. Sorry, sick, perverted mother fuckers. I wish I could kill them all."

The worst part of it all is that I'm trying to deny the duplicity of my own feelings. I truly believe that those men are evil for taking advantage of him, but at the same time I can empathize with them, having felt the same irresistible desire for him myself. I can't say with total certainty that I would not have taken him up on his offer, had I been one of the men he approached.

Corey sits down beside me, so close I can hear his breathing, and he puts his arm around my shoulders and pulls me back so that we're both lying on our backs. Then he rolls toward me and trails kisses down the side of my face and neck. "You're such a good man, Ben. You make me feel safe, like nothing can touch me now that you're in my life."

"That's bullshit, and you know it. I've hurt you myself. I hide you away and deny you like a fucking coward, when you're all in the world I want. I don't keep you safe, Corey. I'm just another source of pain for you. Just another user."

"No, you're not. You're just so used to pretending you have no feelings, you've started believing it yourself."

I let out a harsh laugh. "And you know me so well in such a short time? I think you're deluding yourself. Projecting romantic traits onto me that you only wish I had. It's all a fantasy. I'm just a closed-minded small town doctor, so brainwashed by other people's attitudes that I can't even admit I'm attracted to another man. It's how I *feel*. Why is it anyone else's business to tell me how I'm allowed to feel?"

"See? You do have feelings. Now you've admitted it." Corey stares at the ceiling for a while before he speaks again. "I have a confession to make. I was upset earlier because you don't want to come out in public about me— about us. I told you I understood, but that was only half true. Logically, I did understand where you were coming from, but I was still pissed off as hell. I flirted with that fireman in front of you on purpose, not because I liked him, but because I wanted to make you jealous. It was a messed up thing to do, and I'm sorry."

I sigh and cover my eyes with my forearm, blocking out the light and the world. "You were right, though. If I was even half a man, I'd tell everyone to go fuck themselves."

"It doesn't work that way, though, does it? The fact is, you're part of a community of people who love you, with a really good career going and a lot to lose— a hell of a lot more than I've ever even dreamed of having in the first place. It doesn't affect me that much having people know I'm gay. Who gives a shit, anyway? I'm nobody. But you... If you don't think the community would accept it, and it would hurt your career, then it's the right thing for you to keep quiet. It's selfish of me to want you to risk everything you've worked for just to have my little piece of tail. Like you said, we barely know each other. I could be out of your life in a week or two, and you'd suffer the consequences forever. For nothing."

I squeeze him tightly to me, taking deep breaths to keep the tears from coming again. "I feel like an idiot, blubbering over here. Jeez, I never cry."

"Then maybe you're due. I'm so sorry for everything, Ben. I don't want to be a monkey wrench in your life."

We fall asleep sideways on the bed still in our jackets, arms wrapped around each other, and it's one of the soundest, most dreamless sleeps I believe I've ever had.

16

"HEIGH-ho, heigh-ho." I lock the car and head into work, while Corey makes his way to the ambulance shack. I feel strange entering the ER, as if I've been on a month-long vacation instead of my usual long weekend. So much has happened since I was last here, I'm practically returning as a different person.

The emergency room is hopping with patients already, mostly leftovers from earlier in the day, and I'm still kind of tired from sleeping so much. Neither Corey nor I were very active today, only getting up to eat, shower and watch a little TV.

"Dr. Hardy, you're here," calls one of the nurses who's about to go off shift. "I've got one of your regulars in there with shortness of breath, you remember Mr. Dawson. His O2 sats are in the high eighties, which is actually normal for him, so I didn't put any oxygen on him, but I did order a blood gas. The results should be back any minute."

"Thanks. What else?"

"The lady in room two is about to leave, they're on their way back to take the guy in three to the floor. He's fine, just one of Dr. Hannigan's observations. That boy over there just got stitches, and they're getting his discharge papers done. Half of the people in here are family members, so it's not as bad as it looks." She drops a folder onto the desk and grabs her jacket, heading out to the time clock. "By the way, I love that you and Julie are getting festive in the ER with matching Christmas outfits and everything. I think we'll do that on day shift."

"Um... thanks." Julie is assessing one of the two patients in room one, and she is indeed wearing a red turtleneck just like mine. We've both chosen to pair it with green scrubs, which definitely makes it look planned.

When she's finished with the patient, she returns to the desk and stops cold in her tracks, eying my shirt suspiciously. At that moment it dawns on me what she must be thinking, and unfortunately, she would be right.

"Hi, Dr. Hardy. What's with the turtleneck?"

I meet her gaze unwaveringly. "I could ask you the same thing, Julie. The nurse who just clocked out is under the impression we're showing our Christmas spirit with matching outfits."

She clears her throat and busies herself with tidying the desk, avoiding looking at me altogether.

When she gets close enough, I cover one of her hands with mine. "You don't have to feel awkward. Please don't. Let's just go on like we always have, okay? I don't feel any different about you because of what happened between us."

"And what would that be?" Christina emerges from the hall behind the ER desk that leads to the admin office, which has been closed for over two hours. It makes me wonder how long she's been there listening. "Something happened between you two, and I think I can probably guess what it was, or at least who it involved." She fingers the tall collar of her plush white sweater dress and smirks.

"Chris, this is none of your business. I'm none of your business anymore."

"But we've barely broken up, darling. Your side of the bed isn't even cold yet."

It's my turn to smirk. "That's because Hannigan has been keeping it warm for me."

She gives me a tight little *fuck you* grin and turns to Julie. "Were you sleeping with Ben while we were dating, you little tramp?"

"Hey, that's enough." I jump up between them, trying to shield Julie.

Christina shocks me by reaching out and snatching my collar down, exposing my mark. I feel the heat rise to my face. "Did you do this to him?" she asks Julie. "Was it you?"

Julie stands up and faces Christina with a determined look on her face. "Yes, I did. We made love this weekend at his place. Didn't we, Ben?"

I have to remind myself to close my mouth before I destroy the ruse. "Yes, sweetie. We certainly did." I smile at her, hoping she knows it's genuine, because she's just saved my ass big time.

"You're an asshole, Ben." Christina huffs away toward the

door. "I hope you and your whore will be happy together."

Oddly enough, I find myself wondering if it's really Julie she's talking about, or if she knows more than she's letting on.

"Thanks, Julie," I whisper after she's gone. "But why did you lie?"

Her face reddens. "I didn't think you'd want her to know what's really going on. She's not very discreet."

"And what exactly do you think is going on?"

"Come on, Ben." She rolls her eyes and touches my hand gently. "You may think you're a loner, and that no one knows you, but I pay attention. Plus, I was between you and Corey the other night, remember? I'd have to be deaf and blind to miss the sexual tension there."

"Oh. Does that bother you?" I'm not sure if I want to hear the answer.

"Only because I was planning on asking you out myself, if you didn't ask me first. But I didn't know you were gay."

"I'm not gay."

"You just like *him*?"

"I can't believe I'm saying this, but yeah. Just him. I've never liked a guy in my life… until now."

"Well, for what it's worth, I think you two make a great couple. Both of you are super hot, and you're obviously into each other. But what am I supposed to do now? There aren't that many eligible guys in this stupid little town, you know?"

"Julie, you're a beautiful, intelligent girl. And you're so young. You have plenty of time to find someone amazing."

She smiles, her eyes flickering with excitement. "I did just see a drop dead gorgeous hunk going into the ambulance shack when I got here. Is he new? Maybe Corey can set me up."

"Fuck." I spring to my feet, sending my chair rolling backward to crash into the cabinets behind us. "I forgot about him." I put my hands on Julie's shoulders and look her squarely in the eyes with all the sympathy I can muster. "I hate to be the bearer of bad news, but he's gay, too, darlin'. Now I need to go check on something."

I hear Julie's cry of disappointment from behind me as I bump the ER doors open and sprint to the ambulance shack. How could I let it slip my mind that Corey was going to be staying out here alone with the most eligible gay dude in the county?

The doors are unlocked, but the place is empty. When I re-emerge, I see that the ambulance is gone. I'm not going to be winning any awards for my observation skills tonight, that's for sure.

Julie is readying the main bed in room one when I get back to the ER. "They're gone to pick up an overdose. It's bad. A little kid."

My heart jumps into my throat like it always does when kids are involved. "Little kid? Like how little?"

"Like five."

"Jesus. How does a kid like that overdose? Why can't parents quit leaving their freaking drugs lying around?"

"I don't know, Dr. Hardy, but I'm scared of what we're fixing to be seeing. What if the kid—"

I know what she's going to say. What if the kid dies? It does happen. Has happened here. On my watch. Most of the things that keep me up at night, that plague my dreams so relentlessly, are things that have happened here. Things that I tried to prevent and couldn't.

In the fragile and fleeting game of life, we doctors are just damage control at best, and it's that sense of impotence that haunts me.

The radio clicks to life, and Mike's voice comes across. *"ETA two minutes. Five year old female, suspected overdose on narcotics— uh, Oxycodone?— Yeah, Oxycodone."* I can hear Corey's voice in the background, dictating the status report. He sounds frantic, and that makes me more nervous than anything. *"Patient is unconscious, pinpoint pupils, patient is being bagged with an LMA. We're pulling in now."*

"It's show time." I stand at my spot at the head of the bed. "Don't worry, Julie. Corey's very capable. He's already managing her airway, and that's three quarters of the battle in a narcotics overdose."

Suddenly, Corey and Mike burst through the double doors with the stretcher. I'm dismayed by the small stature of the occupant, but I can't let that affect my performance. I'm the damn doctor, and everyone is counting on me. I consciously drop my ice shield into place.

"She's having trouble breathing, and her heart rate's slowing, Doc."

"Time for Narcan, then. Get it ready, Julie."

Corey is nearly in tears. "Why didn't we do something, Ben? We were too wrapped up in our own bullshit dramas, and now look."

I don't understand what he's talking about until I get a good look at our patient. It's Tyleah, the little girl from the motel. My whole body goes hot with fear and shame as I realize I never even bothered to call child services like I said I would.

Julie hooks up the IV. "Administering Narcan."

I breathe a little easier. "Hopefully, we can head this thing off and avoid having to put her on a ventilator. Where's her mother?"

"She was fucked up as a bat," Corey says. "Possum picked her up and escorted her to jail. Hopefully, she'll stay there until she dies of old age."

Mike pipes up in his deep voice. "That lady's crazy. Corey told me you two had planned to call DFACS and get the kid taken away from her."

"Apparently we waited too long."

"I don't know, Doc." Mike's use of the nickname Corey gave me makes me cringe. "You can't always do the right thing. We all think we have more time than we actually do. That goes for everything."

Mike the Sage. Gotta love this guy.

But he does have a point. We can't go balls-to-the-wall about every little thing, or we'd burn out fast. Most situations tend to resolve themselves without intervention, and we often have no way of knowing which ones are true emergencies. Like playing the lottery, that little girl was just as likely to live a full childhood without incident as she was to overdose— or worse— even with the warning signs. I've personally seen the child of a strict gun law advocate die from a gunshot wound while visiting a friend, but plenty of hunters' children die of old age every day. Ultimately, warning signs mean nothing. It's all down to the luck of the draw.

Still, I feel like shit. I should have done something.

"How many did she take? Does anyone know?" I check her eyes, listen to her breathing and check her heart rate.

"Lucky for us, it was a new prescription. Not the mother's. I don't know where she got it, but there were only six missing, and the mother said she took two herself. So we know Tyleah had no more than four."

"Good. When this Narcan kicks in, I think she'll be out of the woods. We can probably keep her here, thank goodness, because I don't want to let her out of my sight. A few more pills and we'd be sending her to the ICU at County."

By the time morning comes, I'm exhausted. Fortunately, everything else that came into the ER during the night was mundane, and it was a quiet night overall. I spent most of my time in Tyleah's room watching over her. It's heartbreaking that she has no family to visit her, but all of the nurses are obsessed with her, so I know she'll be well cared for during the day while I sleep.

Corey spent most of his time in her room, as well. She's still a little reserved with me, but she's obviously crazy about him. He sat on the side of the bed and let her rest her head on his chest while we watched infomercials and reruns of old Westerns and fifties shows. I don't think Mike minded having the ambulance shack to himself for his first night. They only had one more transport all night, so he was probably sleeping or porn surfing most of the time.

"You're really tired, aren't you?" Corey looks concerned as we pull into the garage and trudge up the steps.

"Yeah, I think I'd just like to sleep all day today. Do whatever you like. What's mine is yours, okay?" I barely shuck my clothes and shoes before falling hard into the bed, reaching over to close the blackouts with the remote. I'm instantly comforted by the cool feel of the sheets and the consummate darkness.

"What I want to do right now is lie down with you and get some sleep. Is that okay?"

"Of course." I yawn and turn my back to him. "Just don't expect me to be much company."

Corey is silent for a few minutes, but just as I'm drifting off, he drags me back to consciousness. "Ben, can I ask you a personal question?"

"Oh, good lord. What is it?"

"Do you get depressed a lot?"

I heave a sigh, wishing he hadn't gone there. Wishing he'd just leave me alone. "I get a little low sometimes. I'm really tired, okay?"

"Okay. Sleep well."

He scoots up close, barely brushing against me, but it feels uncomfortable— like a full-body case of restless leg syndrome. I can't stand to be touched when I'm like this. I've got the urge to shake off his touch, but I don't want to hurt his feelings, so I try to ignore how it makes me want to cringe. I'll be asleep soon enough, and then I won't know the difference.

The sound of laughter wakes me sometime in the afternoon. I hear Corey, but there's also a female voice. When I stagger bleary-eyed into the living room, I find Corey and Allie sitting on the sofa talking animatedly.

"Am I missing a party?"

They both startle and look my way. "Hi, Ben," Allie jumps off the couch and runs over to hug me. "So great to see you again. Hope you don't mind me keeping your boy company while you nap. He's just been showing me around, and I must say your house is amazing. I feel like I'm in a photo shoot for one of those Southern home magazines."

"Thanks." I shift my attention to Corey, who looks slightly apprehensive, as if he's not sure how I'm going to react to him having a guest. "Corey, did you find everything okay? Have you guys eaten? I'm sorry I've been out of it."

He stands and approaches me. "Don't worry, everything is fine. You were dog tired. How are you feeling now?"

"I'm better," I admit, rubbing my head. "Got something of a pain in my gulliver, though."

Allie laughs hysterically, but Corey looks perplexed. "Am I supposed to know what that means?"

"It's from *A Clockwork Orange*," I tell him, smiling affectionately. "There's a copy of it in the library. I'll find it for you before we go to work, and you can read it in your downtime in the ambulance shack this week."

Instead of hanging out with Mountain Mike.

My phone rings, and I rush to the bedroom to find it vibrating across my bedside table. I catch it just as it falls off the edge. "Hello?"

Possum is on the other end. "Hi Ben, how are you?"

"Fine, except for that drama with that little girl last night."

"Yeah, that was bad, buddy. Thank goodness you guys were

able to save her. No telling what would've happened if she hadn't left the room and wandered out. She was looking for your friend, but as you know he'd already moved out."

"Wow. Does Corey know that she was looking for him?"

"Yeah, she was lying right outside the door to his old room. He was pretty torn up about it. Said he never should have left her."

My heart squeezes, but I don't offer any response to Possum's disclosure. I have my own guilt in it that I don't particularly want to talk about, so I change the subject. "To what do I owe the pleasure of hearing your grumpy voice, old man?"

"Old man? Hey, you're not that far behind me, fella. In a few years, I'll remind you of what you just said, and we'll see how it sits with you then."

I have to laugh. Possum has always had a way of lifting my spirits, I guess because he got so accustomed to doing it while my mama was sick. It's a skill he's perfected through years of practice.

"I looked up that tag number for you. I don't know if you're going to like what I found out, though. Can we meet?" My stomach clutches with fear, wondering what he could possibly have to tell me.

"When?"

"Like right now."

Damn. That doesn't sound good.

"Uh, sure. Why don't you come over to my house? I've got guests, but we can have privacy if we need it."

When Possum arrives, his face is so serious it puts me instantly on edge. He shoots Corey a suspicious look. "Quite a bit of drama last night, huh son?"

"Yes, sir." Corey nods vigorously and gets up to shake

Possum's hand. "Good to see you again. Do you know Allie?"

"Seafood Barn." Possum rubs his belly. "Best eating in town. Besides my wife's kitchen, of course."

Allie beams at the compliment. "Thanks, Possum. I appreciate that coming from you."

"So, Ben, I've got some stuff to show you, and it actually involves your… friend. So what should we do about it? I don't want to be airing your business out to the world."

Allie blushes when he glances in her direction. "Oh, don't worry about me, guys. I was just leaving. Got some errands to run before I head back to the restaurant. Call me later, Cor."

She kisses Corey on the cheek, grabs her purse off the counter and beats a quick path out the front door.

When we're alone, Possum sighs purposefully. "Mind if I sit down?" He drops into the middle of the sofa and pats the seats on either side of him. "Join me, boys."

My belly is wound up into my throat right now, choking me. The way he's acting, this can't be good. And what does it have to do with Corey?

We sit on either side of him, and he pulls a digital camera from the fanny pack slung around his waist. "I did a little sleuthing after you gave me that plate number, and I discovered that your peeping Tom is actually a private investigator."

"Huh?" I'm stunned. "Who would want to have me investigated?"

"Out of Atlanta." He looks pointedly at Corey, who swallows and starts chewing the end of his finger. "This guy has been making the rounds, asking all kinds of questions concerning a certain EMT who just moved here from Atlanta. He's spoken to people at the motel, at the hospital, God knows where else."

I can't wrap my head around this. "Why would someone be investigating Corey?"

Possum shrugs. "Your guess is as good as mine." We both look dead at Corey, who pauses chewing his finger.

"I don't know, guys. I have no idea." He seems to think for a moment. "I've done some things I'm not proud of in my life, but I don't know why I'm being investigated. That's the honest truth."

Possum fires the camera up and holds it out straight so that we can both see the screen. "I confiscated this off him. Told him not to come around this town anymore or I'd find a way to keep him out."

On the screen, an image pops up of Corey outside the hospital in his scrubs, talking with his aunt Denise. Another three of them getting ready to go on an ambulance run. One of Corey leaving a convenience store, his Harley waiting nearby. An image of Corey in the door of his hotel room. Christina is with him, kissing him, her arms around his neck and his hands on her waist.

I stare at him, horrified.

"Not what you think, Ben. This picture is taken out of context. She came onto me, and I told her to hit the road. I would never do that to you."

I'm not sure whether to believe him or not. "When was that?"

Possum looks back and forth between us as our discussion heats up.

"Uh, the morning after the… movie… at her place."

"Goddammit, Corey, if it was so innocent, why didn't you

tell me?"

He bites his finger again, his eyes darting nervously from me to Possum. "I had my reasons. Mainly, it was a shitty thing she did, and I didn't want you to know she'd disrespected you like that. Ask Allie. I told her about it days ago."

"I think he's telling the truth, Ben," Possum says. "Look at the pictures." He flips through the next three images, which clearly show Christina pushing against the door and Corey closing it in her face. Their facial expressions tell more of the story than their actions. For good measure, the investigator has captured a shot of Christina kicking the tire of her Toyota.

I slump against the back of the couch. At this point, I don't give a damn whether she tried to cheat on me or not. I'm just relieved that Corey didn't take her up on it.

Possum clicks to the next picture, and I actually choke out loud, my throat seizing on nothing but air. In the photo, Corey is bent over me in the club, my chair leaned back, his tongue shoved down my throat while Allie looks on in shock. If I'd ever wondered what my reaction was to that first kiss, here it is in full color.

Possum doesn't bother looking at either one of us, but continues flipping through pictures. Corey and me ravishing Julie on the floor of the pool house. Corey ravishing me in front of the pool house window. Corey coming out of my house in his jeans and no shirt, taken from the vantage point of my bushes. With every photo that passes by on the screen, the knot in my stomach gets tighter, until it feels like it's closing in on itself.

"You boys have been pretty busy, huh?" Possum doesn't sound like he's chastising us exactly, but there's an unmistakable note of disappointment in his voice. "I don't know what the end game is to this private investigation, but one thing's for sure. When someone hires one of these guys, it usually means some sort of trouble is about to follow. Ben, I don't want you to get hurt because this cowboy can't keep his gun holstered."

"Oh, come on now—" I begin, but Corey interrupts.

"He's right, Ben. I've gotten myself into some sort of mess, and it's not fair to bring you into it. Things are already complicated enough. Some asshole is tailing us and taking pictures of us. He's been here at your home, for Christ's sake. In your back yard. No telling where else. I think it's probably best if I find someplace else to go."

"Now that sounds like a great idea." Possum slaps his knee and slips the camera back into his pack as he stands and prepares to go. "Corey, if that sounds harsh, I'm sorry. But this guy over here is the most respected doctor in town, and he happens to be one of my oldest friends. I feel responsible for him. You, I don't know from Adam."

Corey nods silently, looking down at the floor. It's sad that such a confident man can be put so low.

"Possum, can I, um…" I gesture toward the camera in his pack. "Can I get that camera? I'd like to go back through those pictures and see if I can find any clues or something."

"Sure, Ben." He hands it to me, gives me a strong hug, and leaves.

I don't really have any intention of looking for clues on the camera, because I doubt there are any. I just want the photos, mainly the one of mine and Corey's first kiss. I have a feeling I'm about to lose him completely, and those pictures will be all that's left of us.

17

COREY calls Allie immediately as soon as Possum is out the door, and I can overhear him explaining the situation to her. He's going back to the motel; that much is clear.

Part of me wants to tell him to stay. I like the idea of him sleeping in that disgusting place even less now than I did before. I know him now, and that makes it personal. But I can't be stupid. I really feel like I've been nothing but stupid lately. I definitely haven't been acting like myself at all.

What I need is to regain some normalcy, get back to where I've been for the last five years since finishing med school. I have a life to live, and it doesn't include bohemian gay guys or menage sex or private investigators.

Corey comes into the kitchen where I'm sipping a glass of tea at the bar. "Alright, I've made my reservation for the room. I'll just take my duffel to work with me on my bike and go straight there after I leave work. Mr. Patel is going to let me check in early."

He sets his cell phone on the counter. "Can you get your money back for this, since it's only been a couple of days?"

"No need." I swirl my drink absently, listening to the sound of the ice chinking against glass. "You keep the phone. Use it as long as you need to, okay? I've got a two-year contract and no use for an extra line. It was a gift, anyway. I want you to have it."

"That's very nice of you, Ben." His voice is hoarse, and he clears his throat. "I'll think of some way to repay you. But then there's the age-old problem of what to get the guy who has everything." He tries to lighten the mood by laughing, but it only serves to make me sadder.

I set my glass resolutely on the counter and face him. "Hey, what are we doing? We're not saying goodbye. This is just until we figure out what that investigator wants."

"Then why does it feel so much like goodbye?"

"I don't know. But we're going to see each other around at work, remember?"

"Yeah." He doesn't sound like he thinks that's much of a consolation, and I have to admit, neither do I.

"Well, I'm going to shove off a few minutes early," he says. "Meeting Allie at the Huddle House for coffee before our shift starts."

"See you at work."

He heads out to the pool house, waving over his head without turning. A few minutes later, he emerges with his duffel bag slung over his shoulder. This time when I hear his motorcycle rumbling away, I'm not lying in the bed depressed, but it feels just as bad. I'm left once again in a house that's much too large for me to fill by myself.

The first thing I do when I get to work is check on Tyleah. I've been on call all day for her in case she took a turn for the worse, but no one called, so I already know she's fine.

"How are you feeling today, Tyleah?" I ask, hoping she's warmed to me a little by now.

"Good," she replies in a tiny voice. "Can I have some more toys?"

I look around the room. She's got a Highlights magazine from the waiting room, and a couple of cheap dollar store toys someone probably happened to have in their purse. It's a travesty that this little girl is stuck in a hospital room with no toys.

I buzz the nurses' station. "Someone go to the store and get this child some toys. Come get my credit card."

"Dr. Hardy, is that you?" The nurse on the other end of the intercom sounds shocked.

"Yes, it's me. Someone come get my credit card and go to the store and buy whatever they've got for a five-year-old girl."

When the nurse gets to the room, she takes my card nervously. "What's the limit, Dr. Hardy? How much do you want me to spend?"

"Spend a lot. Pretend it's Christmas."

"It almost is, sir. Three more days."

232

"So it is." That knowledge makes me sadder than it should. "Give her some, but keep some out to wrap for Christmas. And get her some clothes. Pretty things."

After the nurse leaves, I talk to Tyleah for a little while. She's very shy, so our conversation consists mostly of me asking questions and her not answering. It's alright, though. I don't mind. I just want her to know she's safe.

When I leave the room, I put in a call to Blanche Calhoun, the head of child services. She and I know each other well, since we have worked together on many child endangerment cases in the past, and I went to school with her son and daughter. I've even eaten dinner with the family on several occasions over the years.

"I want her to stay with me, Blanche. She's not going back to that woman, and I have plenty of room. What do we need to do to make this happen?"

I know it's a lot easier to cut through red tape in a small town, where people aren't anonymous. I have faith that Blanche and Judge Roberts will come through for me.

"I think that would be wonderful, Ben," she says. "Your mother would be so proud of you. You've certainly got the means to care for a child… and it doesn't look like you're going to be getting married and having your own anytime soon." She chuckles as if she thinks she's made the wittiest observation in the world rather than spouting an obnoxious cliché.

"I'm gay." I blurt the words out before I even know what the hell I'm doing. In the silence that follows my abrupt confession, I try to fathom why in the world I would tell her that, and if it's even true.

Blanche recovers fairly quickly. "I had no idea, Ben. I thought you always dated women."

"I have. You're right about that, but… I've met someone."

"Ohhh… I see. Well, are you sure? Maybe it's just a passing phase. You must be at least bisexual, right?"

"I suppose so." I sigh, wishing I hadn't said anything. "I just thought you should know."

"So you're worried that it might have some bearing on whether or not you can get custody of this child?"

"Yeah, I guess so. Would that be a problem? If I was… with a guy?"

"Oh, no." Her voice is reassuring, cultivated through years of comforting frightened children. "Listen, gay and lesbian couples adopt children all the time. It's commonplace, though not in our community. But I think this town needs to get with the times, don't you? When a change needs to happen, somebody's got to be the first one to do it."

I let out a big sigh of relief. "I thought you might think less of me if you knew."

Her laughter nearly pierces my eardrum through the phone. "Honey, my own daughter is gay. She lives with a wonderful woman up in the North Georgia mountains. They went and had a ceremony and everything. Her daddy had a hard time accepting it at first, but the old coot finally came around. Now he says he's got two daughters."

"Wow, we're both just full of surprises today, aren't we?" I'm feeling awfully close to her in this moment, and I guess it's the closest thing to being able to tell my own mom. If she was still living, I'd love to tell her what's going on in my life. I wonder what she'd think of Corey. If she'd feel like she had two sons.

"Look, Ben, I know it's tough thinking about coming out in this town. You feel like there are a bunch of holy-roller KKK Nazis who would stone you to death if they found out. To an extent, that is true. But trust me when I tell you there are more people who will understand than not. Have faith, give people a little time to sit on it, and remember… There are plenty of folks in this town, like me, who love you to death and will stand by you."

"I can't believe how lucky I am to have friends like you, Blanche. That's one thing I do love about living in a small town." I pause for a moment, not sure what to say next. "I don't know if I'll ever tell anyone else what I've told you, or if anything will ever come of it. I've been straight for thirty-three years, and now one guy comes along and I'm knocked on my ass."

"Have you never been attracted to men before?"

"No, never."

"Well, we can't choose who we love, son. I suppose every once in a while, someone comes along who resonates so powerfully with us that it doesn't matter if they don't fit our idea of an ideal mate. And that means this must be some kind of special man, so you might better hang onto him."

My talk with Blanche has me floating around in a daze. I almost can't wrap my head around the fact that the words *I'm gay* came out of my mouth. It's something I could never have foreseen.

Now I'm being forced to entertain the notion that it may

actually be true. And ironically, my confession has come on the day Corey moved out. This life of mine is getting more convoluted by the day.

If it spins any more out of control, I might have to go away for a while just to take stock of things. I've got so much money from my inheritance and investments that I could quit work and just go to some tropical island if I wanted. I could ogle women in bikinis, drink so much I pass out every night, learn to dance the Merengue...

Mike's voice coming over the radio startles me out of my head, and I listen carefully as he dictates Corey's words. *"Elderly male patient with a history of COPD, presented with shortness of breath and mild chest pains, nitro administered, oxygen at three liters via nasal cannula. O2 sats ninety-six percent. ETA five minutes."*

"Doesn't sound too bad," Julie says.

"I agree. Sounds like a COPD exacerbation, possibly some angina. Go ahead and call respiratory for a blood gas, and the lab needs to draw for cardiac enzymes." I'm glad it doesn't sound like some awful emergency, but my heart rate picks up just the same at the thought of seeing Corey, especially after the bomb I just dropped on Blanche— and on myself.

By the time the ambulance team comes through the ER doors, I'm wound up not from worrying about a medical emergency, but from plain, old-fashioned sexual tension. When I lay eyes on Corey, the sudden welling of emotion in me is staggering. Spilling my secret in such honest detail has had such a profound effect on me that all I want to do is wrap my arms around him and tell him he's my man.

My man.

I feel sorry for the poor sap on the gurney. I don't think he's in any mortal danger, but it's impossible to give him every bit of my attention.

Corey leaves Mike to wheel the patient to his bed and comes to stand beside me. "Ben, he's doing okay. The chest pains are better, but he's still short of breath. His sats are decent, hovering around ninety-six."

When I see who they've got, I know instantly what the problem likely is. "Mr. Baker," I call to the skinny elderly patient as they transfer him onto the bed. "Did you crank up your oxygen too high again?"

"I was trying to cut the grass earlier, Dr. Hardy. Got winded."

"And what did you set your oxygen tank on?" I speak loudly, because I know he's a little hard of hearing. "What number, Mr. Baker?"

He thinks for a moment, his breathing fast. His exhalations are especially long, even for him, and his lips are drawn tight as ribbons. "Uh... six, I think. Did I do bad?"

I chuckle as I place my stethoscope on his chest and listen to the symphony of crackles common in emphysema patients. "Mr. Baker, I've told you time and time again. Even if you get short of breath, you can't turn your oxygen up that high, okay? No higher than three. When you get too much oxygen in your system, it causes your carbon dioxide to go up, as well. Remember me telling you that?"

"Yes, Doc."

"That's what makes you feel this way. Next time you get too

short of breath, call us, but don't turn your oxygen up."

Mr. Baker's eyes moisten visibly, and his throat works with emotion. "I just wanted to get over her to see you, Dr. Hardy. I knew you'd make everything okay. When I get so scared, I just need to see you. Then I can calm down, because I know you'll take good care of me."

His words are a heavy load on my shoulders. Why do people think I can magically take care of them? I'm just a weak, confused man who can't even work out my own problems. I can't imagine what they're seeing in me.

"Thank you, Mr. Baker." I clap him gently on the back. "I'm glad you have such confidence in me. I'm no wizard. I just do the best I can."

He pegs me with his misty, yellowing eyes. "You care. That makes all the difference."

Corey comes up close on the other side of Mr. Baker. "You're right. Dr. Hardy is a very caring person, but he doesn't like to let on."

"Oh, yeah." Mr. Baker laughs so hard he wheezes. "My wife always calls him *Dr. Hard-as-Nails*, but we both know he's got a kind heart."

"Why do people think I'm so hard, or cold, or whatever?"

"Because you never smile," a wavering female voice says from the doorway. It's Mrs. Baker, who has finally caught up to her husband. She shuffles slowly toward us, using a cane to support her weight on the left side, which has been weak since her stroke over a year ago. "You seem so glum all the time... and so particular. But nobody falls for that nonsense. At least none of us who have been your patients. All these other doctors are downright sycophantic with their charming bedside manner. If any of them are on duty and I have another stroke, I'll send someone around to your house to fetch you. I don't want anybody else working on me."

Corey rushes over to help the tiny woman the rest of the way to her husband's bedside. "Here you go, ma'am. Your husband's going to be fine. He's in good hands, as you just pointed out."

He flashes his drop dead gorgeous smile, and I don't know what it does to Mrs. Baker, but it gets my heart pounding like a war drum. I can't help but wish it was directed toward me. He's barely looked at me since Possum showed up at my house today.

"Corey," Mike calls from across the room. "You ready to head out to the shack, bud?"

I can't hide my disgust. "*Bud?* Are you two buds now, after one day?"

Corey rolls his eyes. "Of course not, Ben. I barely pay him any attention."

Respiratory and the lab show up at the same time to draw blood, crowding us out. I glance at Mrs. Baker who is listening to our exchange with undisguised interest.

"Please excuse us, Mr. And Mrs. Baker... Corey, can I speak to you over here?" I gesture toward the corner of the room with the least activity.

"Sure, what's up?"

In the corner we're partially hidden by a curtain, but we're not invisible, so subtlety is key. "How is everything going? Are you... okay?"

"Yeah, fine. I just saw you a while ago. Nothing has changed since then, I guess."

So aloof. Is he over me already?

"So you talked to Allie? What did she think about everything?"

Corey leans in so close I can smell my body wash on his skin, and my mind is suddenly flooded with images of him in my shower. "What is this really about, Ben? I know you don't care what Allie said about it."

His nearness has me so flustered I can't breathe properly or make eye contact. My dick has woken up inside my scrub pants, and I'm feeling so messed up I'm actually considering going home sick. There's no way I can work like this.

He bends even lower, until his lips are close to my ear, and his voice dips down into that intimate register that makes my body hum with desire. "Baby, you're as nervous as a kitten. What is it?"

I whimper. "Corey, I want…" The words won't come.

He nips my earlobe with his teeth before straightening back up and stepping away from me. "Meet me in the doctor's lounge in five minutes."

He saunters innocently back over to the Bakers. "Feel better, Mr. Baker. Nice to meet you, Mrs. Baker. I've got to go now, but I'll try to check on you guys later." He pats the man's frail, spotted hand.

All eyes are on him as he leaves, with Mike puppy-dogging him all the way out. That guy is pissing me off more than I'd care to admit.

By the time I rejoin my patient, the respiratory therapist and lab tech are both wrapping up their blood extractions and heading back to the lab to run the ordered tests. Now it's just me and the

Bakers.

"How are you feeling, Mr. Baker?" I auscultate his chest again, and he jumps at the feel of my cold stethoscope on his bare skin.

"I'll be doing a lot better if you'll get that cold-ass thing off of me." His words are harsh, but he's laughing, and his wife slaps him on the shoulder.

"Stop it, George… Don't mind him, Dr. Hardy. The better he can breathe, the more ornery he gets. You can take that as a sign he's getting better."

"Alright, then. There's something I've got to go do. Just call if you need me, okay? I'm admitting him for observation overnight, so don't worry about a thing."

Mrs. Baker touches me gently on the arm with her good hand. "Thank you for everything." She drops her voice lower. "And for what it's worth, I don't think he's interested in that big blonde fellow. Everything you need to know about a person is in the eyes, you know, and his were focused right on you."

Mr. Baker struggles to sit up. "What are you talking about, woman? Is she running her mouth about all that eyes are the windows to the soul mumbo jumbo? She'll run you crazy with that shit."

"Oh yeah, he's feeling really good now." His wife rubs his arm, soothing him back down onto the bed. "You calm down, George. I was just telling Dr. Hardy that your eyes are looking a lot better."

18

(COREY)

THE back hall is empty leading to the doctor's lounge, thank goodness. An EMT sneaking in the back door and slipping into the doctor's lounge would definitely arouse suspicion, especially among the nosy nurses in this place. Now I know what Ben was talking about. These women think they've got to know everybody's business, and they're not opposed to spreading it around.

Inside the lounge, it's uncomfortably quiet. Coming in here alone feels a lot like breaking and entering, and unfortunately I would know.

"Hello?" I peek into the bathroom, but it's empty as well.

I don't know what's gotten into Ben today, but there's no doubt he's different. The man is all over the map, stoic one minute, crying the next, but the way he was acting in the ER let me know beyond a doubt that it's time to lay him down.

After a moment of pacing, Ben slips in through the swinging door. He freezes when he sees me, as if it's some big surprise that I'm here.

"What a coincidence running into you here, doctor. I was just getting a cup of coffee. Would you like to join me?"

"Forget the coffee. I had something hotter in mind."

That's all I need to hear.

The small round table is still between us, so I move left to come around it, but he moves right at the same time. I immediately dodge right, but he changes direction too, so we're still no closer to getting at each other.

"Fuck it," I growl, propping my hip on the table and sliding across. I make it to the other side, but the table tips as I hit the edge, clattering to the floor behind me. I don't care. I'm going to have Ben if I have to tear the whole place down to do it.

We clash against each other in the middle of the floor, chest to chest, his arms winding around my neck. I widen my stance and band my arms around his waist, cinching him so tightly against me I can feel his cock pressing against mine. I shower kisses down on his mouth, quick and teasing at first, but turning frantic within seconds. His taste, his scent, it's all overpowering me until I'm running on pure animal instinct.

I walk him backward, pushing him against the wall, crushing him with my weight, stealing his breath with relentless kisses. "Touch me," I breathe against his cheek.

He snakes a hand down between us, squeezing and rubbing my dick through the thin scrubs, working my aching mass with a strong hand. "I want you, Corey." He lifts up on his toes and runs his tongue along my bottom lip, covering my mouth in a deep demanding kiss. "I want you to fuck me."

He doesn't have to ask me twice. I grab him by the shoulders and spin him around facing the wall and press my painfully hard cock right up into the crack of his ass. Our clothing and the lack of lube is the only thing saving his virtue at the moment, and those won't be a problem for long.

Suddenly a voice at the door startles us back to reality. "...I think I saw Dr. Hardy come in here a minute ago. Maybe he's already got—"

The door swings open, and one of the nurses pops in. Ben and I scatter like rats from light, and the nurse stops mid-sentence, her mouth gaping. She slowly takes in the tumbled table, our heavy breathing, the way we're both standing half turned away from her to hide our erections, me rubbing my neck while Ben fiddles with his hair. If ever in the history of illicit gay love two men looked guilty, we do.

"Um... Is everything okay, Dr. Hardy?"

"Yeah," he says, his voice a little too coarse.

"Were you two... *fighting?*"

And suddenly we have an out, supplied by the nurse herself.

Why didn't I think of that?

Ben waves a hand dismissively. "Just a little disagreement. Corey thinks it's okay to shock a patient who has no rhythm, when clearly it's not. I set him straight, though. Nothing for you to worry about, Linda."

"Lacey," she corrects. "And he's right Corey. No rhythm, no shock. I would think that's one of the first things they teach you in

EMT school. In fact, didn't we go over that in CPR class on Saturday?"

I glare at Ben. Dammit, he's making me look like an incompetent buffoon.

Actually, Lacey, I was just about to fold Ben over and—

"Did you want some coffee, Lacey?" Ben asks before I can decide what I'm really going to say.

"That's what I was coming to get, if you don't mind. It's a slow night, and the girls at the station are dying for some caffeine."

"Sure, help yourself. Corey, would you please pick up that table you knocked over?" He shakes his head at Lacey. "Such a brute."

Oh, he's gonna get it when we're alone.

She gives me an appreciative once-over and giggles. I don't know how she can miss the huge rod that's still partially tenting my pants, but she doesn't seem to notice. Or maybe that's what she's giggling about, I don't know. She needs to get the hell out of here, though. I'm on the brink of putting her in a sleeper hold so that I can continue molesting Ben.

"We'll leave you to it, Lacey," Ben says calmly. "We need to go check on the ER, anyway."

Ben holds the door for me, and I punch him hard in the arm as I pass.

"Motherfu—" He immediately stifles his cry, covering his mouth with his hand and looking around the hall to make sure he wasn't heard. The coast is clear, so we stagger out the exit door into the cold darkness.

"I'm getting you back for that," he says when he's certain

we're alone.

"Mmmm hmmm… I'll tell you what." I walk steadily toward him, towering over him, and he stumbles backward into the tall bushes beside the door. "You can squeeze me extra hard when I'm making love to you tonight. How does that sound?"

He looks up at me, chest heaving, and I can tell he's as affected by me as I am by him. "Somehow, I don't think that will be much of a punishment. For either of us."

"We'll see." I kiss him quickly on the lips. "Now where are we going to go? I have this raging hard-on I've been saving just for you, and I've officially waited as long as I can. If anyone else gets in my way, they're getting knocked out."

"Let's go to the ambulance shack."

"Oh yeah, we can invite Mike to have a threesome. You seem to like him so much."

"Damn, I forgot about him." He hesitates for a moment, shivering in the gloom. "Are you sure you're not interested in Mike?"

"I'm absolutely, one hundred and ten percent positive." I run a hand over his chest and down his abdomen, reaching around the small of his back at the last second and pulling him into a tender embrace that has nothing to do with sex. He smells so damn good as I nuzzle the spot right below his ear, trailing kisses along his jaw. "You're all I see anymore, Ben. I'm obsessed."

"Really? That's what Mrs. Baker said," he murmurs.

I pull back and stare blankly at him. "She's hot for you, too?"

"Never mind." He lifts up and kisses me on the lips. "You know what? I feel the exact same about you, but… it's cold out here. Can we go somewhere and get naked? We're lurking around in the cold like a couple of teenagers looking for a place to have sex... outside the hospital where I'm Chief of Staff. I have reached an all new low. No way I could possibly be any more irresponsible."

"Guess I'm the responsible one for a change." I reach into the pocket of my scrub top and flash a couple of condom packets.

Ben arches a brow. "Do you always carry condoms around in your pocket?"

"Only when my boyfriend drags me to a corner in the ER and gives me that look... I went and looted my duffel bag."

His face falls at the word *boyfriend*, but this time I'm not letting up.

"Don't give me that look, Ben. You and I obviously can't stay away from each other, so let's just call it what it is, okay? If you want to break up with me in a day, or a week, or a month, then so be it. You can go back to dating women exclusively and chalk this up to a passing phase if you like. But for now, in this moment, you're my boyfriend."

I grab his hand and pull him with me toward the ambulance. As quietly as possible, I pull open the back door, climb up, and take one of the tubes of lubrication from the crash cart. "Where to?"

This time, he grabs my hand and leads me back through the door we exited when we made our escape moments before. "I'm not going to be a chicken anymore," he says. "If someone sees us this time, I don't care."

The door to his on-call room creaks a little when he opens it. Both our eyes are glued to the nurses' station down the hall, and it doesn't appear that we've been spotted by anyone, so we slip inside and lock the door behind us. It's as sterile a room as any in the hospital, used by all of the on-call doctors as a place to rest during a shift, so there are no personal touches here. At least they've sprung for a real bed instead of a narrow, rickety hospital bed.

"I wonder how many other doctors have done dirty things in this room." I wink at him, and he laughs.

"I don't know about any of them, but this will be my first time."

"Good." I reach out and slip both of his shirts over his head, revealing that perfect pale skin I love so much. Then we're frantically undressing each other and ourselves, our desperate fumbling finally leaving us naked and panting.

I bend to suck gently on first one nipple, then the other, rubbing his dick shamelessly with my palm, feeling him grow even harder under my touch. Dropping to my knees, I dispense a large amount of lube onto my hand and take his full length into my mouth, the sound of his moan sending electricity shooting through my own groin. I grasp his ass cheek with one hand and pull him toward me, gagging myself on his cock, swallowing as much of it as I can. Gently, slowly, I work first one lubed finger and then two into his tight hole. His muscles tense in my grasp, his hips moving back and forth, and he's fucking my mouth with subtle movements. I can tell it won't take much to set him off.

"Don't come," I tell him quietly. "I want you hot as hell and on the verge of blowing when I get inside you." I feel how my words affect him, his dick suddenly swelling in my mouth, and he pulls out.

"You'd better hurry up, then, because I want to come so bad it hurts."

I stand and pull him into a tight embrace, kissing him with

every ounce of emotion I have, tasting him, feeling him, unable to get enough. I lower him slowly to the bed, which is a far cry from Ben's comfy king bed in his million-dollar home. But the hospital is where we met, so it's fitting we should make it official here.

Climbing up between his legs, I roll the condom on and lubricate the head of my dick really well. Then I rub some more lube into his ass, not caring what kind of mess we make on the sheets. He's very passive right now, and I'm the most powerful man in the world.

"Are you sure you want to do this?" I lower myself over him, working my fingers inside him, stretching him, kissing his face.

"Yes," he sighs against my ear, running his fingers through my hair, kissing my cheeks, my eyelids.

"If you don't want me you'd better tell me now, because once I get inside you, you're mine. Nobody else's, you hear me?"

He smiles up at me. "But you said I could break up with you in a day, or a week—"

"Fuck that. I lied."

His fingers whisper across my back, sending a smattering of chill bumps across the surface of my skin. The raw surrender in his eyes is something I've never seen there before, and it tightens my heart and my groin at the same time.

He winces as I nudge against his opening, eager to push on in but not wanting to cause him any pain. "Relax, baby," I whisper against his ear, raining kisses onto his cheek before taking his mouth in a hungry kiss. "It's easier if you don't fight against me."

"Corey, I don't think I can…"

His words trail off as I push past that tight ring of muscle,

249

and I'm finally in. Somehow the simple act feels like the most perfect, most important, most heartbreaking thing I've ever done.

I lie still on top of him, kissing him, letting his body become accustomed to my size. By the time I start making small movements, he's so hot he's sucking at my tongue and clenching his muscles around me. His animal side has taken over, and his every exhale is punctuated by a sweet little moan of pleasure and pain.

I bite his lip, his throat, his shoulder as I plunge into him, striving to massage that lovely little prostate. I want to give him the time of his life. I want this to be everything he's never had before, and everything he could want in the future. Desire wells up in me, driving me, and soon I'm pounding into him harder with all of the need and frustration that's been building inside me since the day we met.

When I grab onto his cock between us and mirror my movements into and out of his body, he closes his eyes, his dark lashes fluttering against his cheeks, and sighs out a deep, serrated groan.

"Was there something you wanted to say, Ben? I didn't mean to interrupt you." I regard him with a playful smirk, still moving steadily, working him with my hand.

Watching him lose control is exquisite torture for me. It turns me on so much, I can barely keep from unraveling. But at the same time, it's such a beautiful sight I don't want it to end. His face is completely open, and I can see how much he needs me. There's no pretense between us now, and no mask of indifference. I want to draw it out forever, like that perfect moment before a climax when everything is hitting just right, and your body is reaching for release even as your mind is screaming to hold off just a little bit longer.

Ben opens his eyes, clearly struggling for a moment of clarity. "I was going to say I don't think I can stop what we're doing. I want this to happen." He opens himself more to me, pulling me close, wrapping his arms around my back. Lifting his head from the pillow, he presses kisses onto my chest, tickles his cheek against the smattering of hairs there, rests his forehead over my heart. "Please don't leave."

"Look at me."

He drops his head back onto the pillow, his face flushed with desire, and I kiss his lips tenderly, slowing my body movements to match. I know it's difficult for Ben to admit vulnerability, so I don't want to leave any doubt in his mind about where I stand. This is not some offhand fuck. We're making love.

"I'm not going anywhere." I drop tiny kisses onto his lips and press into his body, lengthening and deepening my motions, fucking him slowly and thoroughly, owning him inside and out. I squeeze him firmly in my hand, stroking him in double time to the languorous rhythm of our love. "I'm yours if you want me."

"I want you... I want you." He gasps out the words, clenching his teeth, biting back the impending orgasm I can feel about to happen.

"Come for me, Ben. Let it go. I'm so ready."

The release is visible on his face even before his hot seed spurts out between us, warming and slicking my skin. He quakes and clenches all around me as I spill out, strained up toward his head, buried to the hilt inside his body.

By the time I come back down, I realize I've been so focused on riding my wave that I'm practically suffocating Ben beneath my weight. I kiss him on top of his head, lifting up off of him so he can breathe easily again. He's quiet, with a goofy little grin on his face that warms my heart.

"You don't regret anything, do you?" I ask after I've disposed of the evidence and begun wiping us both down with a warm wet rag from the bathroom. I think I know the answer already, but I'm compelled to ask anyway.

"Nope." The goofy grin is still in place, softening him, giving him a boyish charm that draws me right in. "I told you I want you, and I mean it. Not just in a sexual way, and not just for tonight, okay?"

19

(BEN)

THE night is creeping by, just as I knew it would. At three fifteen in the morning, the town of Blackwood is dead, but I'm more alive than I've ever been. And deliciously sore.

My head is reeling from the turn of events, and from the fact that I've just lost my virginity for the second time at the age of thirty-three. Most of all, I'm blown away by the magnitude of my own feelings. Earlier, Corey said he was obsessed with me, and I know exactly what he means.

My breath keeps catching in my chest every time I think about him, and it's very much like the panic attacks I used to have after my mom died— only without the debilitating sadness. Being a doctor, you would think I'd be immune to psychosomatic symptoms, but nope. I'm helpless against this. All I can do is try to relax and let it pass, knowing for certain that it will. Otherwise, I'd be huffing into a paper bag, which everyone knows is the official high-tech medical treatment for hyperventilation.

"Somebody's in love." Julie trails her fingers across my

shoulder and drops into the chair beside me at the ER desk.

"And who might that be?" I give a hesitant smile, because as much as I'd like to make light of her comment, it's hitting a little close to home right now.

"You, silly. If you don't want anyone to find out about you and a certain someone, you're doing a terrible job of hiding it. The two of you are like fireflies buzzing around here tonight."

"Is it that obvious?"

She smirks at me. "You ought to look in the mirror, Ben. Jeez, a person would have to be blind not to see it."

I slump back into the chair, letting my arms dangle to the side, and groan at the ceiling. "Why does everything have to be so complicated?"

"Hey, I don't see any problem with it, and I don't think most people around here would. Some of your admirers may, but they'll be fine after they get over the shock of knowing they'll never get a chance at you. They'll pack their mothers' wedding dresses away in the attic, take in a few stray cats…"

"Come on, this is serious, Julie. I don't know what to do."

She spins her chair to face me directly. "Are you happy, Ben? This isn't just some phase that's going to pass in a week, is it? I mean, you seem different to me."

"I'm happy," I admit. "Honestly I've never felt this way before, so ridiculous and irrational, and yet I can't stop myself. It's like I've been living underground all this time, and now I've just come up for air for the first time."

"Then you've got to go with it. Don't worry about what people will think. I'll support you all the way. You're not going to be able to hide it anyway, I've already told you that. And how could anyone blame either you or Corey? Both of you have the best-looking boyfriend in town."

"You're too sweet, Julie. And more importantly, a damn fine nurse. Have I told you lately how much I appreciate you?"

"Actually, never. And you owe me. You've got to help me find a really hot guy... and he'd better be straight. I'm still mad at you for recruiting that fireman into the boy's club."

"Whoa." I hold my hands up in defense. "I did not recruit him. He's a veteran. I'm the one who got recruited."

She crosses her arms and pokes out her bottom lip. "Alright. But you still owe me."

Julie has managed to make me feel so calm during one of the most confusing times of my life, and I do appreciate her— more than I can possibly tell her with words. I lean over and plant a big, noisy kiss on her cheek.

"Well, well... are we looking for a repeat of the pool house incident?" Corey comes in like a whirlwind, followed by Mike, who leans against the back wall and folds his arms across his massive chest like he's Corey's new bodyguard or something.

Corey's tone is light, but there's a hardness in his eyes that lets me know that he's not entirely happy with what he's just walked in on.

"Not a chance, Corey," Julie smiles and gestures toward me. "He's all yours."

"Can I get *my* kiss, then?" Not waiting for an answer, he leans brazenly across the desk and stakes his claim with a kiss that leaves no doubt in anyone's mind as to who belongs to whom. His tongue presses in, exploring my mouth quickly but thoroughly, and I think he's going to take my lips with him as he pulls away. I want more, so much more, but this is not the time or place for that, so I take a deep breath and clear my lust-fogged head.

"Oh, I think your man's got a jealous streak, Ben." Julie smiles at Corey.

"A mile wide," he assures her.

Mike's brows shoot up in obvious surprise. Then he smirks and shakes his head at me as he walks back out into the foyer and stares out the window with his hands on his hips.

Hmmm... Thought you had a chance, did you Mike?

I'm glad he knows the truth now. I don't know what I'd do if he made a pass at Corey, and judging from his reaction to our kiss, it was only a matter of time before that happened.

Corey's got a smug, satisfied look on his face, and I must admit it sends a thrill skittering through me to know that he's so territorial over me.

"Gotta go on a run, babe." He rests his elbows on the desk counter in front of me and leans in close. "Nothing bad, just a simple fall, so it shouldn't take long. Think you can keep your lips off the nurses while I'm gone?" He flashes one of those world-class flirtatious looks he's honed to an art, and I melt.

Julie laughs. "You two are hilarious."

Corey casts a mock glare in her direction. "I'm watching you, girlie. One false move, and you're history." He turns on his heel and follows Mike out to the ambulance.

"He's great, Ben. I think you should just relax and be yourself. Not worry about what the town will think."

"I know. I just… More than anything, I wish my mom was here. I wonder how she would feel about all of this. It would be so much easier if I could just ask her."

Julie considers my words for a moment, fidgeting unconsciously with the stethoscope slung around her neck. "What was your mom like, Ben?"

A big smile steals across my face. "She was very alive. Compassionate, thoughtful, a little nutty." I laugh as a stream of disjointed memories of her flows through my head. "She liked to sit in the rain sometimes— in a rocking chair of all things. And there was this big hill out back of our house that she loved to roll down. She'd drag me out there and we'd lie down at the top of it with our arms crossed over our chests. When she said go, we'd see who could get to the bottom first. She always beat me, because she was much better at staying straight. I never could get the hang of it, and I'd end up rolling sideways across the hill instead of down it. I don't know how in the world she stayed straight."

Julie laughs, and it looks like she's entertaining some memories of her own behind her soft brown eyes. "I know what you mean. Your body just turns for some reason. I always welted up and itched like crazy, because I'm allergic to grass, so I didn't get much hill-rolling practice. I just had to watch my brothers have all the fun."

"Oh, you have brothers?"

"Three big ones. Caleb, Jake and Shane."

"Learn something new every day, I guess. Why don't I know these brothers of yours?"

"Duh. Let's think about this." Julie slaps the desk with her palm and stares at me with an incredulous look on her face. "They

257

haven't needed medical attention from you, Dr. Hardy. That's the only time you see anyone. If you haven't noticed, you're kind of antisocial."

"I am not! Look, you and I are talking."

"Yeah, after a year. Don't try to deny it, mister. In fact, I think Corey has been really good for you, considering you would barely speak to anyone at all before he came along."

I shake my head. "I don't get it. I'm here all the time. I speak. I date."

Julie snorts. "You mean your bi-annual relationship? Ben, everyone knows you only date twice a year, and you never date anyone for more than three months."

I open my mouth to speak and snap it shut again. *Jesus, am I that transparent?*

"Admit it," she says.

"I dated Sheree Alexander for four months."

She fixes me with a stern look that says she's not buying what I'm trying to sell.

"Okay, okay. I'm predictable. And antisocial."

"Very good, doctor. Admitting you have a problem is the first step to recovery."

The desk phone beeps once, and Julie answers, holding up a finger to shush me. "Alright, I'll send him back." She returns the receiver to its cradle. "Mr. Baker is asking for you on the floor, Dr. Hardy."

I'm already getting up to go before she's even finished with her sentence.

After ordering and interpreting another blood gas on Mr. Baker, I give him a breathing treatment. Then I sit down to do my charting at the nurses' station. Everyone is out on rounds except the desk nurse, so it's quiet. Too quiet, in fact, because the lack of sound makes my thoughts run wild, and I don't want to think right now. I'm agitated as hell, ready for this night to end so I can go home and get things sorted out with Corey.

I've decided he's not going back to that infernal motel. *Again.* I'm ashamed that I was going to let him do it. Possum means well, but he's wrong about this. Whatever mess Corey may have gotten himself into, we'll work it out together.

By the time I get back to the ER, it's almost six o'clock. It's that time of the morning when everyone is looking frayed around the edges, but you can see a glint of excitement behind the eyes at the prospect of being free soon. Most people will never learn what it's like to work a twelve-hour shift. And in a hospital as small and short-handed as this one, twelve-hour shifts often turn into eighteen, sometimes even twenty-four hour shifts during flu season or disasters.

"Dr. Hardy." Julie approaches me with a concerned expression when I enter the empty emergency room. "I'm getting really worried. Corey and Mike aren't back yet from that call."

"What? Have they reported anything on the radio?"

She shakes her head. "You think they might just be grabbing a coffee or something? Maybe the call turned out to be a false alarm."

She's grasping at straws, and I find myself grasping a little,

259

too. Hoping maybe that's what it is. "Corey does have a fascination with sweet tea. Maybe they stopped at the Huddle House."

I normally hate talking on the radio, but this time I grab the microphone without a second thought. "EMS, this is Blackwood Community Hospital. Are you there?"

Nothing but static.

"EMS, are you there?"

"I've got a bad feeling about this, Ben." Julie is pacing the floor behind me, chewing on the head of a ball point pen. "They would have at least said something by now. It's been a really long time."

I grab my phone from my pocket, silently chastising myself for not thinking of it first. So far, I've got two numbers on my favorites: Corey's and the hospital. I hit Corey's button, and it goes straight to voice mail.

"I just wasn't paying attention," Julie says. "To be honest, I forgot they went out."

"Don't kick yourself about it. I forgot, too."

"Oh gosh, they didn't even say where they were going, did they?"

"No, but I know where they write it down. I've seen their log book on the desk in the ambulance shack."

I make it out to the empty building in no time. The log book is on the desk, and I skim to the last entry.

5 Friendship Road

With the book tucked under my arm, I return to the ER, calling Possum on my cell on the way. "Hey, buddy, we might have a problem. Someone called EMS over two hours ago to come out for a fall, and they haven't come back. They also aren't answering the radio. Julie and I both have a bad feeling."

"Is your friend out there?"

"Yeah, he is. And there's one more thing. The address of the call… It's out at 5 Friendship Road, down from where you and I used to go fishing. I haven't been back out there since that farming company filled in the pond. Does anybody still even live out there?"

Possum barks a command to someone on the other end of the line. "We're on our way, Ben. That was old man Warner's place, and it's been abandoned since he died."

"More than a year," I mutter, trying to put the pieces together in my mind. "None of this makes any sense. Why would anyone be out there in the middle of the night?"

"Up to no good is all I can think. I'll keep you posted on your cell."

When I slip my phone back into my pocket, my hand is shaking, and I don't even know why. Everything must be fine. There's no reason to be freaking out. They're just a little late. Maybe they just can't get a radio signal way out there.

I try the radio several more times while I'm waiting for Possum to reach the old farmhouse. I also check my phone repeatedly, paranoid that my ringer isn't working or the power has died.

Finally, the radio buzzes to life, and Mike's voice comes across. He doesn't sound quite like himself. His voice is weak, and he's slightly out of breath. *Dr. Hardy…*

I knock over the wastepaper basket trying to get to the radio, sending balls of paper and latex gloves sliding across the floor. "Mike, where are you?"

"On my way back, Dr. Hardy. I'm almost to the hospital. I need you to meet me out at the ambulance, if you don't mind."

"Uh, sure, Mike."

Odd request. Something's definitely up.

Julie looks confused and more than a little worried as I leave the ER, making my way out to the ambulance parking space by the shack.

When Mike pulls in, the ambulance lights are dark, and there's no siren. He parks the vehicle carefully and climbs from the driver's seat, his movements oddly slow and stiff. When I get a good look at his face, my stomach bottoms out.

"Mike, what the hell is wrong?"

His expression is one of pure horror, eyes wide and deranged, lips trembling. He stumbles meekly toward me and offers me a crumpled sheet of paper.

"Where's Corey?"

He shakes the paper at me, and a whimper escapes his throat. "I'm sorry, Ben. I should have known better, but they…" He chokes on the words, struggles to continue. "They tased me from behind. I heard them coming, but I didn't react fast enough."

With my head spinning, I take the note from him and force myself to look at it.

Dr. Hardy,

I recovered my property from your pool house. $100,000 and my favorite Santiago Gonzalez croc bag. Only one problem... Where is the other half?? I want my money. Call me on my cell and I'll tell you where to meet me. Involve the police, and I'll do really bad things to your boyfriend. Worse than I've already done.

There's no signature, but a phone number is scribbled at the bottom of the note.

Numbness starts to spread over my body, a sort of systemic disbelief, and my brain keeps flashing on scenes from movies. Thrillers, most of which end badly. I can't seem to come up with a single one that doesn't kill off the main character's love interest. I'm seeing heads in boxes, fingers in envelopes, bloated bodies dragged out of the river... When my phone vibrates in my pocket, I nearly jump out of my skin.

Shit. It's Possum.

"Hey, buddy." I try my best to calm my heart and steady my voice. "Guess what? I'm sorry I sent you on a wild goose chase, but they made it back to the hospital a few minutes ago. Turns out the bastards were sitting down at the Huddle House drinking coffee."

I can hear the sigh of relief on the other end of the line. "Good, because I was getting really worried. There are some signs of a struggle down at the old house. Some blood, shell casings... Guess it's unrelated. But for what it's worth, I'm glad they're alright. Tell them from now on to answer their damn radio."

"Will do. Thanks for everything." As soon as Possum's call is ended, I dial the number on the paper. I can't afford to waste any more time when Corey's life is in danger.

20

BEFORE I hit send on the phone, I need to find out how much Mike knows. He's so shaken up, I have to ask him a half dozen times. "What happened to Corey?"

"I don't know, man." His eyes are haunted, and sweat is pouring down his face even though it's far from warm in the ambulance shack. "I just don't know. He was walking in front of me, calling out, asking if anyone was there... if anyone was hurt. I told him it didn't look right."

"Did you see anyone? What's the last thing you remember?"

"A man," he whispers. "A tall man in a suit. He didn't look like he belonged there. I only caught a glimpse of him before I heard them behind me. Then everything went black."

"How do you know they tased you?"

"I know what it feels like. We had to do it to each other at work during training. Tear gas, pepper spray, the whole nine yards. They make us go through all that when we sign on."

"Did Corey get tased? Did you see anything at all? Possum said there was blood at the scene. Are you bleeding anywhere?" I'm getting frantic now, my voice rising ever higher until it becomes a shrill ringing in my ears.

Deep breaths, Ben. Keep your cool. This is just like a code. If the doctor loses control, the patient dies.

"I don't think that blood came from me, Dr. Hardy. I'm sorry, but I didn't see anything at all." He's crying now, blaming himself.

"Get it together, Mike," I growl. "You're no good to Corey this way. If you truly want to help him, then be strong and let's do it. You didn't go through all of that hardcore training just to lose your shit the minute it becomes personal."

He takes a big gulp of air, drying his eyes with the heel of his hand, and nods.

I hit the send button on my phone.

"It's about time, Dr. Hardy." The male voice on the other end of the line is smooth and unusually deep, with a distinct Hispanic accent. "I was beginning to wonder if I'd misjudged you. Corey was certainly beginning to wonder, weren't you Corey?" I hear frantic grunting in the background, and the only picture my mind can conjure to go along with the sound is of Corey bound and gagged, trying desperately to communicate something to me.

"Who is this?" I'm surprised at how bland my voice sounds.

"Just call me Ambrosio. I don't suppose Corey has mentioned me..."

"Nope. Never heard of you."

"Of course not. I'm sure he's painted a very pretty picture for you." His voice goes impossibly deeper, and quieter as if he's sharing some dark secret. "Has he told you what he did for a living… before he became an ambulance driver?"

"It didn't come up."

Ambrosio's voice rumbles low like distant thunder, his version of a laugh. "I'm not surprised. He's very good at what he does. I suppose you could call him a professional manipulator. He can't help himself. It's all he's ever known."

"That's bullshit." I can't hold my tongue or keep the emotion out of my voice this time. Not coming to Corey's defense would feel like a betrayal, especially when he's helpless to speak for himself.

"Mmmm... He certainly got under your skin quickly enough, doctor. Tell me, what exactly does a stranger have to do to end up living with the wealthiest man in town in under three weeks? It took him years to get close enough to steal from me, but you... You just handed over the keys to your castle."

The muffled sounds of Corey struggling to be heard comes across the phone again. It terrifies me to hear him that way and not be able to help him, but at the same time it gives me hope. If he can make noise, that means he's still alive.

"Listen Ambrosio, you're obviously enjoying our chat, but I really just want to get this whole situation resolved. Tell me what you want and where you want it. You return Corey to me unharmed, and we'll call it even, okay? I'm not interested in playing vigilante, or involving the police, or anything crazy like that. I understand that this is strictly business—"

"Doctor," Ambrosio interrupts, sounding more agitated than before. "Don't try to fool me. I can hear the slight tremble in your voice. You want me to think you don't care, but you're scared shitless, aren't you? Scared you're not going to see him again." He pauses for a long moment, prodding me when I don't answer. "Tell me, or this ends right now."

"Yes, I'm scared." I'm not sure if admitting my fear is the best thing to do in this situation. The man who has Corey's life in his hands is sounding more unstable by the minute, and I'm not exactly a professional hostage negotiator. It occurs to me that Mike might be trained in such things, but one look at his distressed face and the way he's slumped in his chair tells me I need not bother asking. It's up to me alone to get Corey back, and that means I'd better ramp up my negotiation skills fast.

"You should be scared, Dr. Hardy. If I don't get my money, with interest, I'm going to start removing pieces from your precious boy. And I'll start with the part you like best."

The part YOU like best, asshole. Because you can't cut out a man's spirit.

And suddenly it hits me. In classic Jungian fashion, this smooth-talking creep is projecting his own unwanted feelings onto me. In reality, it is *he* who feels manipulated, *he* who believes he handed over the keys to his castle, *he* who is scared shitless that he's never going to see Corey again.

This isn't about money at all. It's about betrayal, and that fact does not bode well for Corey. I can replace the man's money as easily as dropping by the bank, and he obviously knows it. But there's no way I can fix the damage to his self-esteem, and I can't mend his broken heart.

"How much money do you need?" Though the money is obviously not the ultimate goal, my instincts tell me to keep him focused on it and off of his hostage until I can figure out what to do.

"We can work this out together. I have no problem paying you back. In fact, I feel really bad that this happened to you. I want to help. If you had come to my house and explained the situation, I would gladly have paid you."

"Why don't we do just that, then? Meet me at your house."

Home court advantage sounds good to me.

"Sure, Ambrosio. What time?"

"Hmmm, how about right now? I happen to be sitting in your living room as we speak. Hope you don't mind, I grabbed a beer from the fridge."

Oh, Jesus. They're in my house.

Since there's only fifteen minutes left on my shift, I don't bother arranging for another doctor to cover. I quickly explain to Mike that everything is under control and that he should go home and recover from his trauma.

"Do not tell anyone what's going on," I instruct him. "Absolutely no police. Keep your cell phone on you in case I need your help, okay?"

"You can count on me, Dr. Hardy. I'm sorry I've been so out of it. I'm not quite sure what's happened to me, the way I'm feeling… It's confusing. But I'm starting to feel better now. You sure you don't want me to come along?"

I have to reach up to clap him on the shoulder. "Thanks, but I need to do this alone. As for how you're feeling, you've been in shock, but they may have drugged you as well, Mike. You were gone for hours, with no recollection of anything after you arrived on the scene, so go easy on yourself. I'll give you a good going-over after I get things sorted out, but right now I've got to go get Corey."

"As lame as it sounds, I've got my fingers crossed." He holds his fingers up as proof.

I muster as much of a smile as I can for the battered fireman as he programs his number into my phone. Maybe he's not so bad, after all.

As for Corey, there's no way in hell I'm letting anything happen to him. I'm no badass like the heroes in the movies, and in fact I guess I'm about as far from that as a person can get. I live on the other end of the spectrum— the safe end that ensures I don't get hurt, or touched, or affected by anything. I'm used to carrying my pain home and wallowing with it in the cool dark of my bedroom, confronting it only in the depths of my nightmares where I have no choice but to look.

This is different. For once, I'm driven by something so powerful it makes my fear irrelevant— the feeling that I'm bound up so inextricably with another person that what I'm doing is pure self-defense. Like a hunter struggling with a grizzly, or a diver punching a hungry shark, I know that I'm fighting against the odds. But doing nothing is more frightening than fighting.

The strangest thing in all of this mess is that within a matter of days I've gone from being alone to being something of a unit with a person I barely know. As much as I tell myself it's irrational, that it couldn't happen, that it's all an illusion... it doesn't matter. I'm in love with Corey, and I'm going to get him back or die trying.

My house looks normal from the outside, except for one thing. There's a large SUV parked around the corner in the same spot where the private investigator's car had been, and I know without a doubt whose it is. Matte black in color and styled like a tank, it's got a star emblem on the back that I think I've seen before in pictures.

Is that a freaking Dartz? Who have I got in my house?

I wish like hell my stomach would stop churning, but besides that I'm oddly calm.

"Honey, I'm home," I call as I push open the door. I'm sure the sound of the garage door has already signaled my arrival, but I want to be careful not to surprise or alarm anyone who might have a gun.

"In here, Dr. Hardy." I recognize Ambrosio's deep voice from our phone conversation.

As I move through the kitchen and into the living area, the first thing I see is an enormous bruiser with a buzz cut standing guard by the French doors that lead to the foyer. He has two guns strapped to his body in one of those intimidating double shoulder holsters worn by gangsters and FBI agents in the movies.

When I see Corey, my breathing speeds up, putting me on the verge of a full-blown panic attack. He's sitting on the sofa, but his arms are restrained behind his back, and he's got a black ball gag in his mouth. His hair is more disheveled than usual, hanging lankly onto his forehead, plastered to his skin by a sheen of sweat. His blue scrubs are torn in several places and smudged with dirt and debris. The look in his eyes is what gets to me the most. He looks defeated

271

and ashamed, turning his gaze away from me as I come nearer.

Without a thought for safety, I drop to my knees at his feet and take his face in my hands. "Are you okay?" I can barely speak or breathe through the panic that's seizing my chest.

He nods without looking at me, a tear trickling down his cheek. I wipe it away for him, since he can't to do it for himself.

"Get up off your knees, Ben," Ambrosio says from behind me, and I turn to get a look at him. Tall, handsome, poised, with short dark hair and skin the color of creamed coffee. He wears black dress pants and a white button down dress shirt with pale gray pinstripes, unbuttoned at the collar, sleeves rolled casually to the elbows. He's as comfortable in the formal threads as he is in his own skin.

Again, I have to wonder who the heck I'm dealing with. He's obviously not the run-of-the-mill thug I expected. This man is *somebody*.

"Nice to finally meet you, Ben. I've seen photos, but they don't quite capture the essence."

He holds out a hand to me, several gold rings adorning his slender brown fingers. It pains me to shake hands with Corey's captor, but I do it anyway. Once he's got a grip on my hand, he looks straight into my eyes in a way that threatens to unnerve me, and he doesn't let go for a long, uncomfortable moment.

I meet his gaze as unflinchingly as he holds mine. "You don't seem like a man who would come all this way for such a small amount of money. Why are you really here?"

He cuts his eyes at Corey, and I see a flash of anger that I didn't mean to trigger. "You're right. I do intend to be repaid, but the money is secondary. I don't appreciate being disrespected, and that is exactly what he did to me. He took my generosity and threw it back in my face... and then he stole from me."

Corey shakes his head violently, whimpering, trying to talk around the gag. His body quakes, and I want so badly to get him out of this, but I don't know how.

"Can you please release him, Ambrosio? He's not going to hurt anyone or try to escape."

Ambrosio laughs in that low, rumbling way of his. "You can't stand to see him like this, huh? You care for him? He has really done a number on you, doctor." He looks at Corey struggling on the couch, then back at me. "He likes it, you know. I've had him in these very cuffs, and this very same gag, plenty of times. If I wasn't angry with him right now, I could make him come like a freight train, as you Americans say."

I don't think I've ever wanted to kill anyone before, at least not with such immediacy or intensity, but my mind is conjuring up myriad ways for me to dispose of this asshole. The thought of him touching... I can't even bring myself to finish the thought, it's so revolting.

Corey slumps against the back of the sofa, but carefully, as if he's trying not to mess up my furniture with his dirty clothes. It makes my heart ache to know that he could possibly be concerning himself with my neat-freak proclivity at a time like this.

"Well, can we at least take the gag out? He ought to be allowed to speak for himself. Have you even heard his side of the story? Maybe he knows where the rest of the money is."

"He denied taking it altogether. Then I gagged him before he could attempt to manipulate me with that talented tongue of his. But I suppose you do have a point. Perhaps we can torture it out of him if he's still unwilling to share."

He moves in front of Corey and removes the ball gag with the precision of one who is intimately familiar with the apparatus, using his handkerchief to whisk away the saliva that escapes from behind it. Corey stretches his jaws open and closed repeatedly but doesn't speak. He simply looks at his captor and waits.

"Hmmm, you were so eager to talk when I was telling your new mark what you're really all about. You don't have anything to say now?"

"I didn't take the money, Ambrosio. I swear it." His voice is hoarse from trying to be heard around the gag.

"You look awfully guilty to me, darling. You disappear without even a word to me, and my money disappears at the same time. Then you go into hiding down here in this... *place*." His voice drips with derision for the small town he's been forced to visit.

"I may not have spoken to you in person, Ambrosio, but at least I left a note. I was afraid if I talked to you, I wouldn't be able to go. I needed to go."

Ambrosio narrows his eyes. "What note? You didn't leave a note."

"I did." Corey nods frantically. "I wasn't sure where to leave it to guarantee you would find it, so I gave it to Allister on my way out."

"Allister?"

"Yeah, I didn't want anyone to know where I was going, but when I gave him the note, he wouldn't quit asking questions. That's the only reason I told him and not you."

Ambrosio runs a jeweled hand through his hair and paces in front of the fireplace. "Allister never gave me any note. He said he didn't know where you were. Then after I discovered I had some money missing, he told me he saw you climb into a cab with a crocodile bag like mine and ride away. Said he hadn't told me because he didn't want to get you in trouble."

"Oh my God." My exclamation gets both their attention. "I have never heard any of this, and even I can see what's going on. You've both been played by Allister. Hell, even I got played. I knew there was something wrong about that guy."

Ambrosio whirls to face me. "You've seen Allister? When? He is supposed to be visiting his mother in the hospital in Phoenix. I bought a plane ticket for him."

"He was here a couple of days ago. Right where you're standing. He showed up uninvited, we fed him lunch, offered to let him stay in the pool house…" Suddenly a thought occurs to me that just might end this nightmare once and for all. "Ambrosio, would you mind if I check my security tapes?"

Corey perks up. "Security tapes? I didn't know you had a system, Ben. Why didn't we know the investigator was creeping around here?"

"This is a small town, Corey. Not much crime. I thought the security system was overkill, so I quit using everything except the door and window alarms a long time ago. After we caught the P.I. spying on us, I fired it up again. I've got cameras on all four sides of the house now, and they were running when Allister was here."

"Go ahead and let's see what you have," Ambrosio says. "It's hard for me to believe he was here, but I'll give you a chance to prove it."

"One thing, though." I nod my head toward Corey. "Let him out of his cuffs. I don't want to see him like this anymore. He's innocent, and he needs to walk into the office with us and help us look at these tapes."

Ambrosio hesitates for a moment then leans Corey forward and releases the cuffs. I rush over and help Corey to a standing position, rubbing his arms gently, coaxing the blood, muscles and nerves back to a normal state.

Ambrosio rolls his eyes. "Oh Doctor Hardy, stop being so dramatic. I told you he likes it."

When he turns away, Corey shakes his head and whispers in my ear. "Don't believe anything he says. He's a fucking snake."

I don't want to fraternize too much with Corey at the moment. We're lucky Ambrosio agreed to release him, so I don't want to risk pissing him off. He's got a volatile nature, and witnessing anything akin to intimacy between me and his ex — *lover? employee?* — would be a major trigger.

It's brighter in the office. Floor to ceiling windows line the walls to let in plenty of natural light. We crowd around the antique roll top desk that has been modified to house the computer equipment. My laptop is plugged into the enormous external drive that stores my security backups, and it doesn't take me long to login and begin browsing the security footage from the day of Allister's visit.

"Here he is." I point to the screen, and Ambrosio stares with a mix of surprise and horror.

"That bastard," he whispers. "I always knew he wasn't the most dependable boy, but to be this dishonest…"

I keep flipping through the thumbnails of the footage, but I'm barely paying attention. His comment has me seething inside, and I have to say something. "You're surprised he could be dishonest, but you automatically assume Corey has stolen from you? I only spent a couple of hours with Allister, and I could tell he was a sneaky little bastard."

"You don't understand, Ben. I never thought Allister was intelligent enough to fool anyone. He's always been a drug addict, a fuck-up, nothing more. He always did everything I ever told him to do. Corey was… *is*… different. He has a mind of his own, and a rebellious nature. I knew it wouldn't be much longer before he tried to leave, so when Allister told me his story, I had no trouble believing it."

"Well, looky here," I drawl, zooming in on one of the thumbnails. "It's your boy, caught on tape doing the deed. Never dreamed we could be so lucky."

I hit play, and after a few seconds Allister's skinny body comes into view from around the side of the house. He makes his way quickly to the pool house, which is no surprise. At the moment he's doing this, Corey and I are sharing a particularly steamy moment in the kitchen. The memory of it makes me flush hot, and I want nothing more than for this to be over so I can put my arms around him and pull him close.

What's especially interesting about the security footage is that Allister is carrying what is clearly a large caramel-colored crocodile bag. He slips into the pool house, stuffs the bag under the sofa, and retreats back to the house, where he will interrupt mine and Corey's kiss. Then he will act like a pure asshole and get kicked out of the house, and out of Corey's life for good.

So much for being too unintelligent to fool anyone.

Ambrosio's hands are shaking at his sides. "I don't know what to say. I have made a terrible mistake. Corey, can you ever forgive me? Come home with me, and I'll make it up to you." He drops to his knees at Corey's feet, resting his dark head against his thigh. "Everything you've wanted— it's yours. Freedom to come and go as you please. Money of your own. And no more men, I promise."

Corey tentatively touches the man's head and speaks in a soft voice. "I appreciate the offer, Ambrosio, but I already have all of that. I went out and got it for myself."

Ambrosio sobs against Corey's thigh, rubbing his cheek along the fabric. "I don't think I can take no for an answer, my pet. I came all this way to bring you back. And I'm on my knees."

I see fear in Corey's eyes, and a resignation so profound it breaks my heart.

"He's not going anywhere." I move to stand beside Corey, wrapping my arm around his waist and pulling him close to my side.

There's a man with at least two guns standing in the other room, and I have to assume he will shoot me if Ambrosio tells him to. But I can't stand by and watch him intimidate Corey into leaving. I may not know any details about what has gone on between these two, but a blind person could see that Corey is miserable at the prospect of going back with him. And I don't blame him. Ambrosio is so wrapped up in his own desires, and so obviously used to getting everything he wants in his overly-privileged world, there's no telling how far he might go to win. He's like a spoiled child demanding a toy, but in his case, he's got firepower.

"You don't know me, Dr. Hardy. I can be very persuasive." Ambrosio's face shows no signs of sadness as he climbs smoothly to his feet, looking every bit as poised and intimidating as he did when we first met. His eyes are as dry as the banks of the Chattahoochee in drought season. "Besides, you have no claim. Corey belongs to me. Isn't that right, pet?"

Corey tenses, and I squeeze him closer, letting him know I'm with him no matter what the outcome. It might be a foolhardy kamikaze move, but screw it. From the outside, Corey would probably be seen as a stranger, someone I just met, not worth risking my life over. But to me— a man who's had no real emotional connection with anyone for years— he's so much more. He's the person who woke me from a perpetual sleepwalk and forced me to feel again. I can't think of anyone in the world more worth putting it all on the line for, even if our story burns out right here in this room today.

"It's you who has no claim," I tell Ambrosio. "You can't own another human being. Not in this country, and as far as I'm concerned, nowhere else either."

He laughs, pacing gracefully to the window and back again. "I bought his life. If I hadn't taken an interest in him, he would be dead now. The drug dealer he was working for caught him stealing cocaine from him one too many times. The last time was almost deadly. Lucky for him, it was a dealer who works very closely with my family."

"And I appreciate that, Ambrosio." Corey's voice is pleading, desperate. "I have told you that a million times. But why make me suffer for it forever? It's true, you saved my life. But I've had no life since you did it. Three years is long enough. You agreed to three years, and three years have come and gone."

Ambrosio whirls on him, anger flaring in his dark eyes. "How can you be so ungrateful? I have given you a place to live, food to eat, the very best of everything. All I've asked in return is that you please me. As for the three year term we agreed to, you earned at least another year when you beat one of my most important contacts to within an inch of his life. Do you have any idea how embarrassing that was for me?"

Corey throws his hands up in exasperation, anger eclipsing the self-defeat that had him emotionally weakened only moments before. "You were going to loan me out to him. To a man who is well known for killing his lovers and getting away with it. He's sick. I should have killed him when I had the chance. He's a fucking serial killer, and you people just look the other way like it's nothing."

"His family is very powerful, and you know none of that is proven."

"Of course it's not, or he'd be behind bars for the rest of his life. The fact that you were going to send me with him really bothers me, Ambrosio. Sometimes I wonder if you wanted him to kill me."

"Why should I have cared if he had?" Ambrosio seethes, coming so close to Corey their noses nearly touch. "You refused to have anything to do with me for over a year. Threatened to castrate me with your teeth. I've had drivers and housekeepers more willing to please me than you. I should have forced you." He paces away again, stopping to stare out the window at the nearly empty early-morning street.

"Forcing me is what caused the trouble in the first place," Corey says. "Remember when you started putting me in the sensory deprivation chamber for more than twelve hours at a time? And when you had me bound so tightly I got nerve damage? I still haven't got all the feeling back in my fingers. Trying to send me off with that butcher was the final straw. You people think you're above the law, that you can use and abuse people however you like because you have more money than God, and because your families are powerful where you come from. Can't you see I don't want to be with you anymore?"

Ambrosio turns and pins Corey with a look of unyielding dominance that makes my skin crawl. "You belong to me."

What I do next surprises even me, because I don't actually remember making a conscious decision to do it. I step in front of Corey, between him and the tyrant, and when I speak, my voice has taken on a businesslike smoothness that mirrors Ambrosio's quite nicely. "How much do you want for him?"

Corey gasps from behind me, but I can't see his face, so I don't know if he's just shocked or if he's offended as well. I don't really care, either. This narcissistic Colombian asshole is not going to take him again.

Ambrosio considers for a moment. The scene through the window behind him is so serene, so ordinary. My small town street populated by winter trees, older homes, and the occasional passing car. An odd backdrop for a drug lord who is deciding the fate of a man he considers to be his property. If it weren't so serious, it would be laughable.

"I paid fifty thousand dollars for him. His debt plus interest, I was told." His mouth curls at one corner in a self-satisfied smirk. "But he's caused me nothing but trouble over the years. I think some restitution is in order." He muses for a moment. "I'll let him go for a hundred thousand."

"Done. I'll have someone bring the money."

Corey growls and rushes Ambrosio, pushing against his chest with both palms. "You asshole, he's just a doctor. He can't afford that kind of money. Just stop this game and let me go."

Ambrosio straightens his shirt where Corey has rumpled it. "You don't even know who you're living with, do you boy? Your doctor has a skeleton or two in his own closet, one of which left him with millions of dollars. You're so insulting to me and my family and friends, but have you even bothered to learn about his family? Should I tell him, Ben?"

I stare at the ceiling, wondering who the hell sold me out to Ambrosio's detective and wishing I could have told Corey about my embarrassing family history on my own terms.

Too late now.

I face Corey, whose expression betrays his apprehension. "My grandfather was a bank robber back in the 1950s. He pulled off several robberies, including one that was worth almost three million. It was a very famous case, still considered unsolved because the money was never recovered. Over the course of several years, all of his partners either got busted or killed, but he disappeared without a trace. The general consensus is that my grandfather sold out and even murdered his friends, keeping the money for himself. Only a few people know this, but most of the money was passed down to me. Of course it's worth quite a bit more now, because of investments."

Ambrosio laughs even harder as I finish my tale. "Now you know, Corey. Your upstanding doctor is the grandson of a double-crossing thief— and serial killer, as you so eloquently described my friend. He's been dishonest with you about his heritage and his net worth. What else? One day you'll learn that rich guys aren't nice, darling. Money is dirty, and those of us who have it have dirt on our hands."

I'm afraid to look at Corey as I pull out my cell phone and call the bank, asking to speak to the president. After I arrange it with him, I call Mike and ask him to pick up the money for me. The whole thing takes about five minutes. While we're waiting for Mike to arrive, I rummage in the drawer of the roll top desk and come up with a booklet of carbon-copied bill of sale receipts. "Don't mind if we make this official, do you?"

Ambrosio shrugs in a decidedly petulant manner, and I set about writing out a receipt for my first— and hopefully only— purchase of a human being. To say this is surreal would be an understatement.

Corey sits down in the blue velvet wingback chair in a shadowed corner of the office, but I still haven't worked up enough courage to look at his face. He might hate me for this, but what other choice do I have? Surely he understands that this is necessary to give Ambrosio a sense of closure and to guard against him coming back to defend his misguided sense of honor.

When Ambrosio's armed goon escorts Mike into the office, the silent band of tension that's been squeezing the three of us for endless minutes is immediately broken. "Thank you so much for coming, Mike." I surprise both him and myself by wrapping my arms around his broad shoulders and hugging him.

"No problem, Doc. I told you I'd be waiting." He moves to squat at the foot of Corey's chair, mumbling words of comfort, and I'm thankful he's able to do what I can't at the moment.

I approach Ambrosio with a mixture of trepidation and eagerness, holding out the bill of sale for him to sign. It takes a moment for him to actually do it, his eyes shifting restlessly, and I'm afraid he's about to back out. A disturbing vignette plays out in my head of him ordering his guard to shoot me and Mike as he whisks Corey into his obscenely expensive SUV and takes him back to the sensory deprivation chamber. I shudder when I realize that Ambrosio is probably imagining a similar scenario, and we're balancing on a tightrope between a favorable outcome and a disastrous one.

Finally, he takes the bill of sale from me and scratches out a swirled signature that's just as arrogant as he is. Few things have ever looked as lovely to me, though, or given me as much relief. I take the paper back, give it a perusal, and present Ambrosio with the carbon copy. All three of our names are there, and I'm struck by the fact that our entire sordid story has been told so succinctly on a three-by-eight slip of paper.

After Ambrosio roars away in his SUV, I fall heavily onto the couch. The sudden abatement of stress has left my body boneless, my mind a noisy jumble. I stare up at the ceiling for a long time, hearing Mike and Corey's voices as if from some great distance, unable to discern what they're saying. Relief is all I can feel, all I can focus on.

I don't go to Corey. I don't comfort him or even speak to him, and he doesn't come to me either. Somehow, in trying to draw us closer together, I've merely created a breach.

21

The house twinkles with elegance, decked out from floor to ceiling in gold and silver in honor of the New Year. Flickering faux candles adorn every surface. Tables are covered with crystal glasses, bottles of fine wine, and hors d'oeuvres of all shapes and flavors.

Preparation for the party has been hectic, including a two hour drive to Atlanta to purchase tuxedos, Beluga caviar, and Cristal champagne, none of which were available anywhere in the vicinity of Blackwood.

Corey stands in a corner surrounded by adoring females, tapping his fingers against his thigh to the beat of an understated rap song— one of his choices on the party playlist. He puts me in mind of a roguish prince in his badass midnight blue Armani tux, his unruly black hair curling seductively at his forehead and collar. Not surprisingly, he's eschewed the bow tie, opting instead to wear the shirt slightly open at the collar. As proud as I am of my home and the decorating we did together, everything pales in his shadow.

He is both the brightest and the darkest thing in my life.

Now that the house is full of guests, I begin to worry about the noise level. Hopping over the gate I've temporarily installed at the bottom of the stairs, I head up to the much quieter second floor.

I push open one of the bedroom doors and slip inside. It's dark except for the glow of the pink fairy night light, but I can clearly see the beautiful little girl sleeping in the canopy bed in the center of the room.

"She hasn't woken up yet," says the teenage daughter of one of the day nurses, who is sitting in a rocking chair to one side of the bed. "Such a sweet little thing. I can't wait to babysit her while she's awake."

"Hope you're not too bored up here with all of the partying going on downstairs."

"Nah, got my e-reader." She holds up a cell phone and smiles. "Besides, I'm not much of a partier."

As I approach the bed, my chest tightens with an emotion I'm not yet accustomed to feeling. Tyleah's caramel curls spill across the pillow, her lashes fluttering against her plump cheeks as she dreams. It's hard to believe that only days ago she almost died. Remembering it, I'm awestruck by the way fate has of bringing people together.

My family.

The skepticism in my mind, masquerading as logic, argues with me.

Ridiculous.

It insists that I barely know the other two people in my makeshift family, which has only been days in the making. My heart knows the truth, though. I'm more connected to these two strangers than to any of the people I've known for years.

"She still sleeping?" Corey is suddenly at my shoulder, startling me and comforting me at once with his unexpected presence.

I catch the scent of my body wash on him, loving the way it combines with his body chemistry to create a unique variation of the familiar scent. It boggles my brain, gets me thinking about being wrapped up in his strong arms, skin to skin. But he hasn't even touched me since the night we made love, just before Ambrosio rumbled into town in his tank and poisoned everything.

"She's so peaceful," I whisper. "It makes me happy that we're able to keep her safe now. There are so many children in the world we can't help, but by God we can help this one."

"You're great at keeping people safe." He smiles, but it's not the charismatic, dimpled grin I've come to know so well. It's a wistful little thing that makes me sad, for him and for me.

"Could you step out into the hall for a minute, Stephanie?" I ask the sitter. She hurries out, closing the door quietly behind her.

Unable to deny my instincts, I turn and lean against Corey, wrapping my arms around his waist and burrowing my face into the side of his throat. I inhale deeply of his scent and kiss his neck with trembling lips. There's no way I can get close enough. I want to take him into my body, to go into his, to become one with him.

He pulls away, leaving me bereft, faltering only for a beat before moving to the door. "Your guests… They'll be wondering where you are."

Disappointment settles like an anvil in my gut, but I refuse to allow him to see it. "Let them wonder. There's something I want to give you before we go back to the party."

I'm really taking a chance opening up to him like this, because for days he's been anything but amorous. I'm getting the distinct impression he's not attracted to me anymore, that he's cringing every time I touch him, and it makes me feel empty and desperate inside.

If he doesn't want me, then so be it. I can't make him. But even if he doesn't, I have to do this one thing for him before it's all over.

After I usher the sitter back into Tyleah's room, Corey follows me silently down the stairs, over the gate, and into my bedroom. We get waylaid by a couple of hyper-social nurses who have imbibed a little too much of the bubbly, but they prove easy enough to escape.

Behind my locked door, we have the privacy I've been craving for days. He looks apprehensive, probably thinking I'm going to try to seduce him, but that's not why I've brought him here. I have something much more important to take care of.

A shirt box is hidden beneath my folded boxers in the armoire, wrapped in pale blue paper and tied with an elaborate white bow.

Corey balks when he sees it. "You already gave me so many gifts for Christmas. You bought me a whole wardrobe, for crying out loud. I feel bad accepting another gift, Ben. All I could afford to get you was that stupid tie you hated."

"I didn't hate it, Corey. I loved it. Besides, Christmas was mostly about Tyleah. And yeah, I wanted you to have some new clothes. You came into town with nothing but a damn duffel bag." I sit down beside him on the bed, but not too close. "Would it make you feel better about the gifts if I said I was tired of seeing those same three outfits on you? Really, it was hideous. You were so ugly I almost threw up every time I looked at you. Buying you those clothes was a matter of self-defense."

"Fuck you, Ben." He's laughing now at least, and some of the tension has left his face. "If you think I'm ugly, I'd hate to see how you act around someone you think is hot."

"Okay, I admit it. You could wear Bermuda shorts and gold lamé bedroom slippers and still be the hottest guy in town. I just want you to have nice things, that's all. Now open the box."

He tears into the paper self-consciously, stopping every few seconds to give me an embarrassed smile. Once he's ripped all of the paper away and broken into the box, his demeanor changes. He's quiet for so long that I start to get nervous, wondering if maybe I've done the wrong thing.

He pulls the gift from the box and holds it out in front of him. It's the bill of sale for his purchase, mounted in an expensive gilt frame.

"Maybe I should have given it to you for Christmas, but New Year's seemed the more appropriate occasion, since it signifies a new beginning."

Tears stream out of his eyes, splattering onto the frame, and he struggles to wipe them away. I grab the frame and set it to the side, taking him in my arms and squeezing him tightly. His body heaves with sobs, and I just hold him while he lets it all out. We sit that way for a long time, in our own little world, the sounds of the festivities outside the door barely registering.

When he's finally calmed down enough to speak, his voice wavers. "I've been ashamed of myself for causing you so much trouble... Costing you so much money... I'm nothing but a liability to you, Ben. I'm a mangy stray that showed up on your doorstep—"

"Stop it. You haven't cost me anything. I've been unhappy for so long I forgot that's not how it's supposed to be. Then you came along, and everything changed for me. The money is nothing. It's ill-gotten anyway, and as far as I'm concerned it's finally been put to some good use. That bastard Ambrosio is the bad guy, not you. He made you believe that you were less than a person. That he— or anyone else— could possibly own you against your will is absurd. I'm just thankful I had the kind of money it took to get rid of him." I take his chin gently in my hand and look into his tear dampened eyes. "I didn't buy you, Corey. You're the only one who can own you. That's what this gift is about. I just wanted to make sure you realize that."

He chokes out another sob. "I don't know what to say..."

I didn't expect quite this much emotion, but then I didn't think through all of the possibilities. I just knew I wanted to show Corey that he had his life back.

I kiss his lips with a purposeful tenderness, trying to communicate all of the longing I have for him. "I want you, Corey. And I need you. But I don't own you." When I stand to go back to the party, his eyes are still too wet and bloodshot to be seen in public, so I leave him on the bed. "Join me when you're ready, okay?"

I'm already halfway through the door when I feel a tug at my arm. Corey pulls me silently back into the room and shuts and locks the door.

He kisses me hard, accidentally bumping my head into the door frame, and we laugh all the way to the bed. We don't stop kissing each other for a second, even as we fumble with the shirt buttons and cummerbunds we spent so much time arranging before the party. He nearly destroys my bow tie trying to get it off of me, and it ends up hanging loosely around my neck after my shirt hits the floor.

When the rest of our clothing has gone the way of the shirt, we press our bodies together, maximizing contact. I cling to him so tightly it's a wonder he can still breathe, but he's not complaining. Our kisses are deep and rhythmic now, my cock so painfully hard, I wonder if we'll even be able to do anything before it goes off like a Roman candle.

Corey pauses, breathing heavily. "Are you sure you're not sick of all the drama I've brought into your life?"

"Not a chance. I'd fight anyone to the death over you, and I hope I've proven that already. Can't you see I've fallen for you? So. Fucking. Hard. What can I do to make you believe?"

He lies on the bed, scooting up onto the pillows and pulling me on top of him. "I just haven't had much luck in the past. It seems impossible that you could ever love me the way that I…"

I shower his lips with quick, playful kisses. "Do you love me, Corey? Is that what you wanted to say?" Before he can answer, I claim his mouth, invading it with my tongue, relishing the way his hunger matches my own.

After a moment, he pulls away gasping, reaching into the bedside table. Wordlessly, he offers me a condom and the bottle of lube, and I'd have to be a dimwit not to know what he's asking me to do.

Lounging back against the pillows, he puts his hands behind his head, giving me complete access to his gorgeous body. One leg swings off the bed, the other snakes around me, and he uses it to nudge me closer. The expression on his face is sexy as hell. Confident, even cocky, like he knows he's got me. It's a far cry from the teary emotion of moments before. I'm taken aback by his sudden turnaround, but a flash of concern in his eyes as I move toward him clues me in to what's really going on here.

This is particularly significant to him.

Just as he did in the pool house, he's playing it off like it's no big deal, feigning confidence because what he actually feels is far from it.

I crawl into the vee between his legs and rest my palm on his chest over his heart. It's rattling hard and fast against his ribcage. "What is it? What's wrong?"

He's clearly shocked by my question, but almost instantly his eyes soften and he smiles in that shy way he has that makes my knees weak. "I'm kind of nervous. I… want you to be my first." He blushes and attempts to hide his face behind his arm. "God, it's so stupid. I'm so far from being a virgin, with all the things I've done."

I'm not sure if I've understood him correctly. "Do you mean you've never let anyone…"

He shakes his head. "I always thought if I didn't do that, I'd still be a little bit clean, you know? It was all I had left that I hadn't given away… besides love. Ambrosio tried to force me, but even when he tortured me, I wouldn't let him. I couldn't give him that, too. I swear I would have killed him, and he knew it." He laughs, and a lone tear rolls down his cheek. "Sounds ridiculous coming from someone like me, doesn't it?"

I'm stupefied, wondering if there's any bottom at all to the well of emotion Corey keeps lowering me into. "Please don't apologize for being a romantic. That's one of the things I like most about you. At least you have the courage to feel, and to express those feelings. I've been emotionally dead for years. Right now I'm so ashamed of myself for letting petty fears keep me from showing you and everyone else exactly how I feel. If anyone deserves a fairy tale ending, it's you, and I'm going to see that you get it."

"Are you going to be my prince?" His smile has turned playful, and it's waking me up below the belt again.

"Hell, yes, I'm your prince, and don't you ever forget it."

He spreads his legs for me, a lazy smile on his face, his eyelids at half-mast.

I grab the lube and work it around the outside of the hole I'm about to defile. With the other hand, I work his monster cock, sucking the head gently into my mouth. I massage the shaft with my lips and hand in a slow seductive rhythm while loosening him up at the back with my slick fingers, stretching him out and warming him up. I may not have experience with a lot of the things he's introduced me to, but I damn sure know how to do this.

I glance up to find him watching me intently with a mixture of lust and apprehension unlike anything I've seen on him before. I don't know who is more nervous, him or me. Just days ago, he was initiating me, and now the tables have turned.

I stop what I'm doing and slide up his body, kissing his belly, his chest, his throat, his cheeks, and his eyelids before settling over his mouth. "Are you ready?"

"Yes," he breathes, lacing his fingers behind my neck as I position myself to enter him.

"Don't worry," I whisper. "I love you. This means as much to me as it does to you."

I don't wait for a response before pushing firmly into his body, distracting him with a kiss. Once I'm inside, it's nearly impossible not to move. The romance of new love and lost virtue has put a different spin on things, but when I look down at his amazing body and his perfect face, the animal inside me takes over again. It's as if everything about him was designed to make me want to fuck. That coupled with the way my cock feels sheathed inside his tight ass has me panting for release before I've even started. I wiggle my hips subtly, getting his tender tissues used to the friction.

"God, Ben that feels so good," he gasps quietly. "I have to—" He reaches down between us and takes his dick in hand, circling it with his fingers and thumb in a way that's as unique to him as his fingerprint. I marvel at it, watching him work himself as I move in and out of him, slowly at first but picking up speed as he does. When he slows, I slow, and we go like that for a while, totally in sync with each other's movements. His eyes are closed, his head thrown back in complete abandon, and I lower my head and clamp down gently on his throat with my teeth, unable to control what I'm doing anymore.

The hungry way his body grips me makes me intensely aware of being inside him. The knowledge that I'm the first who's been here is intoxicating, and I intend to make sure I'm the only one. My body and mind unite in one solitary goal— to stake an irrevocable claim on him.

My movements become erratic, and so do his, both of us going where our own instincts take us, striving for an explosive end that hovers just out of reach. Sustaining this level of arousal for long is impossible, and yet it draws on and on, each stroke more stimulating than the last. His body, the way his muscles ripple beneath me, the smoothness of his skin, his manliness, the sweetness of his face in that unselfconscious moment of pure passion…

"I could fuck this sweet ass forever," I whisper against his ear. "But I have to come. You're killing me."

"Don't pull out," he grates through clenched teeth. "I want to feel you finish inside me."

My erection swells, and I pound three long, delicious thrusts into him, riding the crest of a violent climax. Then as he strokes himself to his own climax, I pull out and take his impossibly swollen cock into my mouth, swallowing every bit of it I can, not caring that it's stretching my throat to the point of pain. I feel his seed pumping powerfully up the shaft, but he's buried so deep in my throat it bypasses my mouth altogether and magically disappears.

When we're done, we lie in each other's arms for a long while, basking in the afterglow of amazing sex. Suddenly it dawns on me that we have guests, and we're in the bedroom being very naughty boys.

"What the hell kind of hosts are we?" I jump up out of bed and start trying to get dressed, eying my reflection in the bathroom mirror. "As dapper as we were earlier, this is going to be awkward. Our tuxes are wrinkled, our hair is all messed up, and I don't think there's any way to wipe this just-fucked smile off of my face."

Corey laughs. "Do you really think people will be able to tell?

Is it that obvious?"

"Oh, I think it's very—" I glance his way and have to stop in mid-sentence. He's barefoot with his shirt unbuttoned and hanging open all the way down to his fitted midnight blue pants. "Damn, you look good." I come up against him, sliding my hands beneath the shirt. I run my palms over the muscled abs, up his sides and around to his back, memorizing the contours of his body, kissing his chest, wanting to do more already.

My breathing is ragged as I push back from him, snapping to my senses. "Jesus Christ, I can't think with you looking like that. Button your shirt, for heaven's sake."

The expression on his face is one of pure delight as he finishes dressing. "Sure you don't want me to go out there with my shirt unbuttoned? I kind of liked your reaction."

"Yeah, not a good idea. I can imagine all sorts of scenarios, and every one of them ends in embarrassment. I don't think you understand how amazing you look tonight and what it's doing to me."

He grabs me by the lapels and pulls me close. "Ben, have you seen yourself in the mirror? This jet black tux against your perfect skin and ungodly green eyes… I've wanted to jump you all night. I'm tempted every single time I look at you."

"But you acted totally uninterested earlier tonight. Hell, for days you haven't wanted a thing to do with me. I thought you weren't attracted to me anymore."

He kisses me softly. "It's the opposite." Another kiss on the lips takes my breath. "I was trying to distance myself enough to leave, because I know I'm not worthy."

"You'll hurt me if you go. So don't do it, okay?"

He leans his forehead against mine, and we stare unflinchingly at each other, playing chicken until Corey finally pulls away and laughs. "Okay, you win. Let's get back out to our guests before someone sends out a posse."

When we emerge from the room, we head off in different directions, trying not to look too guilty.

22

My living room is a foreign land with all of these people here. In fact, there are moments I actually feel like I'm at someone else's party. Not all that long ago, this place felt more like a mortuary after dark than a home, but that's all changed now. I smile to myself, thinking of the possibilities, fantasizing about our new life.

"Nice party, bud." Possum steps up beside me looking distinguished in a gray suit and silver tie. "I was wondering when you'd get around to letting anybody in here."

"Thanks, Possum. To be honest, I was a little nervous about people messing things up, but then I realized I was worse than your grandmother, the way she always kept plastic covers on the furniture."

"Shit, you remember that?" He laughs and drains his champagne glass. "That woman… She's the one who gave me my nickname, you know."

"No, I didn't know that. As a matter of fact, Corey was just asking me the other day where you got that name, and I had to admit I was clueless."

299

"Oh, really?" His eyebrows shoot up, and he scans the room. "Where is he? I don't want to tell this story twice."

I spot him across the room, working a crowd of women like he always does. The poor guy is constantly getting accosted. He's shucked the jacket and is even more fetching with his shirt sleeves rolled up. Allie is snugged up to his side, publicly claiming the best friend spot, and surprisingly Julie is at his other side. I'm relieved that she still likes him after the pool house fiasco, which could have gone all kinds of wrong.

When I come up quietly behind Julie, she spins around and throws her arms around me. "Ben, where have you been? You're supposed to be entertaining us." Her words are slightly slurred.

I shrug. "Everyone seems pretty entertained. I kind of like watching from the wings."

Corey glances at me and winks, and I feel an instant tug in my groin remembering what just went down in our bedroom less than an hour ago. When he discreetly shifts his stance, I know he's thinking about it, too.

During a short break in conversation, I lean in and speak close to his ear. "Possum wants you to come over here so he can tell you what his name means."

"Really?" He's genuinely surprised by the news. "I figured he'd rather tell me the quickest way out of town."

I grab his sleeve and pull him toward me. "Don't be that way. He's just protective. Believe it or not, he specifically asked me to come get you."

As we cross the room with Corey in front of me, I rest my hand against the small of his back. It's a natural gesture, a progression of our increasing intimacy, and I don't give it a thought until I notice several people looking. Instead of jamming my hands into my pockets, kissing the nearest female, or something equally lame like I would have done a few days ago, I slip my hand around his waist and hook my thumb into the band of his tux pants.

He looks over his shoulder at me, eyes stretched wide in shock, then breaks into a huge grin. "I'm beginning to think you might like me, Doc." His fingers skim across mine as he covers my hand with his. The simple gesture and the feeling of solidarity that comes with it are enough to make me giddy.

"Oh? If you're not sure yet, maybe I need to step up my efforts."

By the time we've maneuvered the crowd and reached Possum, he's gotten another glass of champagne, and I'm worried that Blackwood's finest will need to catch a cab home. In fact, there are a lot of people in this house who might need to catch a cab, and I believe Blackwood Taxi only has two cars. We'll have to plan better for key checks and designated drivers at the next party, which I'm thinking will be Valentine's Day. In the past I've sneered at the occasion, condemning it as depression-inducing consumer rape, but tonight I'm imagining pink festoons over the transoms and trays of heart-shaped petit fours.

Talk about a change of heart.

"You boys have really outdone yourselves here tonight," Possum says with a hint of a slur. "I don't normally cut loose, but this is nice. And you should feel honored at this turnout. Shows just how many friends you've got."

"Yeah," I reply with a smirk. "Most of them probably just

wanted to see what I've done with the house."

He chuckles. "A few of them, I'm sure."

"I'm here for the free food and champagne," Corey says.

Possum holds his hand out for a shake, as if he's just noticed Corey is here. "Good to see you, man. Look, I'm sorry about the private investigator thing... what I said to you. It wasn't personal, you know. And I see neither of you heeded my advice anyway. Not that I ever thought you would."

"We did for about ten minutes," I admit.

Possum nods. "I know you did. If I was a betting man, I'd say the two of you got all that sorted out anyway."

Corey's eyebrows shoot up. "What makes you think that?"

"You're still alive, aren't you?" He pauses for impact. "The morning you disappeared and got Ben all in an uproar, I drove by to check on things here. Seeing an armored SUV in this town sets my bells to clanging, so I ran the plates, and what I found made my blood run cold. Don't want to be on the wrong side of someone that powerful, if you know what I mean. Especially when dead bodies start popping up the minute they leave town."

"What?" Corey and I both ask in unison.

"Some little skinny fella got pumped full of lead out at that club, the County Line. A bullet in each hand, six in the brain, and one in the pecker for good measure. Atlanta authorities came down for that one. Toted him away all hush-hush, and I knew better than to ask too many questions."

Corey looks at the floor. "Allister... Poor dumb bastard never did have any sense."

"Just tell me we're not about to have a mafia war in

Blackwood." He downs the last drop of champagne and sets his glass on the walnut sofa table at his back.

"It was all a misunderstanding," I assure him. "The guilty party obviously paid for his transgression. Corey had nothing to do with it. Now what about your nickname? We're dying to know where you got it."

"I think it's a travesty that Ben hasn't asked you already," Corey says. "Some friend he is."

"Hey, I was a kid when I met him. I just assumed Possum was his birth name. I've heard stranger."

"Well, if you two will quit running your mouths, I'll tell you the story," Possum interrupts with a chuckle. "You see, my grandma was a laundress. I used to have to help her get the wash in and out, but one day I fell asleep in the grass beside the basket, and she didn't wake me. I heard her tell that story several times, so I cooked up a plan. From then on out, whenever I didn't want to do something I'd play like I was asleep— like a possum plays dead when he's threatened. She caught on and started calling me Possum."

I stare open-mouthed at him, and Corey wears a similar expression. "Wow, that was really anti-climactic. I thought we were going to be hearing about grizzly bear attacks, or attempted murder, or broken bones… Something exciting. You need to jazz that story up before you tell it again."

"Kiss my ass, white boy. Where did that champagne get off to? It's almost midnight."

As Possum wanders off in search of a drink, I glance at the clock. Sure enough, it's only three minutes until the New Year. I grab Corey by the hand and make a mad dash for the stereo system, turning the music down and getting *Auld Lang Syne* cued up to play. My karaoke setup, which I thought I'd never have occasion to use, serves as the P.A. system.

Corey hunts down a couple of glasses of Cristal while I grab the wireless microphone, step up onto the tall hearth at the fireplace, and attempt to get everyone's attention. "Excuse me, everybody... It's almost midnight, and I wanted to say a few words before the big moment."

"Woo, take it off," Julie screams to a chorus of laughter and lecherous hoots.

I spot her swaying in the crowd and give in to the urge to retaliate. "Alright, could someone block Julie from the wine table? I think she's had quite enough." More laughter follows, and it's clear most of the other revelers should be blocked from the wine table as well. It's good, though. Everyone is having fun, and as far as I'm aware, no one has puked on my rugs.

Allie steps over to Julie and throws an arm around her shoulders. "I'll take care of her, Ben." She doesn't look in any condition to be caring for anyone, but I refrain from making that observation aloud.

"Thanks, Allie. Now back to saying a few words... I'm not great at speaking, but here goes." Corey hands me a glass of champagne and stands near me, sipping on his. "I love this town and the people in it. I really do. And I don't think I tell you guys that often enough. I've had the privilege of taking care of many of you and your family members, and I appreciate your trust in me. It's been brought to my attention recently that I can come off as unfriendly or cold—"

304

"Antisocial," Julie yells, and Allie shushes her too loudly. Corey snickers at my side, turning his back to the crowd so as not to call attention to himself.

"Thanks for that, Julie." I give her a smile and a thumbs-up. "Anyway, I wanted to apologize for my *antisocial* behavior. Please know that it's because of my own insecurities. This party is my first step in getting closer, being more a part of the community, and it's only the first of many. Thank you all so much for coming."

Everyone claps and whistles, and I don't mind admitting it makes me feel great. Who knew bearing your soul in a cheesy speech could be so rewarding?

"Time for the countdown," Corey calls to the crowd. I hand him the microphone, and he laughs into it. "Oops... Eight, seven, six, five, four, three, two, one. Happy New Year!"

I hit play on the remote, and the song starts. Party horns and whistles go off, cheers ring out. Every couple is kissing.

I turn to Corey, taking his glass out of his hand and setting it on the mantel beside mine. He looks confused as I lean in and take his lips in a soft, tentative kiss, darting just the tip of my tongue out to taste the champagne on his before pulling away.

"Happy New Year," I whisper.

"Doc, I've got to hand it to you. When you come out, you really come out. With an audience and everything."

I look out into the crowd of guests. Some are still kissing, some are obliviously drunk, and a few of them are staring at us in undisguised shock. I simply smile and turn my attention back to Corey. "Some of them are surprised, but they'll get used to it. And if they don't... fuck 'em."

Corey wraps a hand around the back of my neck and pulls me close, resting his forehead against mine. "You don't know how much it means to me that you just did that. You claimed me right in front of everyone. Because whoever isn't here tonight will hear about it tomorrow, I guarantee you."

"Yep, and I'm glad. Pretending is way too hard. I want the entire population of Blackwood to know how I feel about you, because I'm damn proud of it, Corey. Plus, I don't know if I can handle much more of every single woman in town trying to get in your pants. They need to know you belong to me." I realize too late what I've said. He's just escaped a nightmare of slavery, and here I am claiming ownership myself. "I'm sorry. That was an insensitive thing to say after what you've been through. I didn't mean—"

"Shut up, Ben. I know what you meant, and I feel exactly like you do. You may not have bought me, but I'm yours just the same."

Keeping his hand around my neck, he presses his lips to mine, and suddenly we're the only two people in the room. Everything else falls away. The people, the cares, the stress… All that's left are two broken people who have made a choice to become whole together. If there's anything I've learned from this experience, it's that living to please others is like burying yourself alive. I'm just not willing to do it anymore.

Another thought occurs to me as I lean in to deepen the kiss. All this talk about owning Corey has obscured the fact that he's owned me since the day we met. And you know what? I like it, dammit.

THE END

Thanks in advance for your reviews for *Owning Corey*!
I appreciate them more than you can ever know.

Sign up for new release notifications
at *MarisBlack.com*

About the Author

Like many of my characters, I grew up in semi-rural South Georgia, gorging myself on equal parts classic literature, historical romance, and horror. Back then, it was all about Gothic. Since I've grown up, the dark stuff still has its appeal, but my tastes have changed. After reading and writing my way to three degrees including one in English, the classic literature overstayed its welcome, the historical romance gave way to contemporary, and the horror... well, it just got too darn scary.

These days, I spend most of my time dreaming up new and inspiring ways for men to fall in love on the page. Hey, it's a dirty job, but someone's gotta do it! But the truth is, a story is nothing without a reader, so I really appreciate everyone who has read my stories into being. I just hope I can do right by you.

Find Me:
MarisBlack.com

Like Me:
Facebook.com/marisblackbooks

26808140R00168

Made in the USA
Lexington, KY
16 October 2013